SURVIVOR SONG

wm

WILLIAM MORROW

An Imprint of HarperCollins*Publishers*

PAUL TREMBLAY

SURVIVOR SONG

A NOVEL

Grateful acknowledgment is made to Big Business for permission to reprint an excerpt from "Heal the Weak," words and music by Big Business © 2019.

HarperCollins books may be purchased for educational, business, or sales promotional use. For information, please email the Special Markets Department at SPsales@harpercollins.com.

FIRST EDITION

Designed by Leah Carlson-Stanisic

Illustrations by AnyaPL/Shutterstock, Inc.

Photograph by Stanislav Ronchkovsky/Shutterstock, Inc.

Library of Congress Cataloging-in-Publication Data has been applied for.

ISBN 978-0-06-267916-1

20 21 22 23 24   LSC   10 9 8 7 6 5 4 3 2 1

FOR LISA, COLE, AND EMMA

It's awful and still probably worse
They're biters and rarely alone
And rarely alone.

—Big Business, "Heal the Weak"

AUTHOR'S NOTE FOR THE READER:

When you encounter wide blank spaces and pages, fear not, they are purposeful. Okay, maybe fear a little . . .

SURVIVOR SONG

In Olden Times, When Wishing Still Helped

This is not a fairy tale. Certainly it is not one that has been sanitized, homogenized, or Disneyfied, bloodless in every possible sense of the word, beasts and human monsters defanged and claws clipped, the children safe and the children saved, the hard truths harvested from hard lives if not lost then obscured, and purposefully so.

* * *

Last night there was confusion as to whether turning off the lights was a recommendation or if it was a requirement in accordance with the government-mandated curfew. After her husband, Paul, was asleep, Natalie relied on her cell phone's flashlight in the bathroom as a guide instead of lighting a candle. She has been getting clumsier by the day and didn't trust herself to casually carry fire through the house.

2

It's quarter past 11 A.M., and yes, she is in the bathroom again. Before Paul left three hours ago, she joked she should set up a cot and an office in here. Its first-floor window overlooks the semi-private backyard and the sun-bleached, needs-a-coat-of-stain picket fence. The grass is dead, having months prior surrendered to the withering heat of yet another record-breaking summer.

The heat will be blamed for the outbreak. There will be scores of other villains, some heroes too. It will be years before the virus's full phylogenetic tree is mapped, and even then, there will continue to be doubters, naysayers, and the most cynical political opportunists. The truth will go unheeded by some, as it invariably does.

To wit, Natalie can't stop reading the fourteen-day-old Facebook post on her town's "Stoughton Enthusiasts" page. There are currently 2,312 comments. Natalie has read them all.

The post: Wildlife Services is informing the public that rabies vaccine baits are being dropped in the MA area in coordination with the Department of Agriculture. Baits are also being dropped in targeted areas of surrounding states RI, CT, NH, VT, ME, NY, and as a precaution PA. The vaccine is in a blister pack, army-green. Baits will be dropped by airplane and helicopter until further notice. If you see or find a bait, please do not disturb it. Not harmful but not for human consumption.

The photo: The size of a dollar coin, the top of the bait pack is rectangular, has a puttylike appearance, and the middle leavened like a loaf of bread. It looks like a green, bite-size Almond Joy.

[Natalie and Paul have already stress-eaten most of the large variety bag of Halloween candy and it's only October 21.]

The back of the bait pack has a warning label:

> MNR 1—888-555-6655
>
> Rabies Vaccine DO NOT EAT Live adenovirus vector
>
> Vaccin antirabique NE PAS MANGER Vecteur vivant d'adéno-virus
>
> MNR 1—888-555-6655

A small sample of the unedited comments to the Facebook post, in chronological order:

> What if an animal eats like twenty of these?
>
> This sounds really dumb. There has to be a better way.
>
> Vaccinating as many animals within a population is the only proven way to stop the spread. You can't get ALL animals to voluntarily walk up to the vet for vaccinations. Seriously, the fact that we have effective baits to drop is huge and better than doing nothing.
>
> What if a child eats it? This can't be okay.
>
> That's why there's the warning. And I doubt they're dropping this stuff in the backyards. Only in the woods.
>
> They say its some weird scary new strain.
>
> A rabid animal is more dangerous than eating a vaccine.
>
> Vaccines is what makes you sick. Everyone knows that.
>
> I live in a wooded area and I have cats and grandkids. I don't want them dropping that shit near me.
>
> I ate four baits and now my erection is HUGE and GREEN and it won't go away.

4

HULK SMASH!!!!

This isnt rabies. This is something knew.

I'm hearing you don't even have to get bit to get it.

They don't know.

Regular rabies is slow, usually takes weeks. They're saying this thing moves through you in minutes.

42 confirmed human cases in Brockton. 29 in Stoughton. 19 in Ames.

Where are you hearing this?

What are the symptoms???

Headache and flu-like symptoms but it gets soooo much worse and you go crazy and you get weird and violent and you attack people and you're fucked and everyone is fucked because there is no cure.

That's not true. The original post is about the vaccine. Stop trying to scare people.

We've been quarantined. Nice knowing everybody.

Fuuuuuuuuuuuuuuuck!

My sister said they're closing Good Samaritan Hospital in Brockton. Overrun.

What do you mean by overrun?

I called my pediatrician's office and there's only a message saying go to Good Samaritan. What are we supposed to do???

I live near there and heard machine guns.

You know what a machine gun sounds like do ya?

they cant do anything for any one any way. time to hunker in the bunker until its over. people are going fast.

They don't know what they're doing. We're so screwed.

We have to stay together and share information. Good information. No more wild rumors, and don't use the word zombie, and just obviously false bullshit here please.

None of this is gonna work. We should kill all the animals, kill all the infected. Sounds cruel but if we can't save them kill them before they get us all sick.

The bathroom window is latched shut. The white shade is pulled down, and Natalie keeps both eyes on it. Urine rushes out of her, and though she's alone, she's embarrassed by how loud it is without the masking drone of the bathroom fan.

AM radio crackles through the smart speaker on the kitchen counter as though the poor reception and sound quality are nothing but a special effect from a radio play, its time and hysteria getting a reboot.

One radio host reiterates that residents are to stay in their homes and keep the roads clear, only using them in the event of an emergency. She reads a brief list of shelter locales and hospitals within the Route 128 belt of metro Boston. They move on to reports of isolated power outages. No word from National Grid as to the cause or expected duration of service interruption. National Grid is already critically understaffed because the company is mired in a lockout of a significant number of its unionized field electricians and crews in an effort to eliminate employee pensions. Another newscaster speculates on the potential use of rolling brownouts for communities that are not cooperating with the quarantine and sundown curfew.

Paul went to Star Supermarket in Washington Plaza, which is only a little over a mile from their small, two-bedroom house. He is supposed to pick up a solar-and-hand-crank-powered radio with other supplies and food. The National Guard is overseeing the distribution of rations.

Rations. This is where they are fifteen days before their first child's due date. Fucking *rations*.

It's an overcast, gray autumn late morning. More out of superstition than fear [at least, that's what she tells herself], Natalie has turned the lights out in the house. With the bay window curtains drawn, the first floor is a cold galaxy of glowing blue, green, and red lights, mapping the constellation of appliances and power-hungry devices and gadgetry.

Paul texted fifty-seven minutes ago that he was almost inside the store but his phone was at 6 percent battery so he was going to shut it off to save the remaining juice for an emergency or if he needed to ask for Natalie's "suggestions" [the scare quotes are his] once inside the supermarket. He is stubbornly proud of his tech frugality, insisting on not spending a dime to upgrade his many-generations-ago, cracked-screen phone that has the battery-life equivalent of a mayfly's ephemeral life-span. Natalie cursed him and his phone with "Fuck your fucking shitty phone. I mean, hurry back, sweetie pie." Paul signed off with "The dude in front of me pissed himself and doesn't care. I wanna be him when I grow up. Make sure you don't come down here. I'll be home soon. Love you."

Natalie closes the toilet lid and doesn't flush, afraid of making too much noise. She washes her hands, dries them, then texts, "Are you inside now?" Her screen is filled with a list of blue dialogue bubbles of the repeated, unanswered message.

The radio announcer reiterates that if you are bitten or fear you've come in close contact with contaminated fluid, you are to immediately go to the nearest hospital.

Natalie considers driving to the supermarket. Maybe the sight of a thirty-four-year-old pregnant woman walking to the front of the ration line and dropping f-bombs on everyone and everything would get Paul in front of Piss Pants, into the store, and home sooner. Like now. She wanted to go with him earlier, but she knew her back, legs, joints, and every other traitorous part of her body couldn't take standing in line with him for what they had assumed would be an hour, maybe two.

She's mad at herself now, thinking she could've alternated standing in line and sitting in the car. Then again, who knows how far away Paul had to park, as his little trip to the mobbed grocery store is going on three hours.

She texts again, "Are you inside now?"

Her baby is on the move. Natalie imagines the kid rolling over to a preferred side. The baby always seems to lash out with a foot or readjust its position after she uses the bathroom. The deeply interior sensation remains as bizarre, reassuring, and somehow heartbreaking as it was the day she felt her first punches and kicks. She rubs her belly and whispers, "Why doesn't he text me on someone else's phone? What good is saving his battery if *we* have an emergency here and I can't call him? Go ahead, say, 'You're fucking right, Mommy.' Okay, don't say that. Not for a couple of years anyway."

Natalie hasn't left the house in four days, not since her employer Stonehill College broke rank with the majority of other local colleges and closed its dorms, academic, and administrative buildings to students and employees, sending everyone home. That afternoon camped out at the kitchen table, Natalie answered Development Office emails and made phone calls to alumni who were not living in New England. Only four of the twenty-seven people she spoke to made modest donations to the school. The ones who didn't hang up on her wanted to know what was going on in Massachusetts.

Natalie is jittery enough to pace the first floor. Her feet are swollen even though the prior day's unusual heat and humidity broke overnight. Everything on or inside [*thanks but no thanks, hemorrhoids*, she thinks] her body is swelling or already in a state of maximum swollen. She fills a cup with water and sits on a wooden kitchen chair, its seat and back padded with flattened pillows, which are affectations to actual comfort.

The radio hosts read straight from the Massachusetts bylaws regarding quarantine and isolation.

Natalie sighs and releases her brown hair from a ponytail. It's still wet from her shower earlier that morning. She reties her ponytail, careful to keep it loose. She plugs in her phone although the battery is almost fully charged, and then she hikes up her blue shirt-dress and sends a hand under the wide waistband of her leggings to scratch her belly. She should probably take off the leggings and let her skin breathe, but that would involve the considerable undertaking of standing, walking, bending, removing. She can't deal with *all* the —ings right now.

Natalie opens the diary app on her phone, named Voyager. In her head she says the name of the app in French [Voyageur]; she says it that way to Paul when she wants to annoy him. She's been using the app to keep a pregnancy journal. The app automatically syncs her notes, pictures, videos, and audio files to her Google Drive storage. During the first two trimesters, Natalie had been using the app every day and often more than once. She shared her posts with other first-time moms and caused an amused stir within that online community when instead of posting pictures of her weekly belly growth, she shared pictures of her feet accompanied by her own hilarious [at least she thought so] jokes about how quickly the twins were growing. Natalie slowed down using the app considerably in the third trimester and most of those entries devolved into a clinical listing of discomforts, the saga of the strange red pointillist dots appearing on the skin of her chest and face [including a regaling of her doctor's shrug, and deadpan, "Probably nothing, but maybe Lupus."], work grievances, and a litanylike reiterating of her fear that she'll be pregnant forever. Over the last ten days, she has only mustered a few updates.

Natalie opts to record an audio entry, first marking it as private and not to be shared to those who follow her online: "*Bonjour, Voyageur. C'est moi.* Yeah. Fifteen days to go, give or take. What a terrible saying that is. Give or take. Say it fast and you can't even understand it. Giveortake. Giveortake. I'm sitting alone in my dark house. Physical discomforts are legion, but not thinking about that so much because I'm utterly terrified. So I have that going for me. Wearing the same leggings for the fifth day in a row. I feel bad for them. They never asked for this. [Sigh] I should turn on a light. Or open the curtains. Let some gray in. Don't know why I don't. Fucking Paul. Turn on your goddamn——"

Her phone buzzes and a text from Paul bubbles onto the top of the screen. "Finally out. Bundles in the car. Be home in 5."

She suppresses the urge to make fun of his actually typing the word "bundles." Saying it is bad enough. She types, "Yay! Hurry. Be safe but hurry. Pleeeeze."

She tells the smart speaker to turn down the volume until it's inaudible. She wants to listen for Paul's car. The empty house makes its empty-house sounds, the ones with frequencies attuned to imagination and worst-case scenarios. Natalie is careful to not make any of her own sounds. With her phone she checks online news and Twitter and none of it is good. She returns to Voyager and types a riff on her dad's favorite saying: "A watched clock never boils."

Paul's car and its clearing-of-a-throat engine finally chugs up their sleepy street and rounds the bend of the fenced front yard. His green Forester is a twenty-year-old beater; 200,000 miles plus and standard transmission. Another endearing/annoying quirk of his, claiming he'll only ever drive used standards as though it's a quantifiable measure of his worth. More annoying, he's not a gearhead and cannot fix cars himself, so invariably his jalopy is in the shop and then she is left having to build extra time in her schedule getting him to and from the train station.

As the green machine crunches its way down their sloped gravel driveway Natalie struggles into a standing position. She unplugs and then deposits her phone in a surprisingly deep pocket of her unzipped gray hooded sweatshirt. In her other pocket are her car keys, which she has kept on her person since leaving Stonehill.

Natalie walks into the living room, her footsteps in sync with Paul's march on the gravel. She stops herself from calling out to him. He shouldn't walk so loudly; he needs to be more careful and soft-footed. Arms loaded with bundles [Dammit, yes, fine, they are "bundles"], he emerges from behind the car. The Forester's rear hatch remains open and the little hey-you-left-a-door-ajar dome light shines an obnoxious yellow inside the car. She considers yelling out to Paul again, telling him to shut the hatch.

Paul comically struggles to unlatch the fence's thigh-high entry gate without putting down any of the grocery bags. Only, he's not laughing.

Natalie is on the screened-in porch and whispers out one of the windows, "Can I get that for you?" She has an urge to laugh maniacally and an equally powerful urge to ugly-cry. She opens the screen door, proud that she dares stick her head outside and into the quarantined morning. She briefly imagines an impossible time of happiness and peace years from now, regaling their beautiful and mischievous child [she will insist her child be mischievous] with embellished adventure stories of how they survived this night and all the others to follow.

Natalie returns to herself and to a now of stillness and eerie quiet. Exposed and vulnerable, she's overwhelmed by the tumult within her and Paul's microworld and the comprehensive horrors of the wider world beyond their little home.

Paul mutters his way through swinging the creaking gate halfway open, where it gets jammed, stuck on the gravel [like always]. He shuffles down the short cement walkway. Natalie stays inside the porch and holds open the door until he can prop it open for himself with a shoulder. Neither knows what to say to the other. They are afraid of saying something that will make them more afraid.

Paul waddles through the house into the kitchen and drops the bags on the table. Upon returning to the front room, he over-exaggerates his heavy breathing.

Natalie steps into his path, grinning in the dark. "Way to go, Muscles."

"I can't see shit. Can't we open the windows or turn on a light?"

"Radio said bright light could possibly attract infected animals or people."

"I know, but they mean at night."

"I'd rather play it safe."

"I get it, but put it on just until I get all the groceries in."

Natalie whips out her phone, turns on the flashlight app, and shines it in his face. "Your eyes will adjust." She means it as a joke. It doesn't sound like a joke.

"Thanks, yeah, that's much better."

He wipes his eyes and Natalie leans in for a gentle hug and a peck on the cheek. Natalie is only a disputed three-quarters of an inch shorter than Paul's five-nine [though he inaccurately claims five-ten]. Pre-pregnancy, they were within five pounds of each other's weight, though those numbers are secrets they keep from each other.

Paul doesn't return the hug with his arms but he presses his prickly cheek against hers.

She asks, "You okay?"

"Not really. It was nuts. The parking lot was full, cars parked on the islands and right up against the closed stores and restaurants. Most people are trying to help each other out, but not all. No one knows what they're doing or what's going on. When I was leaving the supermarket, on the other side of the parking lot, there was shouting, and someone shot somebody I think——I didn't see it, but I heard the shots——and then there were a bunch of soldiers surrounding whoever it was on the ground. Then everyone was yelling, and people started grabbing and pushing, and there were more shots. Scariest thing I've ever seen. We're so——it's just not good. I think we're in big trouble."

Natalie's face flushes, as his tremulous, muted voice is as horrifying as what he's saying. Her pale skin turns red easily, a built-in Geiger counter measuring the gamut of emotions and/or [much to the pleasure and amusement of her friends] amount of alcohol consumed. Giving up drinking during the pregnancy isn't as difficult as she anticipated it would be, but right now she could go for a glass——or a bottle——of white wine.

What he says next is an echo of a conversation from ten days ago: "We should've driven to your parents' place as soon as it started getting bad. We should go now."

That night Paul stormed into the bathroom without knocking. Natalie was standing in front of the mirror, rubbing lotion on the dry patches of her arms, and for some odd reason she couldn't help but feel like he caught her doing something she shouldn't have been doing. He said, "We should go. We really should go. Drive down to your parents'," and he said it like a child dazed after waking from a nightmare.

That night, she said, "Paul." She said his name and then she stopped, watched him fidget, and waited for him to calm himself down. When he was properly sheepish, she said, "We're not driving to Florida. My doctor is here. I talked to her earlier today and she said things were going to be okay. We're going to have the baby here."

Now, she says, "Paul. We can't."

"Why not?"

"We're under a federal quarantine. They won't let us leave."

"We need to try."

"So are we going to, what, drive down 95 and into Rhode Island, just like that?" Natalie isn't arguing with him. She really isn't. She agrees they are indeed in big trouble and they can't stay. She doesn't want to stay and she doesn't want to go to an emergency shelter or an overburdened [*they said overrun*] hospital. She's arguing with Paul in the hope one of them will stumble upon a solution.

"We can't stay here, Natalie. We have to try something."

He puts his hands inside hers. She squeezes.

She says, "What if they arrest us? We might get separated. You were just telling me how crazy it was at Star Market. Do you think it's any better on the highways or at the state borders?"

"We'll find some open back roads."

Yes, back roads. Natalie nods, but says, "Maybe we're at the worst point now———"

"I didn't even tell you there was a fox staggering in the middle of the Washington Corner intersection like it was drunk———"

"———the quarantine will help get the spread of the illness under control———"

"———and it fucking dove right at my front tire."

"———everyone will be all right as long as we don't . . ."

Natalie continues talking even though there's the unmistakable sound of footsteps on their gravel driveway. Her ears are attuned to it. She's lived in the house long enough to know the difference between the sustained crunch and mash of car tires, the light, maracalike patter of squirrels and cats, the allegro rush of paws from the neighbor's dog, a goofy Rhodesian ridgeback the size of a small horse [a shooting star of a thought: Where are her neighbors and Casey the dog? Did they leave before the quarantine?], and the percussive gait of a person.

The steps are hurried, quickly approaching the house, yet the rhythm is all wrong. The rhythm is broken. There's a grinding lunge, a lurch, two heavy steps, then a hitching correction, and a stagger, and a drag. Someone or something crashes into the propped open gate and bellows out three loud barks.

After the initial shock, Natalie all but melts with relief, believing [or wanting to believe] what she hears is in fact Casey the dog. Shock turns to worry. She wonders why Casey would be out on her own. The guy on the radio said unvaccinated family pets could be insidious vectors of the suspected virus.

Natalie turns and she cranes her head and looks out the front door and through the porch. A large, upright blur passes by the small row of screened windows. The barks return and they are more like expectorating coughs, ones that sound painful. There is a man standing less than ten feet away from her. He opens the screen door, and says in a dry, scratchy, but clear baritone, "Fall came and it began to rain. Left out in the cold and rain." Then he grunts, "Eh-eh-eh," a vocalization that is all diaphragm and back of the throat.

Natalie and Paul yell at the man to go away. They shout questions and directions to each other.

The white man is large, over six feet tall and closer to three hundred pounds than he is to two hundred. He wears dirty jeans and a long-sleeve T-shirt advertising a local brewery. He steps through the door and fills their porch. With each coughing bark he bends and contorts, and then his body snaps back into an unnatural rigidity. He points and reaches toward Natalie and Paul. Natalie can only see the shape and contour of the man's face as he's silhouetted by the dim daylight behind him.

"Eh-eh-eh."

Despite her all-consuming fear, there's a nagging recognition of those primitive monosyllables buried in Natalie's ancestral memory. Hearing him is enough to know, without the aid of visual cues and without the context of the ongoing outbreak, that the man is sick. He is terribly and irreparably ill.

Natalie's fear morphs into a self-preservation shade of rage. Her fists clench and she steps forward and yells, "Get the fuck off our porch!"

Paul moves more nimbly and darts in front of Natalie. He swings the front door shut with enough force to rattle the frame and wall. His hand momentarily loses contact with the door-knob and he is not able to get the door locked before the man is already forcing it back open.

"Natalie?" Paul shouts her name as though it is a question, a question that is not rhetorical yet has no answer.

The door swings open, forcing Paul back into the house. The bottoms of his sneakers squeak as they slide over the wooden floor. Paul bends his legs, lowers a shoulder, attempting to gain purchase, to find the leverage he has lost forever. His feet stop sliding and they tangle, tripping him up. Paul falls onto his knees and the fiberglass door sweeps him away.

The man pushes the door fully open and presses Paul against the wall. He doesn't stop pushing. The man almost fully eclipses the white door. He is the dark side of the moon.

The man shouts, "I only want to speak! Let me in! Not by!" He yanks the door back toward him and then he smashes it into Paul. The man and the door become a simple machine, then a high revving piston. The impacts of the door into her husband and her husband into the wall make thudding, sickening, hollow sounds. Paul's screams are muffled. The walls and floors shake; the big bad wolf is blowing their little house down.

Natalie dashes the short distance into the kitchen. She knocks over a large blue cup half filled with the water she should've been drinking earlier, and she backhands the smart speaker out of her way while grabbing the chef's knife from the cutting block.

The front door slams closed. The volume of the men's shouting increases.

Natalie yells, "Go away!" and "Leave him alone!" and she runs back into the front room, knife held in front of her like a torch. Her eyes have adjusted to the dark of the house.

Paul is sitting on the floor and scrabbling to get his feet under him. Blood runs down his forehead and leaks from a wound near his right elbow. The man crouches over Paul, looms over him, an object of undeniable gravity. His great hands are clamped on Paul's shoulders and pull him into a bear hug. Paul's left arm is pinned to his side. With his free hand Paul punches and tries to push the man's face away from his. The man shouts indecipherable, plosive-heavy gibberish, and stops abruptly as though suddenly empty of the mad new language, as though he'd correctly recited an arcane ritual, and he bites Paul repeatedly. The bites are not sustained and are not flesh rippers. They are quick like a snake's strike. The man's mouth doesn't stay latched onto any one spot. In a matter of seconds he bites Paul's arm and he bites Paul's chest and he bites Paul's neck and he bites Paul's face.

"Let me in not by!"

The man's shirt is torn and stained red above his left shoulder, near his neck. Tremors wrack his arms and body. He retches and shouts a moaning variant of *no*. He shakes his head and turns away, appearing to be doing so at the sight of the blood, as though it upsets him, or angers him, but he doesn't stop biting.

Natalie charges across the room with the knife raised.

Paul gains his feet and both men stand and straighten. The man still has Paul's torso constricted within his arms. Paul lashes out one last time with his right hand, connecting with the man's eye. The man shrieks and barks and takes two steps forward, lifting and carrying Paul to the corner of the front room. The man drives his weight forward and down, mashing the back of Paul's head and neck into the thick oak seat of Natalie's mother's antique rocking chair. Upon contact there's a wet, pulpy pop and a sharp snap.

Natalie brings the knife down, aiming for the center of the man's back, but he turns, knocking her arm off its trajectory. The knife drags across his left shoulder blade, carving a parabolic arc through his shirt and skin.

The man pivots and is face-to-face with Natalie. He's middle-aged, balding, familiar in an everyman, nondescript way. He might be from the neighborhood and he might not. His face is contorted into dumb, inchoate rage and fear. His mouth is ringed in foamy saliva and blood. He shouts and Natalie can't hear what he is saying because she is shouting too.

She re-raises the knife and jabs at his thick neck. The man blocks the knife with his hands, clumsily pawing at the blade, earning deep slices on his palms and the pads of his fingers. He cries out but doesn't retreat. He grabs her wrist. His hands are hot and blood-slicked, and he pulls her into him, against him. She can feel the appalling heat of his fever through the tights covering her belly.

The man coughs in her face and his breath is radioactive. His cracked lips quiver and spasm, strobing out flashes of smiles and snarls. His tongue is an agitated eel darting between the oval of thick, viscous froth.

He is all mouth. His mouth opens.

Natalie leans away and simultaneously she knees his groin but without her weight under her, there's no leverage and there isn't much force behind the blow.

The man pulls her right arm above her head. He quickly latches his mouth to the underside of her forearm and he bites. Her thin sweatshirt offers no protection. She screams and drops the knife. She wants to shake and yank her arm away but she is also instinctually afraid to move and leave a chunk of herself behind. The crushing pressure combined with a sharp stinging burn at the broken skin, a pain unlike anything she's felt before, runs up her arm even after he lets her go and she stumbles backward and falls into a sitting position on the couch.

The man opens and closes his bleeding hands and he briefly but loudly sobs as though in recognition of what's broken in him and what he has broken. Then that bark. That fucking bark.

The man pivots and returns his attentions to Paul, who hasn't moved, who isn't moving. Paul is splayed on his back. His head is between the wide runners of the rocking chair and rotated toward the wall. The amount of rotation isn't natural, isn't possible. There's a bulge in his neck, the skin taut over a knotty protrusion, a catastrophic physiological and topographical error.

Natalie clambers off the couch, and despite the wildfire pain in her arm and the warning stitch in her lower left side she bends to the floor and picks up the knife. Her bite wound throbs, the pain expanding, radiating with each pulse.

The man lifts Paul and resumes biting and thrashing him about as though rushing through a menial task that must be completed. He bounces Paul's body off the door, the wall, and the rocking chair.

Paul issues no cries of pain. There is no voluntary motion.

Natalie sees a horrifying glimpse of the back of Paul's caved-in, deflated skull. The boneless slack with which his head lolls and dangles demonstrates beyond doubt that his neck doesn't work anymore, will never work again.

Natalie brings the knife down with both hands and half-buries the blade between the man's shoulder blades. She lets go and the knife stays buried.

The man groans and drops Paul between the rocking chair and wall. Some part of Paul's body gongs off the metal panel of the baseboard heater.

Natalie shuffles backward to the open front door. Her left hand digs in the sweatshirt pocket for her car keys. They are still there.

The man spins around unsteadily, reaching behind his back for the out-of-reach knife. He is a wobbling top nearing the end of his rotations. He is out of breath and the man's eh-eh-ehs are weakening huffs and puffs. His revolutions morph into a slow orbital path away from Natalie and the front door. He plods into the kitchen leaving a trail of red handprints on the wall to his right. His heavy, ponderous steps clapping on the hardwood floor become a shuffle and slide, as though his feet have transformed into sandpaper.

Natalie imagines nestling next to Paul's body in the corner of the room while he is still warm, and then closing her eyes and wishing, praying, willing the house to collapse upon them so that she never has to open her eyes again.

22

Natalie doesn't stay with her dead husband. Instead, she steps onto the porch on shaking legs. She holds her wounded arm away from her belly. She stifles the urge to cry out to Paul, to tell him sorry and goodbye. A cool breeze chills the sweat on her face.

As the sputtering big bad wolf disappears somewhere deeper into their little house, Natalie quietly shuts the front door behind her.

* * *

This is not a fairy tale. This is a song.

I.

THEY
BOTH WENT
DOWN

RAMS

Dr. Ramola Sherman has been a pediatrician at Norwood Pediatrics for three years. Of the five physicians on staff, Ramola earns the most new-patient requests. Locally, her reputation has gotten out: Dr. Sherman is thorough, energetic, kind, and imperturbable while exuding the reassuring confidence of medical authority all parents, particularly new ones, crave. The children are fascinated by her English accent, which she is not above exaggerating to pluck a smile from a sick or pained face. She allows her youngest patients to touch the red streak running the length of her long, jet-black hair if they ask properly.

Ramola was born in South Shields, a large port town on the northeast coast of England where the River Tyne meets the chilly North Sea. Her mother, Ananya, emigrated from Bombay (now Mumbai) with her parents to England in 1965, when she was six years old. Ananya teaches engineering courses at South Tyneside and is a polyglot. She mistrusts most people, but if you manage to earn her trust, her loyalty knows no bounds. She doesn't waste words and hasn't lost an argument in decades. She is shorter than her daughter's five-two but in the eyes of Ramola, her mother projects a much larger figure. Ramola's father, Mark, is a white man, nebbish-looking with his wire-rimmed glasses, face often shielded with one of his three daily newspapers, yet he is an intimidating physical presence with thick arms and broad shoulders befitting his lifelong career in masonry. Generally soft-spoken, he is equally quick with a joke as well as a placation. Hopelessly parochial, he has left the UK only five times in his life, including three trips to the United States: once for Ramola's graduation from Brown University, a second time five years later when she graduated from Brown's medical school, and a third time this most recent summer to spend a week with Ramola. The unrelenting humidity of greater Boston in July left him grumbling about how mad the climate was, as though the good citizens of New England had chosen the temperature and dew point. Ananya and Mark's infamous and quite possibly apocryphal first date featured a distracted viewing of *Close Encounters of the Third Kind*, a trip to a notorious pub, and the first match in what would become a playful if only occasionally contentious decades-spanning pool competition between the two. Both parents steadfastly claim to have won that first match.

It's late morning. Ramola finishes eating cold, leftover white pizza that has been in the fridge for four days, before video chatting on Skype with her mother. Ananya's image jumps all over Ramola's laptop screen, as Mum can't help but gesticulate with her hands, including the one holding her phone. Mum is concerned, obviously, but thankfully calm, and listens more than she talks. Ramola tells her the morning has been relatively quiet. She hasn't left her townhouse in two days. She's done nothing but sit on the couch, watch news, drink hot chocolate, and check emails and texts for updates regarding her role in the emergency-response plan. Tomorrow morning at six A.M., the second tertiary medical personnel from Metro South are to report to Norwood Hospital. Thirty-six hours ago all first tertiary were called in and assigned by Emergency Command Center unit managers. Now they already need the second wave of emergency help. Her being called in relatively soon after the first tertiary is not a good sign.

Ananya places a free hand above her heart and shakes her head. Ramola is afraid tears might be coming from one or both of them.

Ramola says she should go and read through the training protocols (she has already done so, twice) and so she can pack. She'll be working sixteen-hour shifts for the foreseeable future, and likely sleeping at the hospital. It's an excuse; her overnight bag is already packed and on the floor next to the front door.

Mum clucks her tongue and whispers a one-line prayer. She makes Ramola promise to be safe and to send updates whenever she can. Mum turns the phone away from her and points it at Mark. He's been there the whole time, off-screen and listening, sitting at their little breakfast nook, his elbows on the table, his meaty mitts covering his mouth, glasses perched on top of his head. His eyes always look so small when he isn't wearing his glasses. He's already been crying and Ramola tears up at the sight. Before she closes out the chat window, Dad waves, clears his throat, and in a voice coming from thousands of miles away, he says, "A right mess, innit?"

"The rightest."

"Be safe, love."

Ramola is thirty-four years old and lives by herself in a two-bedroom, 1,500-square-foot townhouse, one of four row units in a small complex called River Bend in Canton, Massachusetts, which is fifteen miles southwest of Boston. Her well-meaning parents encouraged her to buy the townhouse, telling her she was a well-paid professional and "of an *age*" (Ramola's "Thanks for *that*, Mum" did nothing to deter her from banging on with the hard sell) and therefore she should own property and not insist upon throwing money away on renting flats. Ramola regrets buying the place and feels foolish for allowing her parents, ultimately, to sway her when she knew better. Functionally, the townhouse has more space than she needs, or wants. The dining area of the large common room goes unused, as she eats her meals at the granite-topped kitchen island or on the couch in front of the TV. The spare bedroom/office has become the dusty storage/dumping ground for stacks of textbooks she can't bring herself to sell or let rot in a basement. The monthly association fees in conjunction with the high municipal taxes are more of a burden than she anticipated. With all the open space— the high cathedral ceilings, the second-floor loft overlooking the common area—the heating and cooling utility bills are twice as much as what she paid in her one-bedroom flat in Quincy. If that weren't daunting enough, Ramola faces twelve more years of suffocating medical school loan payments. She has confided in Jacquie and Bobby, two nurses at her office, that she doesn't feel clinically depressed when she goes home, she feels financially depressed. Jacquie and Bobby are her closest work friends despite their only having gone out together socially on a handful of occasions, usually to celebrate a birthday or impending time off due to the winter holidays.

The laptop is closed, the television turned off, her phone in her pocket. She knows she should leave one of the devices on, stay connected, but she also needs a break—even for just a few deep-breath-sized moments—from the news onslaught and its cat's cradle of conflicting information. The house is eerily quiet, making her too-large home feel downright cavernous as though the digital media light and noise fills physical, exterior space.

Should she check in with her neighbors? She doesn't know them well. On her right is Frank Keating, the recently divorced town selectman—the only things more relentless than his conspiracy-leaden political proselytizing are his four male cats who spray everything in sight. In the unit to her left is a late-middle-aged couple, the Piacenzas; empty-nesters with one adult son who frequently visits and referees their loud arguments. The first unit houses Lisa and Ron Daniels and their infant daughter, Dakota. Lisa is friendly enough, but always harried. Ramola has yet to have a conversation with her that didn't involve new-parent worries about the health of their daughter. Her husband Ron is subverbal, barely capable of a head-nod acknowledgment in the parking lot.

Ramola parts the curtains from her bay window and peers out at the small parking lot walled off from busy Neponset Street by a row of trees and evergreen shrub hedges. A breeze sends dead leaves skittering like mice across the pavement. She watches intently for other movement, any kind of movement. She hopes Frank followed the Wildlife Service's first recommendation (Bloody hell, how long ago was that? Seven days? Ten?) to keep all cats indoors. She doesn't realize she's holding her breath until she exhales and fogs up the window.

Ramola returns to the kitchen and wakes her laptop from sleep mode. No new emails. She enlarges the web browser with three open tabs. She refreshes the CDC's website along with mass.gov and CNN.com. The government sites have nothing new on their pages. CNN's panicked headlines and live-stream updates (including bloody images from overnight riots and looting of a shopping plaza in the affluent suburb of Wellesley) are alarming, overwhelming, and she closes her laptop again.

She thinks about what tomorrow will be like at the hospital and her head spins through worst-case scenarios. She closes her eyes and focuses on breathing deeply. She visualizes getting in her car, driving to either Logan or T. F. Green Airport and somehow boarding.

Returning to England has been Ramola's oh-I-give-up plan for as long as she's lived in the United States. She daydreamed about going home when she was stressed about her classes as an undergraduate and medical student, when she was a resident working eighty-hour weeks and came home too tired to even cry, during the fourteen months of her ill-fated cohabitation (his word) with Cedric and their tepid but never cantankerous relationship not so much falling apart as eroding under calm but relentless waves and tides, and whenever she was made to feel like an outsider, a foreigner. Ramola has always fought to persevere, to show herself and to show everyone else she can do it, and she has always fought to win (as her mum puts it). However, there is a small but undeniable part of herself that takes comfort in imagining the detailed journey home: landing in Gatwick, a train to Victoria Station, the tube to King's Cross, another train that rolls through the countryside, small towns, and swelling cities, and eventually to Newcastle, then a forty-minute Metro to South Shields, a two-mile walk (her rolling luggage listing consistently to her left), and it's warm and sunny even though it is never warm and sunny often enough in northern England,

and finally she's standing before their semidetached home with the brick walls and a white trellis, and she walks through the small garden and through the back door, then to the kitchen to sit with Mum and Dad at their ridiculous little table with the ugly yellow vinyl tablecloth and they both glance over the frames of their reading glasses and smile that wan I-see-you-dear smile. The final scene is so vivid that, as a younger woman, she luxuriated in the idea of her return truly having occurred in an alternate reality. As safe and as reassuring as the returning-home daydream is, it fills her with melancholy; a fear of the inevitability of mortality, as though if she allows the daydream to continue, it will speed into the future too quickly, one in which she and her parents remain rooted at the table, and it's there they will molder until the three chairs at the table go empty, one by one by one. All of which is why she has resolved to never move back home, financial stresses and everything and anything else be damned.

Ramola clucks her tongue at herself and says, "Now, that's enough of that," and picks up her phone. She texts Jacquie and Bobby in an attempt to rally their spirits and hers. It backfires dreadfully.

Text message

Oct 21, 2019, 11:37 A.M.

Ramola Sherman

Go team second tertiary tomorrow morning? I think someone should have t-shirts made. A sporting shade of grey, or a lovely shade of blue perhaps.

Jacquie Joyce

Yeah right. Sorry to spread hysteria but this is legit. Just watched the "Personal Protective Equipment Super-Rabies" 15 minutes training vid. Clicked through power point (a fucking power point!!!) This is trained personnel? We need legit Hazmat suits, right Ramola? Plain gowns & boot covers will not protect us.

Ramola Sherman

I'm not comfortable with the level of training either and I'm not comfortable with the conflicting info. Rabies mutation, increased virulence yet still spread via saliva is official word. But saw news speculating a new neurotropic virus? I realise it's an emergency but we should have proper PPE regardless as a safeguard.

Bobby Pickett

Boston's 5 major trauma centers struggling to handle it all but we will at shitty little Norwood hospital??? Yeah, right. I'm going to quit. My life is not worth that place. Especially as they don't even have a plan for us if we get infected.

Jacquie Joyce

I'm with u. feel horrible for two Beverly nurses attacked and infected and the fucking CDC press release saying it's their fault for not following protocol. Those nurses probably had our shit training! They were cardiac care nurses for fuck sake. Not trained for this.

Bobby Pickett

Always blame the nurse. So typical!!!! They didn't blame the doctors (no offense Ramola) in Boston who caught it. They were heroes! Are you all going into Norwood H tomorrow?

Jacquie Joyce

Yeah, I'm going. So fucking scared tho. Heard Good Samaritan in Brockton isn't taking any more patients.

Bobby Pickett

Shit. Norwood will be a zoo. Probably one already.

Jacquie Joyce

We really have cause to not take care of infected pt, we need appropriate gear and training and protection. The sickest ones get violent too right? Jesus fuck. Inf pts should be sent to Emory or Nebraska.

Ramola Sherman

No offense taken, B. Jacquie, you're right but rather sounds like it's too late and there are too many pts to transport.

Bobby Pickett

Even your texts have a brit accent, doc!;) I wonder how scared the ICU nurses are. I hope they at least got better training and PPE than us.

Jacquie Joyce

Friend Lisa at Norwood got a call around 9:30 From MICU. "R u trained for super rabies?" Lisa "no why?" MICU "just taking a poll"

Bobby Pickett

Bullshit! I should've stayed in New York. Where is our raise, btw? You can get infected but we will die before we get a raise! Ha!

Jacquie Joyce

You should've stayed in NY. Maybe we need to refuse as a group until we get right PPE.

Bobby Pickett

I'm on board. What has hosp ntwrk or the state or feds done to show they care about any of us?

Jacquie Joyce

We need to leak our "training" to the media and mention lack of PPE.

Bobby Pickett

It's ridiculous. We aren't equipped like CDC in Atlanta etc.

Jacquie Joyce

Lisa told me one pt of hers is one hour post exposure, fever and aches already. She said CCU is staff tonight, assigned by do-nothing Erin. You remember when she "consulted" at our office?

Ramola Sherman

I do. I would hope Erin is doing more than simply assigning.

Jacquie Joyce

We need to tell everyone that we have no clue how to handle this. That friggin news conference in Boston was all lies! Homeland security guy said area hosps all have appropriate staff and equipment. Jackass president tweeting same.

Bobby Pickett

Yeah we had 30 min "training" and then they made us sign a waiver. Good job in protecting their ass!!!

Ramola Sherman

You signed waivers? Oh dear.

Bobby Pickett

Mary couldn't explain to rest of us if even an observer should be gowned or not. Complete bs. Should let it be known we don't know what to do. It takes about 20 min to gown up. The cuffs on the jackets are permeable. We need serious support and equipment.

Jacquie Joyce

Waiver/sign sheet that u got "trained." She made sure we all signed them. Is Claire still in Cali? (I hope she is). Where's Mags? We ALL need a plan. We should not accept this. I am serious. Fucking assholes . . . Do not let ur kids see these texts, Bobby!

Bobby Pickett

Even though I have a mortgage to pay, my life is worth more. But I'll still go in tomorrow. Fuck. Us.

Jacquie Joyce

Yes it is. (And I know. You know I will too.) Mags doesn't need this shit. She has $

Ramola Sherman

Haha! I elect Jacquie as our team/office rep.

Jacquie Joyce

I elect Bobby as team cap. I swear too much.

Ramola Sherman

Bobby: You mean instead of "hurry up and finish training so we can go to lunch on time"?
I thought I knew you.;)

Bobby Pickett

Normally I'd be okay with that.

Ramola Sherman

Not to worry, Erin will properly assign you.

Jacquie Joyce

Hazmat suit wouldn't fit over her big dome anyway!

Ramola Sherman

That's just wrong, but brilliant.

Bobby Pickett

Bahahahahaha!!!!

An incoming call kicks Ramola out from the group text screen. Her phone fills with an image of herself alongside her dear friend Natalie. The photo is from Natalie's bachelorette party, which was six years ago. They are leaning on a wooden railing at a sun-splashed outdoor bar, their drinks raised and mouths wide with laughter. They are wearing white T-shirts with a cartoon caricature of Natalie's face above the ridiculous slogan "Nats Is Plightin' All the Troths." Ramola was volunteered by the group to explain what the shirt meant to inquisitive passersby, not solely because she is British, but because she is a doctor, which was part of her increasingly elaborate, drunken explanations.

At the sight of Natalie's face on her phone, there's a brief spark of guilt. Aside from a few stray texts, Ramola hasn't talked to Natalie since the baby shower two months ago. Ramola, ever practical, chose from a rather elaborate registry to gift a month's supply of baby diapers and wipes. Post-party, on her way out the door, she also gave Natalie a stuffed Paddington Bear along with a stack of books, joking the extra present was necessary for her to remain on brand.

"Hello, Natalie?"

"Oh thank Christ, Rams." The nickname is a holdover from their college days, and Natalie is the only person who continues using it. "I kept calling 911 and it wasn't going through. I—" She pauses and cries quietly. "Are you home? I need your help. I don't know what to do."

"Yes, of course. I'm here, Natalie. Where are you? Are you all right? What happened?" Ramola has the disorienting sensation of being outside herself, observing this moment from a temporal distance that has yet to be achieved or earned, and it's as though she expected this call and what is sure to be the delivery of devastating news.

"I'm in the car. Halfway there. I'll be at your place in five minutes."

Ramola runs to the bay window, throws open the curtains, exposing the view of the front lot. "Why aren't you at home? Are you having contractions?"

"I had to leave. Something terrible happened. I really need help." Her normally assured, insistent voice loses its force the longer she speaks so by the end of her third sentence she sounds like a timid child.

"I'm going to help. I promise."

Natalie whispers, "Ow, fuck," in a high-pitched voice, one that breaks into hitching sobs.

"What is it? Are you all right, Natalie? Do you need me to come to you?"

"My arm really fucking hurts." Natalie grunts as though attempting to reset herself. "We were attacked by some guy. He was infected. Paul was bringing groceries inside and we were in the living room talking, just talking, and I don't remember about what . . ." She trails off.

"Natalie, you still there?"

"Some guy walked in. He opened the screen door and walked right in our fucking house, and Paul tried to close the door on him, but he fell, and . . . And—and I tried to help Paul, and Paul—" She splinters into shards of tears again, but briefly recovers with a deep, wavering inhale. "The guy killed Paul and he bit my arm."

Ramola gasps, covers her mouth, and staggers away from the window as though she might see the scene described play out in the lot. What can she say? What can she possibly say to Natalie?

After the initial shock of the news dissipates, the clinical doctor in her brain takes over, wanting to know more about Paul, to ask if Natalie's sure he's dead. She wants to ask about the bite on her arm—did it break the skin?—and ask about the infected man, what he looked like, what symptoms he was displaying.

"Oh my God, Natalie. I don't know what to say—I'm so sorry. Please do your best to focus on driving until you get here. We need you in one piece."

"There's a chunk missing from my arm already."

Ramola cannot tell if Natalie is laughing or crying. "Yes, well, we'll get your arm cleaned up and we'll get you vaccinated."

Ramola is aware she's using the royal "we" she often employs with her patients.

"Rams, Paul is gone. He's gone. He's fucking dead. What am I going to do?"

"We're going to get you to a hospital. Straightaway." Ramola runs into the kitchen. From under her sink she pulls out a box of Nitrile gloves. They're from her clinic but she uses them at home for cleaning. Holding her phone against her ear with a shoulder, she puts on a pair of gloves and asks, "Are you close?"

"I just passed under the viaduct."

The granite-and-limestone Canton Viaduct is a two-hundred-year-old leviathan stretching seventy feet above Neponset Street. Ramola lives only a few blocks away.

Ramola says, "Are you feeling light-headed? Do you need to pull over? I can come to you." She plucks her handbag from the kitchen table, double-checks that her car keys are inside. Whether or not they swap vehicles there's no way she's letting Natalie drive anywhere once she gets here. Ramola pins her medical ID badge to the front of her sweatshirt. She's wearing plaid flannel pajama bottoms, her "comfy trousers," but she won't waste time changing out of them.

"I'm not stopping. I can't. I'm running out of time to get help, right? Aren't they saying the virus works fast?"

"You'll be here soon and we'll get you help. I'll stay on the phone with you. Or would you prefer to drive with two hands? Feel free put me on speakerphone or drop me if you need to, if it feels safer. I'm watching out my front window. I can wait on the roadside as well."

"No!" Natalie shouts and sounds to be on the verge of hysteria. "Do not go outside until I get there."

Ramola dashes to the linen closet and grabs two towels and slings them over her shoulder. Then it's back to the kitchen for a bottle of water and the half-full hand-soap bottle next to the sink before returning to the front door. She slips her bare feet into her jogging sneakers.

"Rams, what's all that noise? You're not going outside are you?"

"No. I'm gathering things, waiting by the door, stepping into my trainers."

"You don't still call them 'trainers.'" Natalie's voice goes little again, and it breaks Ramola's heart.

"I do because that's what they are." Ramola unzips the overnight bag, places the water and soap inside and resumes her window watch. "I won't go outside until I see you. That is a promise." Ramola opens her phone's text screen and scans through the group chat with Jacquie and Bobby, and pauses on the message about a patient already being feverish within an hour. The presentation of symptoms with this new virus is astronomically fast compared to a normal rabies virus. A typical rabies patient, when untreated, won't exhibit symptoms for weeks, sometimes even months. Beginning its journey at the bite or exposure site the virus slowly travels to the brain via the sheathings of the nervous system, progressing at a rate of one or two centimeters per day. Once symptoms present (fever, nausea, dizziness, anxiety, hydrophobia, delirium, hallucinations, extreme agitation), it means the virus has passed through the patient's brain barrier, which is the medical point of no return. If rabies enters the brain, there is no known cure, and the virus is nearly 100 percent fatal.

Lisa told me one patient of hers is one hour post exposure, fever and aches already.

One bloody hour. Natalie is indeed running out of time.

There are muffled bumps or knocks coming from the phone's speaker and Natalie sounds like she's at the bottom of a well. "Still there, Rams? I put you on speaker."

"Yes, I'm here."

"Do we need to switch cars? I've kind of bled on this one."

"That's not necessary as—" She stops from launching into an explanation of how the virus is transmitted via saliva and not transmitted through blood. There isn't even a blood test to determine if you have been infected. Multiple tests have to be performed on saliva, spinal fluid, and hair follicles on the base of the neck looking for rabies antibodies and antigens.

Ramola bounces on her heels, willing her friend's car to pull into the lot. "Usually I don't have to encourage you to drive over the speed limit, but you have my permission to do so, Natalie, as long as you—"

"I stabbed the guy. Right between the shoulder blades. I think I killed him, but I was too late to save Paul." Her "Paul" is a sputtering whisper, and then she explodes into semi-intelligible shouting and screaming.

Ramola tries to be reassuring, soothing, without lying that everything will be all right. "I know sorry isn't enough, doesn't come close to covering it, but I am so terribly sorry. You're almost here, yes? Then we'll get you help—there you are now. Brilliant. Park next to the walk and we'll swap seats. I'm stepping out the door now." Ramola does not wait for Natalie to respond and stuffs her phone into her overnight bag. She looks once into her empty townhouse to make sure she isn't leaving something important behind. Her laptop is closed, marooned in the middle of the kitchen table. She doesn't need it but a wave of sadness swells as she has the urge to call her mum and dad to say sorry for giving them the rush off the call earlier.

Ramola opens the front door and darts outside into the overcast and cooling day.

Natalie's white mid-sized SUV weaves through the small parking lot, tires squealing at the final turn, and jerks to a stop perpendicular to the end of the walkway. Ramola runs to the car. There is a consistent breeze and fallen leaves scurry madly in front of her feet.

The driver's-side door opens. Natalie growls with pain and swears.

Ramola calls out, "Do you need help?"

"I got it. I'm out." Natalie stalks around the car's front, her right hand on the hood for balance. Her belly is significantly bigger than when Ramola last saw her at the baby shower. Natalie cradles her left arm, bent up at the elbow. Her sleeve is dark with blood from forearm to wrist. Her face is slack, haunted, and all red eyes. She says, "This is really bad."

Ramola nods and clears her throat of whatever wavering, tearful greeting or response she cannot and will not give her friend. She says, "Come here. We need to get that sweatshirt off and clean where you were bitten." She flips the towels onto the car's roof, drops her overnight bag to the ground, and retrieves the water and soap bottles.

Natalie does as instructed, hissing as she peels the sleeve away from her wounded left arm.

"Bend your arm like this, make a muscle for me." There's a ring of small, ragged puncture wounds, surrounded by puffy, angry red skin. Natalie did not lose a chunk of herself; the man bit and released.

"Do we have time for this?"

Ramola doesn't know, but she also doesn't hesitate. She squeezes soap directly onto the wound and smears it around. "The rabies virus is not hardy and cleaning greatly reduces the likelihood of infection."

"But this isn't a regular rabies virus."

"No, it isn't." Ramola, a full head shorter, flashes a look up into Natalie's tear-stained face. Natalie doesn't return the look. She nervously scans the lot and its surrounding environs.

In the distance, a burst of dog barks is followed by a chilling high-pitched wail of a coyote. Prior to moving to this Boston suburb, Ramola never anticipated that coyotes were animals she might encounter. Their calls are oddly commonplace at night. She's never heard one cry during daylight hours, though.

Ramola chances a look over her shoulder at the townhouse complex. A curtain flutters in Frank Keating's front window.

Natalie says, "A rabid fox attacked Paul's moving car."

Foxes were Ramola's favorite animals as a child. She once famously scandalized a sitting room full of wine-drinking adults (her parents included, though they both were laughing as they admonished her) when she walked out of her bedroom, stuffed-animal fox in tow, intending to ask for a glass of water, but instead inexplicably announcing to the party that all fox hunters were toffs or tossers.

Ramola tries to banish an unbidden image of an adorable red fox, frothing and turned stumbling monster. She says, "We're just about done." Ramola flushes the wound with the bottle of water. She then wraps one towel around Natalie's forearm. "I have a sweatshirt in—"

"I'm not cold. We need to go." Natalie opens the passenger-side door and gingerly climbs inside.

Ramola strips off her gloves and tosses them to the ground on top of the bloodied sweatshirt, denying the urge to gather the contaminated material for proper disposal. She quickly dumps her bags into the backseat, and while doing so, she spies Natalie's own fully packed emergency overnight bag on the floor behind the passenger seat. Ramola grabs the second towel from the roof and runs around the rear of the car to the driver's door and opens it. She does a quick-and-dirty job of wiping the steering wheel, driver's seat, and the door's interior panel. She drops the towel to the pavement and climbs inside. The wipe-down job was not sufficient; the steering wheel feels damp in her hands. She can deal with her own risk of exposure later, after they get to the hospital. She admonishes herself for not wearing two sets of gloves. The exposure risk is minimal, given rabies is not blood-borne and the virus typically dies once the infected saliva dries, but at the same time, she needs to be smart, vigilant.

She's sitting too far away to safely manipulate the pedals. Ramola blindly fumbles with the lever beneath the seat, attempting to slide herself forward. Ramola feels her own level of panic rising as Natalie whispers, "We need to go, we need to go."

Ramola is about to give up and scoot her butt forward and sit at the edge of the seat when she finally pushes the lever down and the seat glides forward. She says, "All right. All right, here we go." She turns the key in the ignition and there's a terrible grinding sound from the engine, which is already running. Ramola's hands fly off the steering wheel as though having received an electrical shock.

Natalie says, "Maybe I should drive."

"Dammit. Sorry, sorry." Ramola shifts into drive and the SUV lunges forward. The vehicle is bulky and unwieldy in comparison to her nimble little compact, but she manages to guide it through the lot and onto Neponset Street. There are no other vehicles on the usually busy road. The Honey Dew Donuts, rows of small businesses, and the residences lining or facing the street are darkened and appear to be empty.

"How are you feeling?"

"Just peachy." Natalie holds her swathed left arm atop her belly.

Ramola pulls the seat belt across herself and buckles it. "Right. Yes. What I mean to ask—"

Natalie says, "I'm sorry. I'm just so scared. Thank you for being here, taking me to the hospital, thank you . . ." She trails off, stares out her window, shaking her head and wiping away tears with her right hand.

Ramola has the urge to reach out and pat Natalie's shoulder or thigh, but she keeps both hands on the steering wheel. "Of course I'm here for you, and I will be here for you all day." The sentiment is as odd and awkward as it sounds.

Ahead, the traffic light at Chapman Street turns red. Ramola eases off the accelerator and Natalie says, "Tell me you're not stopping."

"I'm not. Only making sure it's safe to pass through." Once she's confident there are no cars approaching from their right, she speeds through the three-way intersection. Ramola chances a look away from the road at Natalie, hoping for a comment if not a joke. Natalie continues to stare out the passenger window.

Ramola asks, "Do you have a headache, or any body aches aside from your arm, of course? Any flu-like symptoms?"

"I have a headache and my throat hurts, but I've been yelling and crying nonstop."

"Are you feeling nauseous? Do you feel feverish?"

"No. No. I feel like shit, but—I don't know—it doesn't feel like the 'flu' shit. I'm beat-up, and I'm probably just dehydrated." She adjusts her sitting position, turning her legs toward Ramola, and rubs her belly with her right hand.

"When we get to the hospital, what're they going to do?"

"You'll be examined and given the rabies vaccination."

"They have a new vaccine for this already?"

"They have rabies vaccine but it's not a new one."

"Is it safe for the baby?"

"I think it is safe, but I have to admit I don't know for sure if there are any associated fetal side effects."

"I want to fucking live, so it doesn't matter. That's not true, of course it matters. But I don't want to die for the—Jesus, that's so awful of me to say, isn't it?" Natalie rubs her right hand over her belly.

"No, of course not, and I'll make sure they do everything they can for you both."

The SUV crosses over the I-95 overpass. Below, the six north and southbound lanes are void of traffic. Ramola cranes her neck in both directions hoping to see cars but there aren't any. It's as though everyone has disappeared. A fleeting thought presents as a whispered question, a question not necessarily in search of an answer but instead posed to underscore disbelief at a suddenly unassailable truth: *Is this the end?*

Post-college, Natalie and Ramola roomed together in Providence for two years, during which time Natalie tended bar and seemingly read (*consumed* would be a more accurate verb, here) every YA novel featuring one apocalypse or another. On nights that Ramola visited Natalie at work, the two of them would playfully engage in animated and, judging by the attention of the surrounding bar patrons, entertaining debate about the end of everything. Natalie insisted that civilization was as fragile as a house of cards; remove one and it all will come tumbling down. All systems fail, and she claimed with the air of authority reserved for professors emeritus and bartenders, there was a theorem, one named after a famous mathematician (often, much to the mouthful-of-beverage-spitting delight of Ramola, Natalie casually named the theorem after Ian Malcolm, the fictitious mathematician from the book and film *Jurassic Park*), which proved as more "safeguards" are built into a system, it is not only *more likely* the system will fail, but, in fact, the system will *inevitably* fail. Her go-to example was a confusing amalgam of America's nuclear weapons systems, including the codes within the president's nuclear football, and the 1983 USSR nuclear false-alarm incident. Ramola opened her rebuttal by admitting humans were fragile little things as individuals, but civilization itself was hardy and resilient. Short of an asteroid or all-out nuclear war, she argued, societies have survived and would continue to survive all manner of calamity. Ramola pointed to countless countries/societies (both modern and ancient) that had suffered horrific natural disasters, catastrophic wars, collapsed economies, and/or dissolved governments whose citizens adapted and persevered. Ramola punctuated her rejoinder with a raised glass and a purposefully cheeky "Life finds a way."

The sprawling, empty highway below them is not the marker or portent of the end of everything. Ramola chastises herself for briefly indulging in the paralyzing enormity and hopelessness of apocalypse. It's natural to be scared, of course, but she cannot allow herself to be ruled by fear, which is the source and fountain of irrationality and poor decisions.

Ramola asks, "Do you know at what time, approximately, you were bitten?"

Natalie exhales deeply. Ramola assumes Natalie swallowed a snarky I-wasn't-looking-at-the-clock response. She says, "Oh Christ, a half an hour ago, maybe?" Before Ramola responds Natalie leans forward and grabs something from the cup holders within the center console. It's her cell phone, which remains attached to a battery charger plugged into the car's cigarette lighter. She says, "Paul texted me when he left the grocery store at"—her face glows in the phone's ghostly light as she manipulates and searches the screen—"11:15. He got home about five minutes later. It wasn't long, five more minutes or so, before we were attacked, and I—" Natalie pauses and clicks off the phone screen. "I don't know how long that lasted. It fucking felt like forever, but it was—I don't know—maybe another five minutes, maybe more, maybe less. The guy bit me before I stabbed him. Yes, definitely before. But then he staggered away into the house and I left, and I just left. Paul was—he was gone. So I had to go. Right? I didn't want to leave him there, but I had to."

"Yes, you did."

"I got to my car as quickly as I could and I called 911 a bunch of times but I wasn't getting through. I'd already heard earlier that Brockton Hospital was closed so I started driving toward Canton. It took me three tries before my call went through to you. So, wait, how long is all that?"

"Let's say that you were bitten at approximately 11:30." Ramola looks at the clock on the dashboard. It's 11:56.

"How long before it's too late for me?"

"I'm not sure. No one is. We'll get you treated as soon as—"

"You must know something. Tell me."

"All we know for sure is that the usual timeline of infection has been greatly accelerated. No longer weeks or days. The CDC reports that infection is occurring within a matter of hours—"

"But . . ."

"I didn't say 'but.'"

"You were going to."

"No, I wasn't."

"Rams! You have to tell me everything. What else do you know? What else have you heard?"

"I know of one patient who reportedly presented symptoms within an hour of exposure—"

"Fuck."

"But that quoted timeline wasn't corroborated. I don't know where she was bitten or how she was exposed or how far the virus had to travel within the nervous system to pass into her brain. The time of symptoms onset is dependent upon how close to the head the bite or exposure site is." Upon finishing she regrets allowing Natalie to talk her into sharing hearsay from a harried text exchange. How does that maybe-information help Natalie? She needs to be making better decisions than that.

Natalie says, "Please hurry."

"We're not far away now."

A few hundred yards ahead is the Neponset Street rotary, which passes over the Route 1 commercial highway. There are two state police cars parked at the entrance to the rotary, their blue lights flashing. Two officers standing adjacent to their vehicles are dressed in riot gear and carry automatic weapons. They hold up their hands, motioning the SUV to stop.

"Goddammit, we don't have fucking time for this." Natalie continues ranting and swearing as Ramola stops in the mouth of the rotary. She opens her window.

The officers slowly approach, flanking the SUV. The barrels of their weapons are pointed at the ground but neither removes a hand from the gun.

"Ma'am, I need to ask where you're going. We're under federal quarantine and the roads are to be used in the event of an emergency only." A white respirator covering the lower half of his face muffles his voice. According to emailed procedures Ramola received the previous evening from the infectious disease specialists and chief medical officer at Norwood Hospital, the N95s were to be distributed and fit-tested only to medical personnel identified as being at the highest risk to exposure. What the police officer is wearing is more likely a painter's mask picked up at the Home Depot about a mile down Route 1 South. As nervous as the automatic weapon makes Ramola, she's more bothered by the mask, which doesn't bode well regarding the clarity of communication between local government agencies and emergency-responder groups.

Natalie shouts, "We're going to the hospital! I'm injured and wicked pregnant. Can we go now, please?"

The officer at the window attempts to respond, but Ramola politely interrupts him. "Excuse me, Officer, I'm Dr. Ramola Sherman"—she pushes her medical ID badge toward him— "I'm taking my friend to Norwood Hospital. She's more than eight months pregnant and was bitten by an infected man approximately thirty minutes ago. She needs immediate medical attention. May we pass through?"

The officer blinks rapidly as though having a difficult time processing the information and the dire implications. "Yeah, okay, Doctor. Head to the emergency-room entrance on Washington Street. Do you know where that is?"

"Yes."

"You can take either Washington or Broadway to get there, but you can only use the emergency entrance. All other entrances have been closed." He steps back, says some sort of code into his two-way radio attached to his chest harness, and waves his arm as though there's traffic behind them waiting for the go-through signal.

"Thank you, Officer." Ramola eases off the brake and they creep forward. "Can you call ahead, give them my name, Dr. Ramola Sherman, and tell them to expect us?"

Natalie groans and whisper-shouts, "Just go, come on, let's go!"

"I will but I'm not sure there will be anyone available to greet you."

Ramola accelerates onto the rotary. Three more on-ramps, the remaining points on a compass, are similarly roadblocked by state police. Unlike eerily empty I-95, there is traffic below the overpass on Route 1, its double lanes a glorified path between car dealerships, box stores, strip malls, and themed restaurants. As they pass the on-ramp to their right, cars queue from the highway's southbound lanes.

Natalie says, "You're not stopping again—"

"I'm not stopping."

Officers wearing the same painters' masks wave the SUV through the rotary's west exit and onto Nahatan Street. They pass a warehouse on their right and an apartment complex on their left, a cluster of two-story brick buildings squatting around a three-quarters-full parking lot. Ramola does a double take as someone darts through the lot and disappears among the buildings.

Natalie asks, "How long do you think it'll take to get me in, get me seen? The rinky-dink hospital is probably fucking jammed."

"I can't say for sure, but I'm confident we'll get you in quickly. It won't be anything like a normal emergency room with check-in and then sit and wait, and all that. There is extra staff and there will be a triage set up outside the emergency-room entrance to help with patient screening."

"I don't doubt you, but how do you know this?"

"I received the hospital's emergency-response information sheet last evening. I was scheduled to report there tomorrow morning."

"Lucky you get to go in early for Take Rabies-Infected Preggo to Work Day. It's going to be a shit show when we get there. I know it is."

"I'll personally escort you through the shit show."

"I'd hug you with my bitey arm if I could."

Ramola reaches across the center console and squeezes Natalie's thigh. Natalie covers her mouth with the back of her right hand, still clutching her cell phone. She says, "I-I was going to check my phone for a text from Paul," and cries silently.

They motor past four blocks of tree-lined streets and small Cape houses. The crowded residential area gives way to a shopping plaza. Its sprawling parking lot is vacant but for a dusting of cars. A portable traffic message board sign and trailer squats in the plaza's main entrance. The rectangular display message, in big yellow letters proclaims:

ENTER HOSP VIA WASH ST EMERG ENTRANCE ONLY

Across from the plaza are the Norwood fire and police stations, which marks the eastern border of downtown Norwood. Ahead is a set of lights that normally rotates through the green-yellow-red spectrum, and is instead flashing yellow; proceed with caution. There are no police directing traffic. There is a stopped car in front of them that has yet to pass below the commuter-rail overpass. It is part of a growing line of vehicles at least three blocks long.

Natalie says, "Fucking great. What are we going to do? We're still like a half mile away, right? Is there another way we can go? Are they blocking off other routes? We're never going to get there. What if they already closed the hospital? It's overrun. It's fucking overrun. I know it is."

Ramola attempts to assuage Natalie by saying, "We don't know that. We're still moving. We'll get there." She's feeling similarly panicked. She doesn't know the answers to Natalie's more-than-reasonable questions.

Traffic creeps ahead. Natalie taps the passenger window frame with her hand and chants a *"Come on, come on"* mantra.

Ramola squeezes the steering wheel and she needs to say something, anything, to keep one or both of them from completely freaking out. "How are you feeling? Any change?"

Natalie shakes her head and swears under her breath. She turns on the radio and an AM Boston news station blares at high volume. She says, "We should try the phone. Who can we call at the hospital? You must know who's in charge. Let's call them, and give them your name, ask them what to do, but yeah, we probably can't call because the phones are still fucked, like we're all fucked."

Natalie talks fast and her voice schizophrenically alternates between a low, almost distracted grumble and a manic, high-pitched incredulity. Granted, the circumstances are more than a little extraordinary, but in all the years Ramola has known Natalie, she has never sounded or acted like this. Has the virus already passed into her brain? Could it possibly work that quickly?

Natalie rolls down the window and yells, "Come on, let's go. Drive, you assholes, drive!" She is breathing heavily and her cheeks are flushed red.

Ramola says, "Please, Natalie. You need to try to remain as calm as you can." She thinks about asking if Natalie's blood pressure has been normal throughout her pregnancy, but for the moment it's probably best not to bring focus to other potential ailments. "Let's listen to the radio in case there is new information or instructions."

Natalie closes the window and resumes her tapping on the doorframe. The radio announcer repeats the quarantine protocol and teases an updated listing of emergency shelters and hospitals to be read in two minutes.

They roll slowly between granite walls and then from under the shadow of the rail overpass. Nahatan Street splits and expands into two lanes. Both lanes are full of cars, crawling uphill, into the heart of Norwood Center, toward Washington Street. Perched at the top of the hill is the old stone-and-mortar

Unitarian church, the spire's gray shingles reaching into the grayer midday sky.

"*Come on, come on.*"

Ramola says, "A few more cars and we can turn left on Broadway. Looks like everyone else is going to Washington Street, but the officer said we could—"

An engine revs and the car behind them lunges into the opposite lane. It roars past their SUV and three other cars ahead of them and turns sharply onto Broadway. Ice broken, other cars from behind buzz into the opposite lane and pass them on the left.

"Go, Rams, you have to go. Now!"

"I am. I'm trying." Ramola edges out into the lane cautiously and a continuous blur of cars emerge from the darkness of the overpass and swerve as they pass.

"Go, go now!"

Ramola spies what she hopes is enough of an opening in the passing traffic and darts into the opposite lane, cutting someone off. The grille and hood of a red, full-sized SUV fills her rear-view mirror. Its blaring horn reverberates, but not as loudly as Natalie screaming at them to fuck off.

They turn left, onto Broadway. The other cars that passed them have accelerated on the open road ahead. There isn't a procession of stopped traffic like there is on Washington Street. Ramola says, "Okay, okay, we're almost there." They speed past a McDonald's and a large liquor store on their left. As she takes in the landmarks and spins through quick time-and-distance calculations to the hospital, a black sedan spills into their lane from a side street on their right. Ramola jerks their SUV into the opposite lane, barely managing to avoid a collision.

Two-family homes and small businesses whiz by on the periphery for three blocks but ahead is another dreaded sea of brake lights. They are quickly pinned within the bottleneck.

Natalie looses another expletive-filled tirade.

Ramola says, "We're close. We're so close," which she knows sounds less reassuring and more like a lament of defeat. She cranes her head in an attempt to peer over and around the gridlock. This isn't the slow but steady creep of traffic in the town center; no one is moving. Ahead in the opposite lane are the flashing blue lights from a parked police motorcycle.

They can't wait for the traffic to magically clear. However, their car is almost parallel to a ubiquitous Dunkin Donuts to their right. Ramola says, "Can you walk?"

"Walk?"

"We're only two blocks away."

Natalie nods and adjusts the position of her injured arm. "I can definitely walk. Are we leaving the car here?"

"Not *here* here." Out of force of habit, Ramola flicks on her right directional for a moment but then shuts it off, afraid of starting another rush of cars from behind that would fill the coffee shop's small parking lot, its entrance still more than ten meters away. She turns into a hard right. There's a loud thump and a jostling jolt as the squealing tires climb over the elevated sidewalk curb.

"Jesus, Rams? What are you doing?"

"Sorry, sorry. Parking at the Dunks." Her use of local slang for the doughnut shop is intentionally awkward, as she hopes to elicit, if not a laugh, at least a smirk. She slaloms past a thin metal pole and No Parking sign and navigates the sidewalk for twenty or so feet before turning into the square, half-full parking lot, choosing an empty spot closest to the entrance/exit.

"You stay put until I can help you out of your seat." Ramola opens her door and bounces out of the vehicle before Natalie has the opportunity to argue with her. The world outside their SUV is cacophony and cool air. Ramola was right to worry about setting off a mad rush as the cars behind her joust for space on the sidewalk and in the lot. Determined and with her head down, she dashes around the back to the passenger side, opens the rear door, and retrieves their two bags, slinging them both over her right shoulder. Natalie opens her door, cell phone still clutched tightly in her right hand, and Ramola helps her out of the car and into a standing position.

"You can do this." She hopes the affirmation is prophecy. Natalie is more than a half foot taller and likely fifty pounds heavier; if she is going to fall, there isn't a lot that Ramola can do to keep her upright.

Ramola coaxes Natalie into depositing the cell phone into her bag. With her newly unencumbered hand, Natalie holds her injured arm out in front as though carrying an invisible shield. Ramola loops her left arm through Natalie's right.

Instead of walking through the main part of the lot, which is now full of cars jockeying for spots, they change course and work their way past the front grille of their SUV. They follow a thinning path along the lot's perimeter, shimmying single-file between cars and a chain-link fence, and to the sidewalk.

They link arms again and Ramola asks Natalie how she is doing.

"We're good."

Crowd noise swells, although not the buzz that greets one entering a sporting event or concert that's generally accompanied by a vibe of euphoric giddiness at having peacefully gathered to share a pleasant, if not fleeting, experience, while winking at potential dangers associated with the ludicrous number of people amassed. There's an altogether different feel within this throng of fear-fueled and panicked hundreds racing to Norwood Hospital, one that raises gooseflesh and fills Ramola with the urge to flee screaming.

People abandon their vehicles in the middle of the street. Others lean and pound on their ineffectual horns and shout through cracked-open windows. They plead and they are confused and angry and afraid. Desperation and realization lurk within their collective voices. They don't understand why or how this is happening; why it is that their personal emergency is not more important than anyone else's; why no one is out here helping them.

Worried slinging the overnight bags over her shoulder might've knocked loose her medical ID badge, Ramola double- and triple-checks it is still affixed to her chest and is plainly visible. Finding it in place, she wonders if someone might snatch it from her, thinking they could somehow use it to gain entrance into the hospital.

There are sirens in the distance, approaching from somewhere behind the standstill traffic. Cars hop over curbs and beach themselves on the congested sidewalk. Clusters of people break like cascading waves around the sputtering mechanical carcasses. Everyone moves in pairs or packs, molecules bonded together by held hands, by arms entwined or draped around shoulders. The rhythms of their individual gaits are not in tune and they inefficiently half walk/half jog forward toward a hope they cannot see.

Ramola holds on to Natalie's wrist as they trudge forward.

There is enough space for them to walk side by side. Ramola jogs two steps for every four walked to keep pace with Natalie, who walks faster and with longer strides despite her increased girth and accompanying waddle. They follow Broadway and cross Guild Street, weaving between stopped cars and passing an elderly couple. The hunched gentleman walks erratically and is draped in a blue-and-white fleece blanket. His wife taps his shoulder and repeats his name as though it were an unanswerable question.

Instead of continuing along Broadway, which traces the boundary of the medical campus and leads eventually to the emergency-room entrance, Ramola darts in front of Natalie and leads her through a quick mart and gas station adjacent to the hospital's physical plant and then into the outpatient parking lot. Here they encounter steel crowd barriers plastered with arrow signs pointing left and handwritten signs that read: *Rabies exposure patients via emergency entrance only*. A small group of police and other security personnel stand by the barriers and wave Ramola and Natalie away from the outpatient entrance, which is directly across the lot.

Having the single entrance is an attempt to control the traffic of infected patients and reduce the risk of their spreading the infection to the other hospital populations. Ramola knows better but she is desperate to avoid the crowd, so she shows one of the officers her medical badge and asks to be let into the hospital here. She fumbles through explaining she is reporting for duty, is a part of the second tertiary support, in addition to her tending to Natalie's emergency medical needs, a thirty-eight-weeks-pregnant woman who shouldn't be made to stand and be tossed about by the gathering mob. The man shakes his head the entire time she talks, eventually cutting her off. He points to the left, to a group of blue Zumro tents more than one hundred paces away, erected in front of the emergency-room entrance. He says if either of them has been exposed they must go through triage and screening. As she protests further the man ignores her, and he loudly repeats the instructions and points at the tents for the oncoming stream of people behind them.

Natalie says, "Fuck this, come on, Rams," and walks toward the tents.

Ramola is left openmouthed for a moment, holding her badge out toward the indifferent officer. She says, "Wanker," and then sprints to catch up to Natalie.

They approach the edges of a ring of humanity, ten to twenty rows deep, expanding out from the tents. There are four of them, ten feet in height, each the approximate width of a two-car garage and at least thirty feet long. They are stacked, side by side. Ramola cannot see through the crowd or over the tents to the emergency entrance's sliding glass doors. This morning Ramola gave a cursory read to the hospital's seventy-four-page Emergency Response Plan thinking she would read and reread it more thoroughly later in the evening. The tents are where they've set up triage and where everyone will be screened prior to entering the hospital. Medical personnel and service ambassadors in white coats, gloves, hair caps, N95 respirators, and green scrubs (decidedly not Hazmat gear) carry clipboards and flit from person to person like hummingbirds, serving as pre-screeners. They could be informing patients waiting to be seen for issues not related to the viral outbreak that they are to use a different entrance or perhaps they are being turned away; it's likely that non-epidemic-related services have been suspended.

The crowd grows and presses forward heedlessly. Arguments rage over who is first in the formless line. Everyone is shouting. Bullhorns and police radios crackle with static bursts and unintelligible commands. Off-campus, sirens cry and cars stuck on Broadway and Washington continue to blat their horns. As unnervingly apocalyptic as the desolate, empty lanes of I-95 were earlier, this scene confirms Ramola's worst fears.

"Is everyone here sick?" Natalie asks.

"I don't know." Is it possible this number of locals have already been infected? As Ramola scans the crowd she does not see anyone presenting the most obvious and worst symptoms of rabies.

"What are we—"

Ramola grabs Natalie's right hand. "We're going in."

Natalie's eyes are wide, the skin around her eyes is swollen and so deeply red as to be almost purple. She looks beat-up. She looks sick. Natalie says, "Don't lose me."

"I won't."

Ramola has given up on approaching a police officer or security guard for help, and she does not want to waste precious time in chasing down one of the frazzled medical staff, all of whom have seemingly disappeared. She walks directly into the crowd, sternly projecting in her best schoolmarm voice, an impressive one both in tone and volume. It is a voice Natalie has only been exposed to once, back during their sophomore year when Ramola accepted a late-night bribe (free pizza) to excoriate, anonymously via the telephone, a too-noisy-for-finals-week room on the dormitory floor above theirs.

"Excuse us! Let us through, please. Doctor coming through. I'm here to help but we must be let through. Let us by. Doctor coming through. Thank you. Let us through, please . . ." Ramola steps between people if they aren't paying attention. She taps arms and shoulders of others and if they turn to face her, she doesn't break eye contact until after they step aside. She leverages the bags slung over her shoulders to force a wider opening for Natalie. Stink-eyes and annoyed looks from the crowd soften, some turning to fear, at the sight of clearly pregnant Natalie gamely trailing behind, wounded and wrapped arm held against her chest like a bird might hold a broken wing. There are murmurs and complaints but those come from behind, from people who are not directly in their path.

Navigating becomes more difficult the closer they get to the tents, and some people attempt to engage Ramola, detailing symptoms, pleading with her to examine a loved one. Ramola apologizes and tells them they will be helped soon, and she does so without lingering but not without twinges of guilt. She and Natalie continue to push their way through until they come up against another set of the waist-high, steel crowd barriers that cordon off the tents.

A young police officer, as tall as a folktale, stands over an entry gap between steel barriers. Instead of asking for permission or instruction, Ramola points at the officer, then points at her badge. She shouts, not to him but *at* him, "We're coming through." The officer shrinks under her glare and dutifully drags one end of a barrier back, opening a gap for their passage.

Pausing briefly beneath the wide arch of the tent's entrance, Ramola looks at her watch. It's 12:17 P.M. If one hour postexposure is indeed how long it takes this virus to travel up the nervous system and pass through the brain barrier, they don't have much time left.

Natalie is breathing heavily and looking back at the boiling pot of people behind them. "Are they going to be able to help everyone?"

Ramola says, "Yes," although she doesn't believe it.

They step into the tent's spacious interior. The whir of heated air blowers drone; the air itself oscillates between warm and cold. A lane splitting the tent down the middle is being kept clear for passage and foot traffic. Eight white, square-shaped nylon curtains hang from ceiling beams and partition spaces along both side walls, creating ten patient triage/screening cubicles. Each space has an overhead lamp clipped to a wall joist, a small medical treatment table, and a rolling cart with two shelves loaded with assorted supplies. All the cubicles, as far as Ramola can see, appear to be occupied with patients. Ramola doesn't recognize any of the medical staff in the tent, as she and her coworkers from the pediatric clinic aren't supposed to report for duty until tomorrow.

A skinny, middle-aged white woman with thinning hair, wearing yoga pants and a light, high-end jogger's jacket, emerges from a screening area with her foppish husband in tow. An orderly herds them out of the rear of the tent and toward the hospital proper. Judging by his puffiness, he's gowned to within an inch of his life (a joke from her residency days Ramola can't help but recall, though it was clearly more endearing and humorous in non-outbreak circumstances), sporting at least two sets of scrubs and coats.

The woman's right hand is wrapped in gauze and her face covered in a white mask. She yells to her husband, but purposefully loud enough to be heard by anyone within earshot. "We have to wait three days for the next shot? Can you believe that shit? Three days. Three drops of blood. No room service. Bed-pans and lookie-loos, my ass hanging out of a johnny. I don't want to go in there. I want to go home and die." The rhythm of her sentences is off, landing somewhere in an aural uncanny valley populated by the first iterations of computer text-to-speech programs.

A police officer emerges to aid the orderly in escorting the couple into the hospital.

A short, stocky woman pulling on new gloves steps out from the same screening area and walks toward them. She squints at Ramola's ID badge and says, "Hello, Doctor? Are you just getting here? Have you checked in with the Command Center yet? It's inside, check in at the emergency waiting area—"

"My friend needs help first."

As Natalie walks into the recently vacated cubicle and sits at the edge of the lowered treatment table, Ramola quickly introduces herself to Dr. Laurie Bilezerian (her name is written in script directly on her lab coat as well as the phrase "family medicine"), and the doctor introduces herself to Natalie, insisting she call her Laurie.

Ramola explains that Natalie was bitten by an infected man approximately fifty minutes ago and she's thirty-eight weeks pregnant.

"Okay. Dr. Sherman, can you glove up and unwrap Natalie's arm?" Dr. Bilezerian places the long, tapered temperature probe, which is tethered to her hand-sized electronic thermometer, in Natalie's mouth. "Please hold this under your tongue and keep your mouth closed."

Ramola puts on one glove and then freezes in place as she can't help but watch Natalie and the doctor watch each other as they wait for the temperature reading. Dr. Bilezerian's white mask presses tightly against her cheeks, indenting the bridge of her nose. A tuft of black hair leaks from under her cap, graffiting her wide forehead. Natalie holds her breath without being asked to. All three women are motionless. Chaos churns outside the tent.

The thermometer beeps three times.

Dr. Bilezerian removes the probe and reads the digital screen, "Ninety-nine point two." Her voice clipped, sharp. She turns away and disposes of the probe's plastic cover.

Natalie says, "I'm fine. That's not a fever. I tend to run hot."

"It's within the range of normal," Ramola says, and puts on her second glove.

Dr. Bilezarian nods, says a solemn, "Yes, it is," and returns the thermometer apparatus to the supply cart and prepares a needle.

Natalie shivers as Ramola unwraps her arm. They lock eyes and Natalie offers a preemptive explanation. "It's cold out. I'm cold. I only have this thin, damp shirt-dress on."

"I'm sorry, I should've given you my sweatshirt earlier."

"Don't be sorry. You don't have to say sorry to me for anything ever again after today." Natalie wipes tears. She flinches and grimaces as the last of the towel is pulled away from her arm.

Ramola says, "Laurie, prior to wrapping the wound I cleaned with water and hand soap. It should be cleaned again with Povidone."

From her spot hunched over the supply cart, Dr. Bilezerian says, "We'll get you all cleaned up and tended to, Natalie. Have you ever been previously vaccinated for rabies, pre- or post-exposure?"

Natalie shakes her head and says, "No, never." Her right leg bounces up and down nervously, right foot tapping on the step-stool below the examination table.

"Roll up her sleeve, expose her shoulder for me, please, Doctor. Okay, Natalie, this first shot is human rabies immune globulin; it slows the virus down, keeps it from attaching to the nervous system until the vaccine can get in there and help your body make its own antibodies. Both the globulin and the vaccine are safe for you and your baby."

"Oh, good. Great. I'm . . . Thank you, Doctor. Sorry, um, Laurie." Natalie looks at Ramola and then away, and away from her belly, down at her jittery leg. Ramola assumes she's feeling guilty for what she said earlier about not caring if the vaccine was safe for the baby. Ramola wants to shout, *No!* and hold Natalie and tell her that she is the one who doesn't have to apologize, doesn't have to feel sorry for anything, not after all that's happened to her.

In a screening area across from theirs, a medical staff member has a needle in her hand while another grapples with a small, late-middle-aged man. His tan oxford shirt is dotted with blood, so too the mottled skin of his neck. He shouts, "No!" and as he loses the wrestling match, his shouts become mewling cries. Whether it's intuition or that dastardly enemy, fear, taking the reins again, Ramola believes, for the first time today, that it is too late for Natalie, they won't be able to help her, and in a matter of hours, she'll be gone.

Dr. Bilezerian says, "This is going to hurt, I'm sorry, but it's most effective when administered in and around the wound. Try to keep your arm as relaxed as you can."

Laurie swabs the puncture wounds, most of which have

already scabbed over, with iodine, staining Natalie's forearm a coppery brown. Ramola offers Natalie the crook of her arm instead of her gloved hand. Natalie takes it. She turns her head and looks away as the doctor inserts the needle and injects globulin at three sites. Natalie squeezes Ramola's arm with each stab of the needle, but otherwise doesn't react until it's over, and then she releases a large, wavering exhalation.

The doctor covers the wound with a gauze pad. "We're all done with that. You're doing great, Natalie."

Natalie releases Ramola's arm, pats her belly, and exhales deeply again.

Dr. Bilezerian swabs Natalie's shoulder with an alcohol wipe and holds up a second needle. "Next is a shot of vaccine. This won't hurt as badly. I promise. It feels more like a flu shot."

"Ooh, those are my favorite." Natalie half laughs and half cries, and her mischievous smile remains. Natalie already appears less vacant, less hopeless. Ramola has never felt more proud of her friend, or more bone-crushingly sad for her.

"Right? You could do this all day," the doctor says as she injects the vaccine. "And we're done."

Ramola swaps spots with Laurie and sets to affixing the pad and wrapping Natalie's forearm with more gauze. She considers asking the doctor what the efficacy of this treatment has been during the outbreak. Have they had many or any successes in preventing exposed patients from succumbing to the viral infection? She doesn't want to ask in front of Natalie, not yet anyway. Ramola has always believed physicians should be forthright in sharing information with the patient, or in the case of her charges, their parents, no matter how dire the prognosis or uncomfortable the conversation. As Ramola's sinking, hopeless feeling can be measured in fathoms, perhaps it's not Natalie she's protecting from hearing potentially devastating news.

Dr. Bilezerian removes her gloves, picks up a two-way radio, and asks for an available orderly to bring a wheelchair.

Natalie says, "I don't need that. I can walk."

"I think you've walked enough. You need to rest, get some fluids, and think healthy thoughts." She hands Natalie a piece of paper. "This lists rare but potential side effects you might experience. It's marked with the date and time, and that barcode sticker corresponds to both the globulin and vaccine you received. You'll be given a bracelet inside, too, with the same information but you definitely should hold on to this as a backup. I'm sure you noticed things are a little hectic out there. If all goes well, which I'm confident it will"—at this her voice increases in volume, she turns to look at both Natalie and Ramola, and she places a hand on Natalie's shoulder; with the mask covering all but her eyes, it's impossible to tell if she's smiling or frowning or any one of a thousand complicated expressions in between— "you'll be back here or be assigned to go to another treatment center for the follow-up vaccine booster in three days. You cannot get one before then, okay? Getting the second shot too soon will compromise the immune response. Now, you may need that paper to ensure you get the second shot. They'll explain this process to you again inside. Do you understand? Good. And while we wait I need to take down some information as well."

Natalie gives her name, address, date of birth, cell phone number. When asked for an emergency contact she says, "I don't— my husband, Paul, was killed. He died less than an hour ago."

The doctor pauses typing on her medical tablet computer. "Oh my God, I'm so sorry."

Natalie shakes her head, silently saying no to everything. She points at Ramola and sputters through a flash flood of tears. "She's my emergency contact."

Dr. Bilezerian asks what their relationship is.

"Friend," Natalie says.

As Ramola digs through her overnight bag, hunting for her yellow zip-up hooded sweatshirt, she recites her cell phone number.

"Is there anyone else you'd like to list as an emergency contact? Any immediate family or—" Dr. Bilezerian peters out as though coming to the too-late realization that there is no good or happy answer to her queries.

Natalie shivers and gingerly flexes her left arm. "I don't know if any of this, any of what we're doing, even matters. I'll pretend it does."

Ramola says, "It very much matters, and we're going to keep you healthy. And the baby, of course." She stumbles over herself to include the nameless child.

Natalie says, "I'll add my parents as contacts. They are in Florida. They sit in their condo all day and watch Fox News and complain about the humidity when they're not arguing or forgetting to eat."

Dr. Bilezerian asks for their names and information and Natalie obliges.

Ramola drapes the sweatshirt across Natalie's back and over her shoulders. "You can take that damp jumper off once we're inside."

Natalie says, "I don't think I can squeeze into this."

"It's surprisingly roomy. I swim in it."

"Yellow, huh?" Natalie laughs.

"Well, it's my—"

"I know yellow is your favorite, but this is really fucking yellow. If I zipped this up I'd look like a pregnant banana."

"Only if you wore matching bottoms. I'd say you look more like a lemon."

"Don't argue with the pregnant banana."

An orderly appears in the cubicle with the wheelchair, and without missing a beat, says, "I'm here to help a, um, pregnant banana get in out of the cold."

Natalie says, "All right, I'm the only one who can call me that." She slides off the table and settles into the chair.

Dr. Bilezerian helps Natalie put on a white respirator mask, explaining that exposed patients are wearing them out of an abundance of caution. She reminds Ramola where the Command Center is, instructs the orderly to take good care of her patient. She says, "Goodbye, Natalie," and wades back into the tent's bustling concourse.

The orderly says, "It's ugly out here. Think they'll let me stay inside with you ladies?"

As they wheel Natalie from the screening area Ramola notices the middle-aged man in the cubicle across from them is gone and has been replaced by an older one, pointing at the back of his hand. She overhears the doctor—who un-gloves and crosses his arms—saying, "I don't see any broken skin. I know—but you're the one who told me she's an *indoor* cat. . . ."

Outside the tent and its numbing drone of the heater, the

chilled air nips at exposed skin. The surging roar of the crowd returns, angry at having been ignored for the duration of Natalie's screening.

Inside the hospital they run a frenzied but well-organized gauntlet through checkpoints and hallways. Ramola is identified, briefly screened, and allowed to accompany Natalie after donning scrubs, gloves, and a lab coat. She does not remain behind in the ER's waiting area, which has been reserved for visitors and family members of patients in which the infection has taken hold. Those patients are being treated in an isolation ward.

Ramola and Natalie are brought to the second floor and the department normally reserved for patients recovering from hernia and weight loss surgeries, procedures that were the first nonessential services suspended by the hospital. This ward is one of four areas reserved for monitoring people who have been exposed to the virus and have received the globulin and vaccination but have yet to exhibit symptoms of infection. They wheel Natalie to a private room, though a nurse tells her that it might not be private for long. The nurse takes her temperature again and tells Natalie they are going to continue to take her temperature every fifteen minutes until she is symptom-free for six hours, at which point she'll be released. Her temperature remains at 99.2 degrees. Her blood pressure is 125/85, which is slightly higher than normal.

When Natalie asks what will happen if she begins to present symptoms, the answer is: try not to worry about that unless it happens. Natalie says that isn't good enough, as she's speaking for two. The nurse apologizes and promises Dr. Kendra Awolesi, who is working directly under the incident commander and chief medical officer, is on her way up to meet with them and discuss such protocols.

The nurse and the orderly leave. Natalie and Ramola are by themselves.

Ramola looks at her watch. 12:43 p.m. Natalie is now over an hour post-exposure, if their original estimate is accurate. Despite her having received the prophylaxis, this time marker has the ominous weight of both possibility and inevitability; from here on out, anything can and will happen.

Natalie asks, "Aren't you going to wear your mask?"

"When I checked in I was informed the mask was not compulsory in this wing. And I'd prefer you see my smiling visage."

Natalie slides her mask off her face. She parrots Ramola's "visage," elongating the soft *g* of the last syllable. She repeats the word again, as though reminded of something.

"Accent needs work."

"You're so mean. My French is impeccable."

"Oh, that's what that was?" Ramola smirks and wanders to the windows, which overlook a gridlocked Washington Street: flashing blue-and-red lights, National Guard troops working to keep one lane open for emergency vehicles, more and more people walking.

"Nice view?" With a mechanical whir, Natalie raises the head of the bed so that she is in a semi-upright position.

"Not particularly." Ramola fusses with the curtains.

Natalie lowers the bed, then raises it again.

"Having difficulty getting comfortable?"

"I won't be comfortable until after the kid is birthed—God, what a painful-sounding word—and isn't sitting on my bladder or kicking me in the kidneys."

Ramola is pleased she references a time after her child is born. Any positive talk of the future is a good thing.

Natalie grabs the side rails and pushes up as she twists her hips. She winces and grabs her left forearm. "Fuck, that hurt."

"Want me to put a pillow behind your back, would that help?"

Natalie waves her off. "No. Well, okay. Let's try it. Thanks, that's actually better. Hey, when this other doctor gets here we'll talk about what to do for my baby if I get sick, right?"

"Yes, of course."

"Do you know—"

There's a knock on the partially closed door and Dr. Kendra Awolesi walks briskly into the room. She has brown skin and is in her mid-to-late forties. While about the same height as Natalie, she is more slightly built. She wears a blue hair net and her respirator mask dangles around her neck. After a courteous but brief introduction she matter-of-factly informs Natalie that she is recommending they perform a cesarean section to deliver her baby within the next two hours. If Natalie were to begin presenting clear symptoms of infection, they would still perform the procedure, and remain reasonably confident that the baby would be not be infected.

"'Reasonably confident'? Is that like a medical shrug?" Natalie asks.

Dr. Awolesi is direct and does not break eye contact with Natalie. "The latest from our area's infectious disease specialist is that we are dealing with a rabies or rabieslike virus, one expressing increased virulence by the greatly shortened incubation period. Normally, the virus advances along at one centimeter per day as it travels up the nervous system to the brain. This one, as I'm sure you know, is moving exponentially faster. Regardless, the virus is not blood-borne and it will not pass through the placenta to the baby while you are infection-free. We know the post-exposure prophylaxis you received is safe for both the mother and fetus, but there isn't a lot of medical literature out there regarding what happens if a woman at your stage of pregnancy succumbs to rabies, or this rabieslike infection, and begins to shed the virus in her saliva. As I said, we are confident the baby would remain free of infection, but we don't know for how long, as there are no case studies available to refer to."

"Okay, okay, let's get the kid out as soon as we can, yeah?"

Dr. Awolesi nods. "As of eight A.M. Norwood Hospital ceased providing all other services beyond accepting patients who have been exposed to the virus. Right now there are two general surgeons in the building, and they are both occupied with cases they cannot leave. We have contacted Dr. Danielle Power, an obstetrician, and have sent a police officer to pick her up and escort her to the hospital. She should be here within the hour. While it's preferable for Dr. Power to perform the procedure, either general surgeon is certainly more than capable and qualified if one of them is ready before she arrives."

"Yes, of course. Whoever is ready first, I'll be ready. Thank you, Doctor."

Dr. Awolesi says, "Don't tell anyone, but you and your baby— does the baby have a name?"

"No, I mean, we have names, but we—we didn't find out the sex."

"You and your baby are our number-one priority today. We've already given you a private physician to be by your side." She smiles. "Is it okay if I steal Dr. Sherman for a minute? I would like to give her today's briefing and cover the highlights of our general emergency response, especially as she is due to officially join us on staff tomorrow morning."

"Yeah, okay. Please don't go far."

Ramola says, "We'll be right at the door, and we'll leave it open."

"Oh, hey, Rams, can you give me my cell phone? Or you can just put my bag up here, because I want my charger too."

Ramola says, "Yes, of course. Are you going to call your parents?" She places the night bag next to Natalie.

Dr. Awolesi says, "A text is much more likely to get through. The cellular network is getting crunched with the surge in calls."

Natalie says, "Right. Believe me, I know. Maybe I'll text them, I don't know." She lifts the phone out of her bag, holds it up. "I have this pregnancy diary app thingy on it. Voyager. *Voyageur.* See, there's my impeccable French, Rams. And yeah, anyway, I'm going to talk to my kid on it."

NATS

I've recorded and deleted four tries at this. This is number five. Math, right. Five is not my lucky number, by the way. It's nineteen. That'd probably be a weird thing to remember about your mom, but also kind of cool. Maybe.

If I'm not around to play this for you, which is probably the only reason you'd ever listen to this, then I'm sure someone will give you a, um, fuller explanation as to what this is, or why I'm recording messages for you. Sorry, but there's no good way to intro this, to explain why I have to do this. I mean, I'm doing this because your dad was killed and I'm sick. I might get better but I might get awful, terrible sick, and very quickly. I'm not even a mom yet and I'm already not telling you things to protect you, but if you're listening, those things have already happened. Let me try again: Your dad was killed by a guy infected by a weird new super rabies and the same guy bit my arm. There's a good chance I'm going to die from it, maybe even before the day is out. There. I said it.

You're squirming all around as I'm recording this. Good timing, kiddo.

I'm doing this because I want you to hear me. I want you to know my voice. Maybe even know a little bit of who I am, you know? And I want you to know my lucky number, apparently.

So, yeah, hi there. It's me, Mom. That sounds so weird and fake to me. I haven't had any chance to get used to me being called that, so it doesn't seem real. I have been talking to you for months now. We have excellent conversations. They're one-sided, but you're a great listener. And I haven't once referred to myself as "Mom." This wouldn't really apply to you until you're older, like, at least a teen, but don't ever refer to yourself in the third person. Only assholes do that.

I totally planned on making you call me "Mom." Wait, is "making you" too harsh? How about, "encouraging you," then? Hey, look at me being all nurturing.

Anyway, I'm cool—yeah, so cool I have to tell you that I am cool. That's almost as bad as talking in the third person. But I wasn't going to be one of those, like, too-cool moms with kids who call her by her first name. I can't stop you, but I'd prefer you not call me Natalie. Or Nats. I do like Nats though, especially when your dad or Ramola says it, but for you, I'm Mom. And definitely not "Ma." Nothing worse than "Hey, Ma!" in a Boston accent. And I insist you have a Boston accent.

Here I am, going on about what to call me and I'm not calling you by your name. That's messed-up. I'm sorry you don't have a name yet. Well, you have one now, whenever it is you're listening to this, but you don't have one in my now. Shit, I'd be so bad at time travel.

That's another thing you should know about me: I like to swear. I won't give you a fake example of me swearing, it'll just come out I'm sure.

I'm sorry about your dad. We were, um, attacked—I tried to help him but I couldn't. He's a beautiful man. The kind of man who would crinkle up his face like he smelled something bad if someone told him he was a good man. He always said he was still a kid. I wanted to be there to call BS on him still saying that when he was an old man; he totally would've.

Two months ago I got all fired up to take a bath. I texted Paul from work that I was going to take the bathiest bath. He asked why I was "taking the bath and please bring it back when you're done." Not funny but funny. At dinner we talked nothing but bathing and *the* bath. Then it was time. I had on my fluffy robe and everything, but I sat on the toilet crying because the tub suddenly seemed so dirty. Normally I don't care about that stuff and, please, I'm more of a slob than Paul is, but right then, I was convinced the tub was dirty, like unhealthy filthy, and it meant that we weren't ready, we weren't capable of being parents, or doing right by you, and I didn't want Paul to hear me so I cried into my hands, but he heard me, and he came in and held me and I don't think I explained myself very well because I could barely speak. He led me out into the kitchen and made me a cup of hot chocolate, and then he cleaned the tub and the rest of the bathroom, cleaner than it had ever been, and then he ran a bath for me, which I didn't even want anymore.

I hope you look like him. I hope you look like me, too, but him especially. He was a beautiful man.

I'm back, sorry. I don't want you to hear me crying. Judging by how you're kicking me, you don't want to hear me crying either. I know I have limited time and space, and whatever, and I don't want to take up any of it with me crying. Not that there's anything wrong with crying, please don't think that. It's way healthier to share your emotions and not bury them—like my mom and dad, your grandparents; shit, can you even follow this? Don't think I'm cry-shaming you. Please, I'm a crier. Full-on ugly-crying, tears and snot everywhere. I'm like a sprinkler. Say it like this: sprink-lah. Do you even know what the hell that is?

There's some other alternate universe where you and I are together, and I'm crying in front of you all the time, like once a day minimum. I'm not saying I'm a mess, I just don't hide how I'm feeling. Okay, swearing and crying, maybe I am a mess. But I mean who doesn't cry at kids' movies? The first five minutes of *Up* kills me every time.

So in the other universe, the one where we're together, we'd be laughing a lot too, don't get me wrong. There are all these times where I'm saying or doing the silliest things to get you to laugh. Like my mom used to randomly say "sassafras and lullabies" to get a laugh out of the baby me. I don't remember it, but I kinda do. And there are times where I'm singing you goofy songs and you and I are laughing so hard that I'm crying too.

Goddammit.

I hope you're in a good place. I hope you aren't scared.

I didn't plan this very well. This is a spur-of-the-moment decision. I'm just going to keep talking until Rams or Dr. Awolesi comes back in. They're still outside the room talking about stuff they don't want me to hear. I don't feel very good, physically, but as long as my temperature stays normal, I'll pretend I'm okay. My arm hurts and my head is fucking pounding.

Sorry, I shouldn't drop the f-bomb, but that's exactly how my head feels.

Hey, speak of the Rams. Say hi, Rams.

"Hi."

That was exciting, wasn't it? We'll talk again later. I won't promise, but I promise. Hey, I love you. I do. Don't forget that.

RAMS

Ten years ago Ramola was in her second year at Brown Medical School and Natalie tended bar at the Paragon, a trendy Thayer Street restaurant one block from the Brown University bookstore. They shared a two-bedroom apartment, a second-floor unit of a three-family house on Hope Street. None of the rooms had doors (only curtains), and the floor of their small kitchen was pitched, sloping distinctly, if not alarmingly, downhill toward the rear of the apartment. On quiet nights they sat on placemats on the kitchen floor, drank wine, ate sharp cheddar cheese, raced runaway rolling coins down the linoleum pitch, and talked. Sometimes they talked about the meaningless and ephemeral, which turned out to be—for Ramola—the more memorable nights; Ramola playing devil's advocate and setting Natalie on rants about iced coffee (coffee should be molten hot), the toe that does the least amount of work (the one next to the baby toe, of course), and a short-lived campaign to rename one of the seven days without using the word "day." Some nights they discussed more serious subjects, including careers and their families. Ramola most often voiced her anxieties concerning the pressures of medical school, the financial insecurities of what lay beyond, and fearing she would allow the pursuit of her career to narrowly define who she is and would be. Natalie's fraught if not outright toxic relationship with her mother was her recurring topic. Both women would offer advice, when needed, but more often than not, their shared roles as the supportive listener was enough and was, ultimately, what both parties wanted. Ramola is more homesick for those wine-laughter-and-occasionally-tear-filled nights on the kitchen floor than she ever was for her childhood home.

Natalie had been dating Paul for about six months when he showed up unannounced at the apartment one night. Natalie was at work, but Ramola was home studying; her books, notes, and an array of highlighting markers and pens were spread out on her bed. Paul walked into the apartment carrying a wilted and wet fistful of daises. He gave Ramola a side-eye and a smirk, one that was somehow cocksure, nervous, and totally Paul, as he announced he was there to talk to Ramola, and, surprise, the flowers were for her, not Natalie. Years later Paul admitted (to no one's shock or surprise) to liberating the flowers from a window box he passed on the walk over. Ramola didn't know what to think other than whatever it was Paul had to say couldn't be good. They sat on the sheet-covered couch and he stammered through an aimless recounting of his relationship with Natalie. Ramola demanded he get to the point, as she had to get back to her studies. Her tone was harsher than what was warranted, but it reflected a sinking dread she couldn't control, much less recognize. He was there to ask Ramola's blessing for Natalie and him to live together. Ramola without hesitating or even blinking said, "Christ, I'm not her bloody mum. You don't need my permission." Ramola was annoyed; she knew this meant she would have to find a new place or a new roommate. What she wanted to say was, *No, you can't have my Natalie.* She never did, technically, say yes or give her blessing, something Paul pointed out years later. Truth be told, at the moment he asked, she wanted him and his stupid flowers to go away and she wanted to pretend the discussion hadn't happened. She wanted to tell him it was a bad idea, that he was moving too fast and he might scare Natalie away, which wouldn't have been true. After the initial shock and jealousy were beaten back and inner-monologued away, Ramola was able to express happiness for Natalie and Paul, who indeed made a lovely couple.

It's impossible for Ramola to imagine the awkward but charming young man from that bittersweet night in her favorite place on earth, and the wry, only slightly older one he became, is dead.

Ramola remains in the doorway to Natalie's room, the gatekeeper, the half-closed door resting against her hip. She says to Dr. Awolesi, "I haven't pressed Natalie for details. She is adamant her husband, Paul, was killed by the infected man who bit her."

"How did Natalie get away?"

"She fought him off with a knife. She thinks she might've killed him."

Dr. Awolesi stands in the hallway. The radio in her front coat pocket crackles and she pauses to listen, but does not retrieve the radio or respond. She pulls another handheld radio device from inside her coat. "There are only two channels. One is open to all staff and security personnel. Channel two is direct to me and other members of the coordination center. You can switch channels with this knob up top. And you press this button to speak."

Ramola accepts the radio, turns it over and back, inspecting it as though she is well familiar with its circuitry.

Dr. Awolesi says, "There was another option for Natalie and her baby: sending her to Ames Medical Clinic, which is where pregnancy services for Norfolk County are currently being routed. Our infectious disease specialist ultimately decided against moving Natalie, worried the risk of introducing the virus within that clinic's population is too great. I disagreed, and if we aren't able to perform the cesarean section within the hour, and if she remains symptom-free, I might stick you both in an ambulance and send you there."

Ramola says, "We had the radio on and didn't hear about the Ames Clinic or the cessation of services within this or any other hospital."

Dr. Awolesi doesn't respond but holds Ramola in her gaze.

Ramola says, "I'm not saying it's your or anyone else's fault, of course. I'm only telling you—"

"Communication between government and emergency-response agencies has been less than ideal. Everything has been happening so rapidly, but the lack of clear communication with the public has been making the coordinated efforts less efficient, shall we say. Up until the last twelve or so hours, the vast majority of the people arriving here were not infected, had not been exposed, and were sent home. Because of what they're reading online we were inundated with people who believe the virus is airborne, who believe this is some kind of Hollywood zombie apocalypse, thinking their headaches and colds are proof of infection, or that they caught it because their dog sneezed on them. I'm not making that last one up."

"I'm sure you're not."

"Most of the information being broadcast has been focused on fighting general misinformation about the virus and the response, and it's almost impossible to keep up.

"While the speed with which this virus infects is terrifying, it shouldn't prevent us from containing it. If anything, given how quickly people succumb to the virus, if we can maintain a proper quarantine and isolation, we should be able to contain the outbreak. But that presumes people do not panic, that correct information and instruction are disseminated efficiently to the public, that the federal government follows the CDC's recommendation to be proactive with vaccine, and not reactive. Animal culls and other reactive rabies approaches are not nearly as effective as vaccinating populations prior to infection. We should be offering prophylaxis to whoever comes through these doors."

"Do we have enough vaccine to do that?"

"No, we don't. We're almost out, in fact. And to my knowledge the federal government has yet to enact an emergency vaccine-production protocol. I am going to send someone up to give you a pre-exposure dose, however."

"Save it for someone—"

"Keeping staff healthy is a priority. Particularly as we're probably an hour away from shutting the doors and quarantining the building. Which is another reason I'm tempted to send Natalie to Ames. If the building is quarantined, she cannot be moved."

"Right." Ramola nods. "Right. Well, we'll all do our very best with what we have then." She jumps as her radio spews a blast of static followed by a terse message in medical coding.

"Do you have any questions, Dr. Sherman?"

"Yes, I do. How many beds in this hospital?"

"Officially, two hundred sixty-four."

"How many patients are currently in the building?"

"We're approaching four hundred."

"Where are you keeping infected patients?"

"Third floor."

"Any particular department?"

"The entire third floor." As though anticipating the follow-up questions, Dr. Awolesi tells her given the level of violence that infected patients present, for their own safety and the safety of others, they are administered sedatives as soon as their fever spikes.

Ramola asks, "Of those who have received the vaccine, how many have not succumbed to infection?"

"There are upwards of fifty patients on this floor, including Natalie, being monitored for infection."

"Yes, but have you discharged any exposed patients, confident that the vaccine prevented infection?"

Dr. Awolesi says, "Not nearly enough."

"Can I have a number?"

"Two," Dr. Awolesi says, and then exhales sharply. "Two. Both patients were bitten on the lower leg. The virus had the longest possible distance to travel and they received shots within thirty minutes of exposure."

Ramola floats unsteadily into the room, Dr. Awolesi's words and their implications a fuzzy white noise in her head. She is not sure what to do with the radio in her hands. After everything she heard, she wants to shut it off and stomp it to pieces.

Natalie says, "Hey, speak of the Rams. Say hi, Rams."

"Hi." Ramola waves, flustered, unsure who the greeting is

for. She cannot recall why Natalie wanted her phone, though remembers she did state it was for a reason other than contacting her parents.

Natalie's mask sags limply on the table tray. She holds the phone away from her ear and faces the screen. "That was exciting, wasn't it? We'll talk again later. I won't promise, but I promise. Hey, I love you. I do. Don't forget that." She jabs the screen once, places the phone down on her bed. "They gave you a new toy?"

"What? Oh yes." She pockets the radio as though embarrassed to be holding it. "Who were you talking to?"

"I told you. I was recording messages for my kid. Just in case I don't make it. I feel better saying that out loud. Is that weird? I think it is, but it doesn't feel weird."

"Please don't talk like that. You're going to beat this—"

"Rams, your brown skin has gone whiter than mine. I'm guessing Dr. Awolesi didn't have much in the way of good news. But listen, I'm emailing you my username and password for the app while I can. Wireless still works here at least."

"All right, but you don't have to—"

"This is fucking important to me, okay? I'm sorry, I'm not swearing at you. I'm swearing at"—Natalie waves both arms in the air—"everything. Ow." She eases her left arm back down to the bed. "Anyway, if I die and the rest of the fucking world doesn't, which it probably should—yeah, I'm saying that out loud too—if I go, then, fuck yeah, why not everyone else? Except you, if you want. I don't need to take you down with me. Just everyone else."

"Natalie . . ."

"I need you to make sure my kid gets to listen to my messages.

And my maybe-dying wish is for you to call me Nats, please. You sound *so proper* when you say Natalie." She mimics Ramola's accent when saying "so proper."

"We're going to fight, and the rest of the world isn't going to die. Dr. Awolesi and I were in fact discussing how—how containable the virus is."

"Containable."

"Yes, that's a word you use, isn't it?"

"Oh sure."

"Yes, well, things are darkest before the dawn."

"Oh, Jesus, we're so fucked." Natalie is smiling and appears to be on the verge of laughter. The earlier muting of her personality has swung one hundred eighty degrees into manic levels of Natalie. Is this how she is coping? Is her hyperactivity a symptom of infection?

"Natalie."

"Nope."

"My dear Nats, is that better?"

"Much. Hey, did you read this list of vaccine side effects?" She waves around her vaccination information sheet. "Pain, swelling, redness at the injection site. Check. Headache. Check. Nausea, muscle aches, abdominal pain, dizziness, fever. Something to look forward to? Um, aren't all those the symptoms of infection?"

"Those side effects are exceedingly rare."

Natalie rescans the page and points to its lower half. "It says 'rare.' Nowhere does it say 'exceedingly.'" She tosses the paper toward a plush visitor's chair and before it lands, she says, "Can you get me some water? Sink water is fine."

Ramola goes to the bathroom, shares a despairing look with

herself in the mirror, and fills a small blue plastic cup. Water dribbles over the rim as she carries it out to Natalie.

"Sorry, I shouldn't have filled it to the top."

"Okay. Watch me, please." She holds the cup at an arm's length away from her body. She glowers at it, like she wants to give it a talking-to. She brings it up to her mouth, leaving it there only an inch or so away from her lips. She lifts the cup to her nose, cocks her head, and side-eyes the water. She finally takes two small sips, and then large, greedy gulps, spilling water down her front. "Oops."

"What are you doing? Should I be concerned?" Despite herself, Ramola laughs softly.

Natalie wipes her chin and neck with a corner of the bedsheet. "Testing for—what do they call it?—hydrophobia. I read all about it last week. People with rabies get freaked out by water. Like they can't even go near it, never mind drink it."

"Drink-management issues aside, you don't appear to be hydrophobic."

"The water tastes and smells like hospital sink water, which is to say, not good, like water that's had pennies soaking in it, and I'm not happy my shirt is wetter than it was, but no hydrophobia."

"Let's get you into a dry shirt."

"Shouldn't I just change into a johnny? They're going to prep me soon for the C-section, right?" Her two questions are contained in a single breath. She doesn't give Ramola a chance to answer. "Wait, I have to pee first." Natalie clambers out of bed and walks to the bathroom.

With the bed and room newly empty, Ramola wipes her face with both hands. To prevent parting the curtains, staring out the window, while repeating the feckless mantra of *What are we going to do?,* she sets to searching the room for hospital gowns. She mutters instructions and observations to keep herself company. Sometimes new gowns are stacked above the dirty-linens hamper, but there are none. She opens two swinging doors of a tall, thin wardrobe locker on the wall across from the foot of the bed, which is bare but for a small stack of folded pillowcases.

A nurse raps hard twice on the door and enters, announcing she has vaccine for Dr. Sherman. Though most of her face is obscured by a respirator, she appears to be young, likely under twenty-five years old. Ramola has been recently noticing the decreasing ages of newer staff within her clinic, or more correctly, noticing her own increasing age. Ramola asks for gowns for Natalie. Nurse Partington says she'll ask at the nurses' station on her way to the elevators.

Ramola sits at the edge of the bed, removes her coat, and rolls up a sleeve. There is no chatter or banter as Nurse Partington twice tells Ramola to relax her arm, then administers the shot with a tremulous hand. Ramola holds a square of gauze against her shoulder as the nurse prepares a bandage. She wants to ask what's going on in other areas of the hospital, what's the morale of the staff. She fears the tightly wound, fatigued younger nurse might break apart at the questions. Or maybe it would be Ramola who would crumble in the face of the answers.

Intent on breaking the awkward silence, Ramola asks, "Will I need a second shot in three days like Natalie?"

"Pre-exposure vaccination follows a different course: a booster in seven days and a final one twenty-one days after that."

Ramola says, "Seven days." She cannot imagine what will have happened seven hours from now, never mind seven days.

Ramola thanks her and puts her coat back on. Nurse Partington nearly jogs to the door, throwing it open. She almost collides with three people sprinting down the hallway toward the nurses' station and elevators. Nurse Partington falls in behind them and the door swings closed but doesn't latch. There's inarticulate shouting somewhere on their floor. Ramola estimates the source is five to ten doors down from this room. It's a man, shouting in anger, not pain, and there's a crash, and more hurried footfalls on the linoleum.

Natalie emerges from the bathroom. Her eyes are red and her cheeks flushed as though she has been crying. "What's happening?"

A quick message bursts from Ramola's radio: "Code Gray, third floor. Code Gray, third floor."

Natalie asks, "What's Code Gray?"

"It means a combative person."

A man announces over the intercom: "Paging Dr. Gray to the third floor . . ."

Ramola says, "Same announcement. Sounds less scary for patients when broadcast over the intercom that way."

"Third floor? Um, sounds like there's a combative person on *our* floor. We are on the second floor, right? I'm not delirious yet am I?"

"Maybe he announced the wrong floor."

There's a room-shaking crash directly above their heads. Ramola and Natalie drift toward the bed, their eyes on the ceiling as though expecting it to crack open and reveal its secrets. Ramola jumps when her radio squawks again; security personnel speaking in numerical codes with which she is unfamiliar.

"What do you think that was?"

Ramola can only imagine something as large as a wardrobe locker being pulled from the wall and tipped over.

A different voice comes over the intercom. "Paging Dr. Silver to the second floor . . ."

Natalie says, "Silver?"

"A combative person with a weapon."

"Fucking great."

Outside their room the shouting continues. Metallic clangs and jolting thuds add to the cacophony.

Natalie asks, "Is our door locked?"

Ramola rushes to the door, but she opens it first, daring to peek down the hallway. From this vantage, only half of the nurses' station is visible. A short and stout man with a long, thick beard is behind the main desk. The beard (and the distance) obscures most of his mouth but the teeth. The teeth are bared. He brandishes and swings an IV stand. He snorts and shouts as two officers circle, their stun guns drawn. Ten feet away from the desk and at the mouth of the hallway, a young woman thrashes about on the floor. She's pinned on her stomach, a scrum of security and medical staff grapples with restraining her hands behind her back. She screams and growls, whipping her head from side to side, her long brown hair spraying in every direction. The woman looks up, hair partially obscuring her face. Ramola can see the woman's eyes though. Her gaze locks onto Ramola and her features soften, eyebrows arching into an everyday expression of recognition, of I-see-you-and-do-I-know-you, but then her eyes roll back, showing whites, and her lips curl into an animal's snarl, a single-minded statement of purpose. She stretches and cranes her neck, hair pasted to cheeks and chin. Her mouth opens and snaps shut, over and over, teeth clacking.

Foamy drool darkens her hair, runs down her chin, pools on the linoleum.

Ramola shuts the door, pressing her weight against it for an extra beat as the woman on the hallway floor barks and shrieks. Ramola attempts to think calmly in clinical terms; her locking the door means they are sheltering in place, which is a rational part of emergency procedure, and not a hopeless act of blind fear.

She walks into the room and announces, "There are two infected patients on our floor but they are being tended to—what are you doing?"

Natalie sits propped with one leg on the bed and the other on the floor. Her opened overnight bag is up against her hip. She holds a white handheld device. The tapered nose is pointed at but not touching her forehead, which is colored with a glowing red dot. A green digital display screen faces out toward Ramola. Natalie is using an infrared thermometer, not dissimilar from ones Ramola has used in her practice.

Natalie says, "I'm taking my temperature again."

Sounds echo from the struggle outside the room. The woman in the hallway continues shrieking.

Ramola says, "Again?"

"I got one hundred point seven the first time." Natalie turns the thermometer around and reads, "One hundred point five this time." She drops the thermometer in her bag. "Shower gift. Paul got sick of me randomly zapping his forehead with it and making *pew-pew* sounds. I left it in this bag, like, two months ago. Forgot it was there until I saw it when I got my phone."

Ramola says, "You can't go by that. Forehead scanners can be wildly inaccurate."

In the hallway, the woman's shrieks abruptly cut out.

Natalie shakes her head. "I don't feel good. My throat hurts. And not because I've been yelling and crying. It's an I'm-sick kind of throat pain. I know the difference."

Frenzied chatter and call-and-response on the radio. Intercom announcements plead for Dr. Gray and Dr. Silver to make their appointed rounds.

Natalie says, "I was feeling okay but then I crashed hard in the bathroom. I got dizzy and nauseous when I stood up from the toilet. That's why I was in there so long, splashing water on my face, leaning over the sink. I thought I was going to puke."

"Like I said earlier, you're most certainly dehydrated. We really should have you hooked up to an IV to replenish your fluids."

"I feel hot, like I have a fever. Put your hand on my forehead. Come on. Please. You tell me I'm not hot."

On the floor above them, there is more banging and shaking, as though there are giants up there stomping, searching for bones to grind for their bread.

"My hand cannot divine temperature."

"I'm not asking. I'm telling you to feel my forehead." Natalie gets off the bed and walks over to Ramola.

Using a tone reserved only for the most obstinate parents of patients, Ramola says, "Natalie, dear, I will take your temperature with a proper thermometer as soon as our floor is secured. I—"

Natalie grabs Ramola's hand and slaps it over her forehead.

"I can't feel anything through my gloves."

"Take them off."

"You know I don't go around feeling foreheads at the clinic. This is hardly—"

"Just tell me. Do I feel warm?"

Ramola sighs (Natalie returns her sigh) and shakes her head. She takes off both gloves and puts her right hand on Natalie's forehead. And it does feel warm; it feels warmer the longer her hand lingers. When Ramola was sick as a child, her mum would consult the oral thermometer but would not diagnose a fever until after she pressed the back of her hand to her forehead and cheeks. Mum would then announce in an exaggerated English accent, "You're a little boiler, you are."

Ramola says, "Perhaps you're a tad warm." She flips her hand over briefly. Looking up into Natalie's face, it is difficult to not read infection in the redness and glassiness of her eyes, the red splotches on her skin. "Not outrageously so. My hands are cold from being in the gloves." Ramola pulls away and rubs her hands together. They are not cold. "It would be perfectly normal to have an elevated temperature given the stress."

Natalie groans and goes back for her bag. She plucks out the thermometer and aims it at her head again.

Over the intercom: "Paging Dr. Firestone to the cafeteria."

Natalie lowers the thermometer without looking at the temperature reading. She says, "Seriously? Dr. Firestone?"

Strobing lights flash, followed by the automated, rhythmic wail of the fire alarm.

Natalie says, "This isn't good."

"No, it's not ideal." None of this is ideal. None of this is good. Ramola closes her eyes for a moment and rubs her hands together and they are as clammy as Natalie's forehead. *You're a little boiler, you are.* Ramola pulls the radio out of her pocket.

Natalie is standing and turning from side to side, as though searching for an escape route. She rattles off a blur of questions. "Do we stay? Do they make us go stand outside? What about my C-section?"

Ramola hasn't worked in a large hospital since her residency, and their fire-alarm drills have become fuzzy bits of marginalia. She remembers that if evacuations are necessary, most staff help ambulatory patients to the exits, while only a skeleton crew remains with the patients who are not so easily moved. Ramola halfheartedly (and not very convincingly) explains that hospitals are "defend in place" buildings that have fire protections built into them. They likely won't have to evacuate the building. They might be moved to another area within the wing, or to another floor, however. She knows her calm recitation belies the panic and despair she feels; all the best-laid plans of incident commanders and infectious disease specialists and chief medical officers—their rigorous emergency-response logistics and government protocols—cannot prevent disaster, cannot save everyone, and perhaps cannot save Natalie.

Natalie slumps and sits on the edge of the bed. She wipes her eyes with the back of her right hand and then rubs her belly. She says, "Are they still getting that obstetrician to help me?"

Ramola tunes the radio to channel 2, presses the button, and says, "Hello, Dr. Awolesi, or Central Control? Hello? This is Dr. Ramola Sherman in Room 217. Are we evacuating ambulatory patients? Please advise."

"That's me. Ambulatory patient." It's a Natalie-style wisecrack but is cold and inflectionless.

Dr. Awolesi answers almost immediately. "Dr. Sherman, only visitors and kitchen staff on the first floor are being evacuated currently. You are to remain in your room for now, but we may be moving you. The situation is—" The long pause becomes a break.

Ramola drops the radio away from her mouth and says, "Fluid?" unable to resist completing the sentence.

"Fucked," Natalie says. "Ask her if they're still going to do the C-section."

Ramola does as asked. Dr. Awolesi responds with, "I'm working on it. Hang tight."

The alarm stops. The lights continue to flash.

Natalie grabs the empty blue plastic cup from the bed tray table, stands, and shuffles past Ramola. She says, "I'm going to drink more sink water. Or throw up. Or both." She ducks inside the bathroom, does not shut the door, and turns on the sink.

"Do you need any help?"

"No, I can manage both."

Ramola paces and tunes the radio to the open channel. From the harried chatter she determines the fire in the cafeteria is not the main concern, but a second one at a nurses' station on the third floor is. She tunes back to the second channel so as not to miss a message or instruction from Dr. Awolesi.

Natalie walks out of the bathroom holding the cup of water, her face scrunched up. "Ugh, I need, like, some regular, non-sink water. This tastes so gross. Almost like old eggs. I can smell it. Disgusting." She puts the cup on the table tray.

Ramola intends to say something about getting her bottled water soon but does not. She goes to the bathroom sink, fills her own cup, and takes a sip.

Natalie calls out, "It's awful, right?"

There is that overly chlorinated taste one associates with unfiltered tap water, but it's not overbearing. There's none of the sulfur odor or flavor Natalie described. Is Natalie expressing dysgeusia, a drastic change in sense of taste that many pregnant women experience? That usually only occurs during the first trimester. Is her taste aversion to the water instead a manifestation of the classic rabies symptom of hydrophobia?

The staccato two-note fire alarm blares again. Ramola steps out of the bathroom, turns right, and almost knocks into Natalie. She has her bag slung over her right shoulder.

Natalie says, "We can't just sit here in this room."

"Yes, I know, but—"

"Tell the doctor they need to try something, something new. Anything. Give me the booster early, like now."

"We can't. The booster doesn't work like that."

"How do you know that? How does anyone know that? It's a new fucking virus, so they should be trying or testing new treatments. We're just sitting here and I don't have the time. I don't. And I don't want to die. Don't let me die. It's not fucking fair, not fucking right . . ." Natalie turns away.

Ramola can't tell her she isn't going die. She can't tell her everything will be okay. She doesn't say anything. How could she possibly say anything? Ramola places a hand on Natalie's back. The fire alarm squawks and the lights flash, their rhythms not synced but unyielding; it's easy for one to imagine these broadcasted warnings continuing through the darkest of ages, ceasing only when there is no one around to heed them.

Natalie turns around. "Okay. We need to do the C-section now. Right now. Get one of the surgeons, anyone, I don't care. Give me an orderly with a penknife. Get an operating room, lock it fucking down, and get it done."

Dr. Awolesi says Ramola's name repeatedly on the radio.

"Yes, yes. I'm here."

"Open your door, please."

Ramola opens the door. Dr. Awolesi rushes inside and says, "Change of plans, Natalie. We're transporting you to Ames Medical Clinic. Oh, I see you're already packed and ready to go."

Natalie cocks her head and pulls at Ramola's yellow sweatshirt, stretching it over her belly. It falls away when she lets go. "Why can't we just do it here?"

"Both of our surgeons have been injured. The obstetrician has not arrived, and I don't know her ETA. Most importantly, I cannot guarantee the procedure could be performed safely here at this time. You'll be sent via ambulance. The Ames Clinic is less than twenty minutes away and they'll know you're coming. But you need to leave before this building is quarantined, which could happen at any moment, and that would mean no one will be allowed to leave until that order is lifted." Dr. Awolesi speaks loudly to be heard over the alarm. Unlike earlier conversations, she gesticulates while talking, but instead of aiding in communicating and projecting calm confidence, her traitorous hands are held low, at her side, and palms-up, as though pleading. Her shoulders slump and shrug.

Natalie looks past Dr. Awolesi to Ramola, watching for her response.

Ramola hides her ungloved hands in her coat pockets, as though they might betray their thermometer ways. She says, "All right. We should move quickly then." She walks past both women and retrieves her bag.

Natalie says, "I—I'm not feeling well. Should I take my temperature—"

Dr. Awolesi holds up stop hands (or are they surrender hands?) and says, "Stop. Natalie. I didn't hear you say that. . . ." She pauses, looks down, defeated, and shakes her head.

Ramola instantly extrapolates from this shocking statement, questions avalanching within her head. Is the doctor implying Ames wouldn't take Natalie if she were infected? Would the clinic break protocol (and federal quarantine law) for her emergency case? Is the clinic willing to risk exposing their patient population (presumably healthy mothers and babies) to a potentially infected Natalie and her child? Where do they go if the clinic refuses Natalie, high temperature or no high temperature? Are things so dire here that this is their best or only option?

Dr. Awolesi looks back up at Natalie and says, taking care to enunciate as though each word were a story: "You are well enough to get on that ambulance. Isn't that right?"

Natalie says, "Yeah. Okay, I'm fine." She doesn't break eye contact with the doctor. Her expression is blank and, for Ramola, worryingly indecipherable.

"Good. We need to go now," Dr. Awolesi says, and before Ramola asks any one of her questions, the doctor turns and walks out of the room, adding, "You can take your temperature on the ambulance if you feel you must."

A security guard is waiting in the doorway to escort them. He is a young white man, about six feet tall. His patchy, thinning black hair is buzz-cut short. A respirator mask dangles from around his neck and he touches it with a gloved hand as though it were a talisman. He wears a blue vest, SECURITY written in bold yellow across the midsection. He is armed with a Taser, holstered at his hip.

Dr. Awolesi hurriedly introduces the guard as Stephen. He

nods and flashes the variation on a smile where one's lips disappear entirely. He motions for everyone to follow. Dr. Awolesi walks with him, stride for stride.

The hallway is not empty. Medical staffers duck in and out of rooms, buzzing from patient to patient. There are no signs of the struggle with two infected patients Ramola briefly witnessed. She wonders what happened to them and where they were taken, and she can't help but imagine the woman with the rolled-white eyes, the one who in her stressed memory now looks like Natalie, is waiting behind any one of the doors they might pass. The alarm reverberates, echoing from one end of the hallway to the other, made more piercing by the distance traveled.

Refusing an offer to have her bag carried, Natalie trudges forward, following the doctor and guard. Ramola shuffles behind Natalie, sidestepping left and right in an attempt to see through and beyond the group; she is too short to see over them. Every other step, she throws a look over her shoulder, the hallway behind them expanding with each flash of light.

At the nurses' station a late-middle-aged man argues and pleads with a police officer and a nurse. His hunter-green flat cap held in hand, he's a stooped and grayed Oliver Twist, weary from all the years of begging for more. From what Ramola can piece together, he is not a patient but a visitor who, in the newer chaos ushered in by the alarms, managed to sneak up to the second floor to either be in the room with a family member or to help his loved one evacuate the hospital. Both the officer and nurse shake their heads and say sorry as they attempt to herd him wherever it is the healthy are supposed to go and go alone.

Once through the open area of the nurses' station, their group quickly huddles around Natalie in the elevator vestibule and in front of the exit stairwell. She grimaces and slowly flexes her left hand as they ask her how she's doing and if she can walk down one flight of stairs, as they should bypass using the elevator. Natalie says she is fine to walk and still stubbornly won't allow anyone else to carry her bag.

The guard, Stephen, opens the door to the stairs and the four of them step onto the cement landing. Contained and compressed within the cold metal-and-concrete stairwell, the alarm is again transformed, cruelly mimicking human vocalization, growing more weary and desperate with each ricocheting call. Smoke gathers around the recessed emergency lighting as though the wisps are moths. The smell is not the pleasant roast of wood at the campfire or fireplace but the cloying, sickening tang of melting plastic and other substances that shouldn't be burned.

Natalie says, "Jesus, aren't there other stairs?" then covers her mouth.

Stephen says, "We're okay going down. The smoke is coming from the third floor."

Ramola is the last to step off the landing and onto the stairs. She can finally see over the others' heads from her elevated vantage, but she can't see around the turn to the landing between the first and second floor. From above, a percussive bang almost sends her tumbling into Natalie. Everyone stops. Ramola turns, looks behind and up; the third-floor landing and door are not visible. The alarm still cries. There's a click and a whoosh before another exploding bang. The same sounds repeat, caught in a loop. Someone is opening and then slamming closed the third-floor door.

Dr. Awolesi urges everyone to continue on. "Keep moving. Keep moving."

A woman shouts from above, "She had great power and was dreaded by all the world." The door slams shut and then swings open without pause. "Surrounded by a high wall," she says sing-song, lilting at "high" and separating "wall" into two syllables. Her voice is the same tone and pitch as the alarm and it sounds like there are two of her. The woman continues shouting between the pistonlike opening and closing of the door. "Let it cost what it will cost."

Ramola eases down the stairs, a reluctant swimmer stepping into freezing water, one hand on the railing, neck craned, trying to locate the shouting woman, to see if she's following. Ramola reaches too far out with her last step and stumbles onto the landing. The others have stopped walking.

"In the desert she has to live in misery."

Natalie has her back pressed against the far wall. Dr. Awolesi shields her and speaks rapidly into her radio. Stephen has his Taser gun pointed at a teenage boy standing a few stairs below the platform. The boy wears a fitted gray hooded sweatshirt adorned with a sneaker-brand logo and black skinny jeans, both showing off his wiry frame. Gauze bandaging is visible, a secret peeking out from under the sweatshirt at the base of his neck.

"The beautiful bird isn't singing in the nest," the woman says. She has stopped slamming the door and her heavy, descending footfalls vibrate throughout the stairwell's exoskeleton.

Stephen scoots to the edge of the landing, talking to the boy, telling him to turn around, to walk downstairs, telling him they can get him help if he goes downstairs.

Wild-eyed and as twitchy as a short-circuiting electrical panel, the boy snaps and growls, atavistic in his new animalness.

He does not turn around or walk down the stairs. He holds his ground. His legs are spring-loaded. His fists are rocks, his teeth bared in deimatic display, broadcasting the threat of our most primitive weapons.

"The cat got it." The woman jumps onto the platform between the second and third floor. She cries out as she thuds and crashes, landing on all fours judging by the sounds of her scrabbling hands and feet, but quickly gathers herself and continues progressing down the stairs.

The boy leaps and wraps his arms around the guard's legs. Stephen cries out and falls backward, onto his butt. There's a pop and rapid ticking from the Taser gun. The boy and Stephen stiffen and then convulse in thrall to 1,200 volts. As the ticking slows and ceases, the boy slumps, slides off Stephen's legs, and rolls into a fetal ball. Dr. Awolesi rushes to Stephen's side. His eyes are closed and he is groaning. The boy unfurls and lies facedown on the platform, crying.

"It'll scratch out your eyes too!" The woman rounds the corner onto the second-floor landing above them. Her feet are bare and dirty, and her hospital johnny hangs loosely around her shoulders and chest. Her forearms are streaked with blood. She points at Ramola, rooting her to the spot. The woman laughs; a terrible hitching, grinding gears within her chest, and her sputtering, sickly engine springs a leak and she hisses and spits, flailing one arm as though it is a trebuchet.

Ramola backs away until Natalie grabs her arm and says, "Let's go."

Stephen is sitting up and shaking out his left hand. Dr. Awolesi has his right arm draped across her shoulders, urging him to get on his feet. Natalie and Ramola scoot by and descend the flight of stairs to the first floor, pausing at the fire door.

Ramola calls out to Dr. Awolesi, "Where are we going? Which way?"

The guard and the doctor slowly make their way down the stairs. Their three-legged race is awkward and out of rhythm.

The boy remains on the landing between floors, whimpering and belly-crawling in aimless circles. The woman crash-lands on her knees next to the boy and rains two-fisted punches down on his head and back. She spits in his face and pulls his hair, lifting his head off the platform. He squeals a younger child's squeal, one of heartbreaking shock and despair at the physical realization of the pain and horror of the real world.

Natalie yells, "Fucking where? Come on! We need to go!" but she doesn't move to open the door herself.

Dr. Awolesi is at the base of the stairs and says, "Take a right, follow the main hallway to the other side of the hospital. Central Street exit. We're right behind you. Go."

Holding his head up, the woman leans in, spits in the boy's face, and bites his ear. He screams and writhes, twisting out from underneath her. He briefly holds a hand over his ear before launching shoulder-first into her chest, bending her backward, her legs pinned under her, driving her into the stairs. The woman arches her back, thrusting out her torso, but then sags, slides, and pools at the bottom of the stairs. The boy blurs with his own attack. The uninhibited ferocity is breathtaking. He punches her head repeatedly, hopping into the air with each strike. He grabs and pulls and shakes her, and he alternates those terrible, full-body-weight strikes with bites of her arms and shoulders and face, latching onto the same area with two quick strikes before moving to the next and the next. There's no apparent strategy or reason or order to the violence beyond the existence and the instance of the acts themselves.

Ramola opens the door to the first floor and leads Natalie by the hand.

Standing within the ground-floor elevator vestibule is an EMT, the name of his ambulance service written in script across the chest of his white button-down shirt and the company crest patch on his right shoulder. He's a lanky man, built like a puppet with extra joints and hinges in his limbs, with shaggy brown hair and facial features crowded together but not in a wholly displeasing way. Looking at Natalie and Ramola but shouting into his lapel radio, "This is her? The pregnant one, right?" and then he looks past Ramola and says, "Hey, are you Natalie?" sounding more stern than he looks, like a new mathematics teacher students instinctually know they do not want to piss off.

"That's me."

Any air of authority or expertise he has dissipates as he exhales and deep-knee bends with a celebratory fist pump. "Thank Christ. I'm your ride." He shakes the hair out of his face and strides into the main thoroughfare running the length of the hospital from the ER entrance across to Central Street on the opposite side of the structure. Staff, security, and two soldiers in camouflage fatigues wash past him without regard. He settles against the far wall, holds up his hands at the height of his head and points down the hallway to their right, his long index fingers flipping up and down, a human directional signal.

Dr. Awolesi and Stephen spill out of the stairwell door. Stephen is walking under his own power, but gingerly, as though each step is a new experience in pain. If he has suffered a wound or physical trauma beyond the electric shock, none are visible. He is not in possession of his Taser gun.

Dr. Awolesi says, "Where did the driver go?" She spies the EMT in the hallway and rolls her eyes and shakes her head. She says to the group, "Quickly now, or they won't let you out."

Everyone moves at once. Ramola picks up her pace so as not to be in the rear this time, pulling on Natalie's arm a little, goosing her forward. Within the wider space of the main hallway is a cacophony of shouts, cries, barked orders and questions, crackling radios, individual voices. Dr. Awolesi sprints ahead. The EMT still points and Ramola can't help but briefly imagine him as the *Wizard of Oz* Scarecrow ineffectually directing Yellow Brick Road traffic. He flashes Ramola a crooked smile, perhaps a traitorous one born of shock or nerves, or one that speaks to incompetence and incongruity given the graveness of their situation, or it is a wholly appropriate and commiserative *Can you believe this bullshit?*

There is no parsing which comes first; the sights and sounds are simultaneous. The EMT's head jerks to Ramola's right and toward a garish splash of blood and gray matter scarring the wall. The gunshot crack is followed by a second, or is it a third? He accordions into a boneless, grotesque collapse, his body pooling on the tile. What a world, what a world.

More gunshots, and Ramola instinctively ducks but then straightens, shielding Natalie as much as she can with her slight frame. They drift up against the wall. Dr. Awolesi rushes to the aid of the EMT. The fire alarm changes its rhythm and pattern, from two short blasts to a single protracted one with a heavier weight of silence between, the length of which is almost impossible to anticipate.

A man jogs from the direction of the ER waiting area, indiscriminately firing a pistol. One bullet burrows into the drywall a foot or so above Natalie's head. Behind him, other people are motionless, huddled or splayed on the tile floor, and Ramola cannot tell if they're taking cover or have been shot. The man is shaved bald, older, and wears a tight T-shirt that shows off his considerable upper-body musculature. His forward movement slows and he weaves and wavers, weight shifting left and right randomly, as though he's fighting against hurricane-force winds. The flashing lights blur and muddy his movement.

He fires off more shots without aiming, then he talk-yells, like he's delivering a sermon. "You want to be a sickle you must bend yourself. I can't help you. I won't be burnt with you."

Instead of sidling away from the man and heading deeper down the hallway, Ramola considers going forward and back into the elevator vestibule, where Stephen crouches and carefully peers around the edge of the hallway. They would be covered but also potentially trapped. The stairs offer no safe exit (Is that boy still there waiting for them on the platform? Is he moments away from opening the fire door?) and she's unsure if the elevators are operable.

A commotion approaches from the other end of the hallway; clacking boots and shouts of "Stay clear!" Three members of the National Guard in full fatigues: one carrying a gun-metal-colored shield, the other two clutching automatic weapons. They quickly overtake and pass Ramola and Natalie. The soldiers shout unheeded commands at the man, each soldier taking a turn, as though singing in rounds. A hail of gunfire drowns out their infinite canon. The man with the pistol screams and falls to the floor. Most of Ramola's view is blocked by the circling soldiers, particularly the one with the shield, as the man uses his hands and arms to crawl forward on his stomach, his motionless legs trailing red smears. He hisses and gurgles, and drums his lips together like a child might when imitating a car engine. His bloody, foaming mouth is a leer and he lashes out with a hand, reaching for the ankle of the shield carrier. A single gunshot discharges from one of the soldiers' guns. The man goes still. After the briefest moments of silence, that end of the hallway explodes into argument and recrimination between approaching medical staff and the soldiers.

Dr. Awolesi has flipped the EMT onto his back. She explores his midsection for a reason Ramola cannot determine. He is most certainly dead; the left half of his head is a sizable trapdoor left ajar, hair and scalp misshapen and jellied with gore. Dr. Awolesi climbs out of her crouch, dangling a set of keys in one hand.

Ramola and Natalie follow the doctor down the hallway, swimming upstream through waves of more soldiers and, now, firefighters. Stephen the guard doesn't continue with them. He stays behind, leaning on the corner of the elevator vestibule and hallway, talking to soldiers and pointing, presumably, at the door to the stairwell.

Ramola walks side by side with Natalie while looking every direction at once. They do not talk. She tries to catch Natalie's eye, to give her a nod or a smile, whatever either expression is worth, an opening to perhaps ask the dreaded *How are you doing, how are you feeling?* Natalie grimly keeps her gaze pointed forward, to the finish line they cannot yet see. Her gait is hitched and her right arm is scaffolding under her stomach. The overnight bag bounces off her hip with each step.

A few paces ahead, Dr. Awolesi talks into her radio. The keys jingle as she gesticulates, flashing her right arm out to her side and pointedly jabbing it forward.

Natalie asks, "Who's driving us? Is she driving us?"

"I don't think so. EMTs work with partners, don't they." Ramola doesn't mean it as a question, but as emphasis. "How are—"

"I'm fine." Her eyes fixed on the hallway horizon, Natalie shakes her head no as though her physically taxed and possibly catastrophically compromised body cannot tell a lie. They pass intersecting hallways and signs with arrows pointing to the ICU, cafeteria, Psychiatry, and the Washington Street entrance, which is closed, and Natalie repeats, "I'm fine."

The Central Street exit/entrance is a service and employee entrance, one not generally used by patients or visitors under normal circumstances. Two armed and masked soldiers guard the glass double doors.

Dr. Awolesi shows her ID and identifies herself as acting chief medical officer. This is news to Ramola, and her use of "acting" and its implications floods her system with pulses of unease. Dr. Awolesi tells the soldiers, with permission granted by the incident commander, she is transferring Natalie and her attending physician to another clinic.

There is no argument as Ramola anticipated there might be. One soldier nods, says, "We know," and mumbles something about minutes to spare. The other opens the door and closes it as soon as they pass through. Outside the hospital, the wail of the fire alarm is muzzled (but still audible), and the cool air is bracing on Ramola's sweat-slicked skin. The parking lot is significantly smaller than the sea of blacktop by the ER. A skinny rectangle that winds and tapers by the entrance has only thirty or so parking spots for staff, currently filled with military trucks and other vehicles. Two trucks, parked tail to head, block access from Washington Street. Soldiers guard and maintain one-lane access to and from Central Street.

A large white ambulance with the company name writ in blue cursive on the side panel is parked at the walkway curb in front of the exit. Dr. Awolesi jogs ahead and pounds on the passenger door with an open hand and stands on tiptoes, peering into the window. When no one answers, she opens the unlocked door, pulls herself up into the main cab, and visually inspects the rear of the vehicle. She hops back onto the sidewalk, looks around, and throws up her hands.

She says, "This is alarming to admit, but I cannot locate the other EMT. She might be inside helping. But I don't know, and now it doesn't matter." She hands Ramola the fistful of keys she lifted from the dead EMT. "I'm conscripting you into driving, Dr. Sherman."

Ramola holds the loose pile of jangling metal in her left hand, out and away from her body as though cupping a handful of sleeping bees. "Are you sure . . ."

"Yes, and before you can ask, I have that power. Come on, Natalie, let's get you in."

Natalie snorts a hard laugh. "Yeah, why not?"

Dr. Awolesi walks away from the front cab toward the rear.

"I'm not sitting back there all by myself," Natalie says. "I'm sitting in the front with Ramola. She'll need my help navigating."

Dr. Awolesi, speaking for the first time without her air of authority, says she'd feel better having Natalie in the four-point harness in the back and, more sheepishly, something about regulations against patients being up front.

Natalie says, "Right. Well they can sue me later," and goes to the open passenger door. The two doctors help Natalie step up into the cab. She settles into the chair and allows Dr. Awolesi to fasten her seat belt. Natalie stows her overnight bag on the floor between her feet.

After they shut the door Ramola asks, "Will I be allowed through checkpoints, roadblocks? I'm clearly not the intended driver."

Dr. Awolesi assures her that the communications team has already sent alerts and will continue to spread the message throughout state and emergency networks.

They walk around the front of the ambulance. Ramola opens the heavy driver's-side door, which creaks on its hinges, protesting her coming aboard. Part of her wants to say, *I cannot do this. This is too much.* "Well, I drove a moving van once," Ramola says aloud, though she's really talking to herself. She returns the handheld radio to the doctor.

Dr. Awolesi stares at the device and blinks, empty of expression. She says, "Ames Medical Clinic is on Depot Street, right near Five Corners. Do you know where that is?"

Natalie shouts, "Yes!"

Ramola says, "Yes, I do."

Dr. Awolesi hands Ramola a small card. "My cell-phone number. Calls have been iffy, but texts have a better chance of going through should you need to contact me." She says the last sentence like a question for which she doesn't have a proper answer. "Good luck. Not that you'll need it. I'm sure she'll be fine but—keep an eye on her."

Ramola says, "Thank you, Doctor, I will." She climbs into the cab and stows her bag behind the seat, and mumbles, "While keeping the other eye on the road? Fucking hell."

Natalie says, "You and your eye will do great. And use both for driving, please." She now has her bag in her lap and is rooting through it.

"Do you need—"

Natalie doesn't look up. "No. Nothing. Drive."

The ambulance's design more resembles a tall, skinny delivery van than a truck. Other than its dramatically spacious headroom and the center console with its radio and two rows of chunky black buttons or switches, the front's interior is similar to a typical automobile. Ramola is sunken into the too-large bucket seat that was not designed with the Goldilocks principle in mind. She roughly slides the chair forward until the tops of her knees are almost brushing the steering wheel. Inserting the key, its hard plastic sleeve as thick as her hand, she starts the engine.

Ramola checks her side mirrors, shifts into drive, and rolls away from the curb.

Natalie lets her bag drop between her legs and down to the floor again. She holds her phone with both hands. She says, "I hope someone calls that obstetrician, tells her to go back home," using her this-is-Nats-being-sarcastic voice, which, at first blush, isn't perceptibly different from her regular, conversational tone. Instead of employing hammy, exaggerated inflection peppered with head tilts and eye rolls, Natalie holds eye contact, so direct as to make her target self-conscious, and drops into a slightly lower, more serious register, speaking with the hushed wisdom of an expert or authority. It took Ramola years and more than a handful of misunderstandings before she could consistently identify Natalie's sarcasm. "She'll be very put out, I imagine, when she shows up and I'm not here. Not to mention the money her police-escorted hospital jaunt will cost the state. What a terrible mess."

Ramola won't look at Natalie directly. She needs to concentrate on getting them out of the hospital lot, through downtown Norwood, and pointed in the direction of the clinic before she'll dare to keep that other eye on Natalie. The questions about symptoms and the increasing possibility of infection will simply have to wait. If she could put those questions off forever, especially now that it's just the two of them again, she would. Ramola nods as though agreeing with something she said to herself.

The ambulance floats through small but tight turns within the lot, swaying and dipping like a dinghy in choppy waters. Knowing it's a paranoid thought, Ramola is convinced the ambulance's high center of gravity is actively conspiring to tip.

Natalie says, "Remember where we parked. Hope we don't get towed."

Soldiers remove the white-and-orange-striped sawhorses blocking Central Street. Ramola pauses at the exit, offering a last chance for someone to give her instructions, tell her what to do, what to expect, how any of this is going to work out. A half block to her left, hemmed in by cement barriers, Washington Street boils with activity: police and military herd and direct people away from the hospital; people shout and they honk horns; they wander aimlessly between stopped and abandoned cars, unsure of where to go or what to do; they wave arms and fists but not in a threatening way, instead, it's a someone-please-see-me-and-help-me plea; everyone's face shows confusion mixed with terror and incredulity, and perhaps most frightening, an odd look of recognition/resignation, and it's a look Ramola fears she'll find on her own face if she stares into the rearview mirror.

Dragging the tail end of the ambulance fully out of the lot, Ramola turns right. Central Street is empty of traffic, the curbs lined by a blockade of military and emergency-response vehicles. Packs of soldiers cluster around individuals attempting to cut across the road and funnel the interlopers back onto Washington Street or Broadway.

A Jeep pulls out ahead of the ambulance, a single flashing red light perched on its roof, and leads them away from the hospital.

Natalie presses one of the console buttons, turning on their own flashing red lights. She says, "No siren. My fucking head is killing me." She clears her throat twice, and then a third time.

Ramola has the irresistible urge to snap at Natalie, to yell at her, to tell her to stop carrying on like a phlegmatic old man, to say she is exaggerating her headache and the scratchiness of her voice, all of which is making it impossible to drive, to concentrate, to not think and imagine the worst.

They follow the Jeep through a bend, past the post office, past Olivadi's Restaurant & Bar, and to a straightaway section of the road, and past Norwood Cooperative Bank and Mak's Roast Beef. Two blocks away is a fire engine, a leviathan floating across Nahatan Street and then up Central. Falling in behind the red truck wider than the lane it straddles are three coach buses, each one able to accommodate more than fifty passengers.

Natalie asks, "Are they quarantining the hospital or evacuating? Do they even know?"

Ramola shrugs and says, "Come on, let's keep it moving," even though no one has stopped the Jeep or their ambulance. They pass between the Norwood Theatre and the green space of Norwood Common. They cross Nahatan Street, where the traffic they were sitting in an hour ago hasn't abated. They go straight for two more blocks and turn right onto Railroad Avenue. The Jeep pulls over to the shoulder, adjacent to the mostly empty Norwood Depot parking lot, and the driver rolls down his window and waves them on.

Ramola slows the ambulance as though hoping to communicate *No, you first. We insist.*

Natalie says, "So much for our escort."

Ramola says, "We'll be all right," and regrets it as soon as she says it.

Natalie knocks on the dash. "Pretend it's wood. That was for you, by the way. Just because you're not superstitious—"

"Doesn't mean I want to be a jinx."

Natalie finishes the punch line, one born of obligation to tradition, but not without warmth. "You are a woman of reason and science."

A shared joke from one late night when the two of them were at the Brown University Sciences Library studying for freshman first-semester exams. Both were hypercaffeinated, loopy from stress and nearly a week's worth of lack of sleep, and unabashedly silly and awkward in the way young people are when they are comfortable within their own skin for perhaps the first time in their lives. The study session deteriorated into laughing fits as Ramola loudly shushed and repeatedly knocked on wood whenever either of them speculated on how they would perform the next morning. The following afternoon, celebrating the completion of their exams, the two of them wandered Thayer Street searching for a ladder for Ramola to walk under or a black cat with which to cross paths so she could prove she was not superstitious; she was a woman of reason and science. Being a cold and blustery mid-December there were no cats to be found and the only ladder was the rolling one within stacks at the University bookstore, swollen with students purchasing last-minute holiday gifts. Ramola tried gamely to shimmy between the cranky, clanging ladder and the bookshelf, but got pinned between. She was in nonfiction/history—Ramola remembers the section clearly—her eyes inches from the faced-out cover of *The Devil in the White City*, a book that Natalie bought her as a cheeky graduation gift. A clearly unamused graduate student working one of the registers had to stand on a chair to detach the top of the ladder from its track in order to free a giggling but mortified Ramola. All the while, Natalie sat on the floor and with the straightest of faces asked Ramola if she needed water or a blueberry muffin from the café. She read aloud from the opening chapter of *Into Thin Air* until the grad student monotoned that she wasn't helping.

Ramola creeps the ambulance past the Jeep, hoping, willing the driver for a change of mind, if not heart. The hand continues to wave, cruelly implacable, without pause or impatience.

She exhales and stomps on the accelerator. The ambulance lurches forward. Within two blocks, the commuter rail station, commercial properties, and congestion of the large suburban downtown give way to trees, rolling sidewalks, landscaped lawns, picket-fenced yards, and front porches of residential neighborhoods.

Ramola turns, sparing both eyes for Natalie.

Natalie stares into the mirror of her darkened phone. Her mouth clenched tight, the muscles in her cheeks pulse and quiver. Is she grinding her teeth? She clears her throat two more times without opening her mouth.

Ramola snaps her head back to the road as though having witnessed something she should not have seen. The ambulance's flashing red lights reflect off the darkened windows of houses they pass.

Natalie says, "I don't feel great. I know there has to be a thermometer in the back, but we're not pulling over to get it. I just—I don't feel great."

"You're thirsty and hungry and beyond exhausted—"

"I'm not trying to be a dick, I swear, but please don't explain it away. All you have to say is you know: you know I don't feel well. That's all I need. I mean, that's all *we* need, I think. I'm sorry I don't know what the fuck I want or need or what to do."

"When one says one is not trying to be a dick, it generally implies the opposite."

Natalie laughs. "I can't believe you're calling a rabies-exposed preggo a dick. That's gotta go against your Hippocratic Oath."

"Nats . . ."

"Oh, please tell me you call some of your other patients dicks. That would be amazing. Let me pretend—"

"Nats."

"What? What?"

"I know you don't feel well."

"Thank you, Rams. Thank you. I mean that." Each word gets quieter, like a song fading out instead of ending abruptly.

"Doctors don't say the Hippocratic Oath anymore."

"No?"

"I did recite a modern version of the oath rewritten by Dr. Lasagna."

"Ooh, yum. Lasagna." Natalie is again at exaggerated volume and exuberance. "Hey, I like your sweatshirt. Yellow is my new color."

"You pull it off."

"So I don't look like a giant rubber ducky? I'm glad."

After shared, restrained laughter, they drive in silence, passing through this new ghost town, where the ghosts are reflections of what was and projections of what might never be again.

The urge to say something, anything, to keep them talking becomes a compulsion. Ramola says, "This windscreen is rather large, isn't it," knowing Natalie won't be able to resist commenting upon the Anglicism.

"'Windscreen.'"

"Sorry. Of course, it's a windshield."

Natalie says, "I like windscreen better. And yeah, it's huge. You can see the whole world. You can see everything."

Ramola keeps her eyes on the road, afraid of looking at Natalie and seeing a ghost.

II.

FILL YOUR KNAPSACK FULL OF THE SWEEPINGS

NATS

Hi, I'm back. I love you.

It's only been, like, thirty minutes since recording my last message and it seems like I did it two weeks ago. Rams says "fortnight" when she means two weeks and still can't get over that no one in this country says the word unless they're talking about a video game your dad and other children are obsessed with. Yes, I just called your dad a child. He would've laughed at that, and totally agreed. I can't believe he's gone—

Hey, you won't be listening to any of this until years from now. From my now. So I shouldn't talk about fortnights, weeks, and time. It's too much. Time is too heavy. It really does have weight you can feel but you can't measure.

Jesus, I'm talking in shitty riddles like I'm Rabies Yoda.

We're back on the road. We've been forced to leave the hospital. It was on fire. And there were zombies—

"Natalie, they're not—"

I know, I know. Okay, fine, they're not really zombies. You probably already know that because the goddamn history of this will have already been written since you're able to safely listen to this. I'm dreaming about you being safe right now.

So, they're not zombies. No one is rising from the dead. Sounds silly to have to say because it's so obvious, right? Dead is dead. There's no coming back.

This is getting dark. And I'm getting way off track. . . .

I was kind of joking when I said zombies, but not joking at the same time. They're sick people and they turn delusional and violent and they bite, but it's easier to say *zombie* than "a person infected with a super rabies virus and no longer capable of making good decisions."

I'm not making fun of this. I'm not. It's either I say it this way or you get a recording of me screaming and crying.

Not for nothing, I hope you make good decisions in your life. It's okay to make bad ones too, of course. No one makes all good decisions, and it's often difficult to know if your decision was good or bad or likely somewhere in between, and you might never know. I mean, don't sniff glue, right? Doing so would be an obviously bad decision. Don't microwave a hardboiled egg. Don't drink milk past its expiration date. The sniff test isn't reliable enough on milk.

When I was in high school and going out with friends my mother used to say, "Make good decisions, Natalie." She'd be so proud of herself for being different from the moms who said "be smart" or "be good" or "don't drink and drive" or "be safe and don't talk to strangers or get attacked by zombies."

Can you hear Auntie Rams tsking me each time I say "zombie"? She's here next to me, on the correct side of the road, driving us in an ambulance to another hospital that hopefully isn't on fire. I'm not making any of this shit up.

So let's say hi to Auntie Rams again.

"Oh, I'm to be Auntie Rams, now, am I? Don't I get name approval?"

No. Say hi, Auntie Rams.

"Hi, Auntie Rams."

Isn't she so clever? You missed her calling me a dick, like, two minutes ago.

"I did not say you were—"

You totally did. Don't lie to my kid.

Auntie Rams isn't my real sister, but she's even better than a blood sister because I got to choose her. We got to choose each other. That sounds cheesy but it's true. She's the best, and she'll be an amazing auntie. You'll be able to count on her. I mean, she's risking her life and her driver's license for me right now, driving a stolen ambulance—

"It's not stolen."

Totally stolen—and driving us—expertly, I might add!— through a *Fury Road* wasteland, only much less dusty and way more suburban. You can watch that movie when you're four- teen. Or maybe twelve if you think you can handle it.

I have no familial sisters or brothers. I'm a partially spoiled only child. The full-on spoiledness inherent to being an only child was kept in check, mostly, because my parents were im- possible to deal with. Maybe that's not completely fair and I don't want you to think your grandparents were mean or ter- rible people, because they weren't. They were a little cold, not always there even when they sat in the same room as you, if that makes sense. They loved me sometimes and they tolerated me the rest of the time. Some of that was my problem too, and I'll freely admit I was a bit of a monster as a teen. I ran away from home three different times my freshman year. My parents were older, in their mid-forties when they had me, and I don't know if that was the reason for their distance. They tried their best, but sometimes trying isn't good enough.

I shouldn't be wasting what little time I have telling you this stuff, but what else am I going to say? I don't have a lifetime to do this. No one does, I guess.

These recordings are me grieving for you and your dad, grieving for us, for the moments that won't ever happen, the memories we won't be able to make.

"Natalie, please don't talk like this. You can't give up—"

Sorry, Auntie Rams, I have to. I need to. And I'm not giving up.

You need to know that too. I am not and have not given up. No way. These recordings are the break-in-the-event-of-emergency glass, just in case I become a zombie.

Doesn't that sound better than saying "just in case infection blooms and I die a horrible, painful death"?

I am sorry to do this to you. Maybe this is selfish of me. See, I'm a typical only child. You have my permission to fast-forward past any of this if you want to.

Yes, I realize odds are you are an only child. Maybe I am a dick.

You'll be *my* only child no matter who you live with. But I think I can confidently say that you won't be spoiled. I mean, how can you be, knowing that your dad and I are gone? I'm sorry you'll never meet him. He would've been great at dadding.

Hey. Took a moment to regroup. And we passed through the same rotary checkpoints we were at, like, an hour ago. The police were confused by our new ride and Auntie Rams threatened to run them over if they didn't let us pass.

I'm joking. Ha-ha, right? My jokes are usually better and I'm way more fun when we're not navigating the zombie apocalypse—that was for you, Rams.

"Thank you. Please stop saying 'zombie.'"

Za-om-bay, Za-om-bay, Za-om-bay-ey-ey-ey!

You're kicking me like crazy right now. You do that when I sing. Or when I try to sing.

What else? I'm trying to think of stuff that no one else will tell you about me. I'm five-eight and I was that height in fifth grade. That wasn't fun. I wonder if you'll be tall or short. Sorry if you're either and, um, you'd rather the other? Middle school was worse than fifth grade, but middle school is worse for everyone. I had a dog named Pete when I was a kid. He was a sweet, slobbery goof, as big and soft as a beanbag chair. My first job was scooping ice cream at a dairy farm. I love driving with the windows down, even when it's cold out. I hate flying. To distract myself during takeoff I make up names and stories for the people around me. It's weird but I remember a few of those random strangers because the stories got so big. Not big like action-movie big, but big in the . . . I don't know, human way; the people they knew and loved, and the secrets they had to keep. I miss music being as important to me as it was when I was in high school and college. And I do and I don't miss *everything* being as important to me as it was when I was in high school and college. I'm a terrible dancer but I loved dragging Rams to Stupid Dance Party on Thursday nights when we were sophomores. Rams had moves. The best night was when my Chuck Taylors exploded and the toes on my right foot were sticking out. Someone had a Sharpie and I got as many people as I could to draw on the sneaker and my toes. I would rather eat cookies than cake, or pies. I don't really like pies. I wish I could draw better than I can. I read for at least twenty minutes before bed each night. If I fall asleep with the book on my face (which happens a lot), I'll read two pages when I wake up to make sure I meet the reading goal. I'm agnostic but I have this fantasy of me as a cute old lady going to all different kinds of churches, mosques, temples just to hear people talk. If you couldn't tell I like to talk and to listen to others talk. I don't believe in ghosts but I'm afraid of them, or the implications of them. Maybe I'm more afraid of being wrong about ghosts. I initially kind of hated the house Paul and I bought. It was expensive and I was freaking out and it was too quiet and I just wanted to stay in Providence and live in an apartment. Neither one of us was very handy, and we knew nothing about home improvement and upkeep that didn't come from a YouTube video. There was one fall weekend we pried the hideous wooden paneling from the porch walls and put up clapboard all by ourselves. I was so proud of us and it was our house after that. I never told Paul or anyone else that. So that belongs to you now. And Rams, too, since she's eavesdropping.

We're almost to Cobb's Corner. That means we're really close to our house now, and getting closer.

I—I'm going to stop now, I think. We'll talk again later. I promise. If I break the promise, please know I didn't mean to. It sucks, but promises get broken all the time. Promises are like

wishes. Yeah. They're great as long as you know they won't always help and won't always come true.

"Now you *are* Bummer Rabies Yoda. I'm sorry, I'm sorry, I
couldn't resist. You can edit that part out, correct?"

I told you Auntie Rams is the best.

I love you. Sassafras and lullabies.

RAMS

The first half of the trip toward Ames retraces their earlier drive, including passing over I-95, which is as still as a stagnant river. Ramola experiences a dissociative feeling of going backward—not quite déjà vu, but a sense of rewinding, of going nowhere. Listening to Natalie dictate her hey-in-the-event-I-die messages to her unborn child—a child with no guarantees of their own health or survival—isn't helping. She worries they are moving further away—both in terms of time and distance—from getting Natalie the help she needs.

They approach River Bend, Ramola's townhouse complex. Her bay window is a dark rectangle. The parking lot has the same number of cars as it did when they left. She wonders how the Piacenzas and Danielses are faring. Is Frank's cat inside his house or will she see it, haunches slouched, drunkenly stumbling in the middle of the road, fated to be the grease under ambulance tires? As Neponset Street snakes away from her new home and under the Canton Viaduct, Ramola's scattered thoughts go deeper into her past and she wonders about the ex-neighbors from her apartment building in downtown Quincy, a mix of townies and people her age, all white, and all of whom were guarded (to be overly kind) in their initial interactions with her. By Ramola's force of cheer and goodwill, the neighbors and locals were eventually friendly enough to engage in hallway chats and share a drink on the front porch in the summers. She hopes someone is checking in on Mr. Fitzgerald, a rascally sparkplug of an old man who lived alone on the first floor, argued with his visiting nurse, hobbled around on a bum hip that needed to be replaced, and smoked a cigar while perched on the front stairs every Saturday afternoon.

Natalie says, "I'm joking. Ha-ha, right? My jokes are usually better and I'm way more fun when we're not navigating the zombie apocalypse—that was for you, Rams."

"Thank you. Please stop saying 'zombie.'"

Natalie sings the chorus to the Cranberries' "Zombie," and not very well.

Ramola's thoughts briefly travel from Mr. Fitzgerald in Quincy to the flat in Pawtucket, Rhode Island, she had shared with her ex-partner, Cedric. They started dating while in medical school, one month after Natalie and Paul got their own place. She remembers Cedric with neither malice nor fondness. He was plain but handsome, gentle but never warm, maddeningly demure only when he wasn't. He was intractable if he dug in on a topic or position. Most notably, their date-night schedule was so rigidly mapped and unmalleable in his eyes, he took to hanging an otherwise blank calendar on the refrigerator door with DATE NIGHT slashed onto a scatterplot of dates, the handwriting desperate, accusatory, childish. Her memory of their relationship is neither enhanced nor distorted by the haze of nostalgia; their time together represents a signpost of where she once was and nothing more. She idly wonders if Cedric is still in New England. Her mum took their breakup and Ramola moving to Quincy much harder than Ramola did. In the immediate aftermath Mum insisted Ramola move back home to England and do so immediately. She stammered through saying the America experiment was a noble miss and was incredulous that her daughter didn't agree. She would not hear of how Ramola was almost done with residency and was preparing for a second interview with Norwood Pediatrics. At the height of the contentious, one-sided (or Mum-sided, as Ramola thought of their occasional spats) argument, Ramola said, "Mum. Listen to me. I cannot say it more plainly: I am not moving back to England. Not ever." Ramola had never before stated this to her mum. The shocked and hurt hiss of silence on the phone was a hard-won victory, but it came at a cost. Ramola attempted to soften the blow with "I will visit you and Dad, of course, but I will not be coming home in the way that you want me to." Mum didn't call Ramola back for eleven days. Ramola refused to be the first to break the embargo and held out. She talked to Natalie every night instead. On the eighth day, she admitted Mum not calling made her sad in a way that felt irreparable, as though this sad (Ramola referred to "this sad" as if it were an object, something to be probed, dissected, but delicately) might diminish or fade into the background, but would always be there. Mum was the first to relent. She never apologized directly but did so in her way by calling every other day for the next two months. She demanded a detailed recounting of the third interview that became the job offer, and she wanted to know everything about Ramola's new flat and city. There were, of course, subtle digs coded within her catching Ramola up on the lives of her friends' children, the ones who were married and had children of their own. It went unspoken when talking to Mum, but Ramola was as resolute about never having children as she was about not moving back to England. She was content to help and to serve other people's children as their doctor. Not that being a pediatrician was a substitute for a lack of children in her life; quite the opposite. There was no lack as far as she was concerned. Mum would occasionally ask if Ramola was seeing anyone. Ramola dismissed the queries by saying she was far too busy and by the time she got home most days she was exhausted. During one memorably wine-fueled conversation, Mum asked if Ramola missed "physical intimacy." By then Ramola had begun to think of herself as asexual but would not admit this to her mum. She said she was impressed by Mum's vocabulary choice, and added she enjoyed the idea of sex like she enjoyed the idea of riding a bike, but both involved too much prep work, or leg work, as it were, and she was all right forgoing both for the foreseeable. Mum surprised her by saying, "Cheers to that," and they both broke up laughing. There would always be a point during their conversations when Ramola would tell Mum not to worry, because she was happy, which was more or less true, although happiness was never Ramola's ambition. Happiness held no nuance or compromise, did not allow for examination, did not allow the hopeful, hungry will that fills the vacuum of failure and what-might've-beens, nor did it allow for the sweetness of surprise. Happiness was as rigid in its demands to adherence as a calendar shouting about compulsory date nights. Happiness was for dogs, lovely creatures though they were. Ramola yearned for something more complex, something earned, and something more satisfying. If she ever felt lonely, it was a passing storm, not one she brooded upon, and it was easily banished by resolving to be better about seeing friends, seeing Natalie and Paul. What Ramola yearned for was not a gormless vision of happiness or a dewy romantic relationship but a future when she was financially stable enough to travel wherever she wanted on holiday. In some daydreams she traveled with friends, in others she traveled alone. That was the life she desired to live. As a promise to herself, she decorated the bedroom of her Quincy flat with travel posters and those posters multiplied and moved with her to the townhome in Canton.

The ambulance rumbles to the end of Neponset and turns right onto Canton's version of Washington Street. On the corner, the 7–Eleven's lights are extinguished and the front window is cracked down the middle, the glass intact for now but as doomed as the calving Antarctic ice shelf. Across from the convenience store, a row of local shops and businesses is dark. Farther down the street a funeral home and its parking lot is vacant. As terrifying as the panicked mob of humanity in and around Norwood Hospital was, the quiet desolation of Canton center—whether its populace has fled, is in hiding, or has suffered a catastrophic collapse—is more disturbing and feels like a permanent condition, one from which there will be no recovery.

Natalie says into her phone, "We're almost to Cobb's Corner. That means we're really close to our house now, and getting closer."

Cobb's Corner is where the borders of three towns (Canton, Stoughton, Sharon) converge, meeting at the intersection of Washington Street and Route 27. Sprawling networks of strip malls layer both sides of the street with the largest to their left, a single-level labyrinth of chain restaurants, corporate retail stores, and a dwindling number of independent mom-and-pop shops and businesses. The supermarket demarcates the rear of the shopping area, set back four or five hundred yards from the road. Cars and military vehicles are amassed in the lots closest to the supermarket. From this distance it is impossible to determine if the market is still open. Ramola is careful to not stare in that direction too long, irrationally fearing the act of her looking will attract unwanted attention to the woman driving an emergency vehicle she is not meant to drive.

Natalie says, "I—I'm going to stop now, I think. We'll talk again later. I promise. If I break the promise, please know I didn't mean to. It sucks, but promises get broken all the time. Promises are like wishes. Yeah. They're great as long as you know they won't always help and won't always come true."

Ramola says, "Now you *are* Bummer Rabies Yoda. I'm sorry, I'm sorry, I couldn't resist. You can edit that part out, correct?"

"I told you Auntie Rams is the best. I love you. Sassafras and lullabies." Natalie puts the phone on her lap, screen down. "She's a girl, you know."

"I thought you didn't find out—"

"I didn't. And I wasn't getting any vibes until a few weeks ago. But now I know. She's a girl."

The traffic light at Cobb's Corner is blinking red, which it isn't normally. Ramola slows the ambulance to a crawl but does not come to a complete stop. She speeds through the intersection as soon as she's confident there is no oncoming traffic. Washington Street morphs into Bay Road, a much less densely populated house-and-forest-lined border running between the towns of

Stoughton and Sharon before leading into Ames. Cobb's Corner fades away quickly in the rearview mirrors, replaced by a blur of trees with red and orange leaves. In approximately five miles are Ames's infamous intersection Five Corners and their ultimate destination, Ames Medical Center.

Natalie says, "We're so close to my house."

"I'm sorry. I should've gone a different way."

"No, this is the quickest. I wonder if Paul is still there, but of course he's still there. I know he's not a fucking zombie. But—I don't know. Did someone else show up? Try to help him? Move him? Take him away? Our neighbors must've heard me, heard us. No one came to help. I hope—I hope I killed that fucking guy. He better not be doing anything else to Paul."

Natalie goes quiet and covers her eyes with her right forearm as they pass Woodlawn Street. As the crow flies, Natalie's house is less than fifty meters away, close enough that someone standing on Bay Road might've heard Natalie and Paul's yells and screams when they were attacked.

A gray squirrel darts in front of the ambulance but changes its mind and returns to the road's shoulder and its blanket of red pine needles. It rubs its front paws together, a worrier wringing hands.

Natalie drops her arm, sighs, and twists and adjusts in her seat. "I might have to pee. I think I can make it though. If I don't, sorry to the ambulance." She lifts her left arm, bent at the elbow, and swears under her breath. "My arm hurts. Really hurts all of a sudden. Like a stabbing, and then burning, and a wave of numbness. Fucking ow. Back to the stabbing. Shooting up into my shoulder."

"I'm sure you jostled it when you climbed into the cab—oh, right, I'm explaining again, aren't I. I'm sorry, I know your arm doesn't feel good, Natalie. How's that?"

"Don't patronize me. Actually, do patronize me. This feels like it did when the guy bit me. It's kinda weird." She tugs at the yellow sleeve of her sweatshirt.

Bite-wound pain returning is a classic symptom of rabies infection in humans. Of course, normally, it takes weeks for that symptom to appear in patients. There's no way for Ramola to know if Natalie's arm hurts because she was bitten two hours ago or if it's a sign of infection.

They round a curve, and ahead on the right is the Crescent Ridge dairy farm and its locally famous ice-cream stand. During the summers, from noon to evening closing time, queues are fifteen-to-twenty people deep at any one of the eight service windows. Now there are no lines, no cars in the parking lot (the front of which is paved, the back lot is dirt), and no cows lazily grazing in the fenced-off fields and meadows.

A skinny dog emerges from behind the ice-cream stand and patrols the blacktop. Its chest and belly fur is white; brown and reddish fur color the back and legs. The tail's length and bushiness is outsized, exaggerated, as though a child drew it.

"I hope someone hasn't lost their dog," Ramola says.

Natalie says, "I think that's a coyote."

The animal's face is more vulpine than a dog's. Fur is matted and rough. Ears are pointed, sharp triangles. Ramola says, "I think you're right," without ever having seen a coyote in person.

The coyote is less a confident, vigilant predator canvassing the area than a confused animal listing and wobbling through repetitive arcs. Tail and shoulders are drooped. Legs tremor and shudder. Neck telescopes the weary, swaying snout, hovering parallel to the pavement. White, stringy drool leaks from its mouth.

Natalie asks, "Why are you slowing down?"

"I'm not," Ramola says, but a quick look at the speedometer reveals her speed has dropped to 25mph. She presses the gas pedal and the engine grumbles.

The coyote explodes into a sprint, one it didn't look to be physically capable of only a second ago. Its gait is graceless and without rhythm, legs moving of their own accord, heedless to what the other legs are doing, as though running is ancillary to the goal of repeatedly smashing paws against the pavement. An inefficient tornado of movement and momentum, the coyote careens toward the road.

Natalie says, "Holy shit, holy shit. Don't hit it, don't hit it . . ."

Ramola jerks the ambulance into the opposite lane. The sudden shift of the vehicle's top-heavy weight wants to sway them farther left and onto the shoulder and someone's front lawn. Ramola maintains control and their current velocity. She cannot slam on the brakes, as rapid deceleration would dangerously tighten the seat belt around Natalie and her belly. She squeezes the steering wheel and winces preemptively, anticipating impact with the animal but hoping for a miss.

The front grille noses ahead of the charging coyote. She gives the ambulance more gas, aiming to surge past without the creature mashing into them. It's running so quickly it appears to be bouncing and rolling, a tumbleweed in a gale-force wind. Ramola loses sight of it, dreading the sickening thump of the tires rolling over the animal.

There's a loud, jarring bang as the coyote broadsides the ambulance, just behind Natalie's door. She yells, "Fucking fuck!"

and recoils from the door but then presses her face against the window, mumbling indecipherable commentary or judgment.

Ramola doesn't slow, doesn't stop, and pilots the ambulance back into its proper lane.

Natalie, still looking out the window, says, "I can't see it. Is it dead?"

Ramola checks her mirrors. Reflected in the large rectangular passenger side-mirror, the coyote is a lump of writhing fur, flailing more limbs than its four, before flipping onto its paws. It opens and closes its mouth rapidly but if it issues cries or calls, they can't hear any. As the coyote's reflected image diminishes in the expanding distance, it limps after the ambulance, following the center yellow lines.

Ramola says, "It got up and is loping after us."

"Jesus. If I go full rabies, please don't let me launch myself into ambulances."

"That would be inadvisable."

Natalie turns away from the window, lifts her phone, looks at it, puts it back down, as though confirming it is still in her hand.

Despite knowing it's impossible for the sick and injured coyote to keep up with them now at 45mph, Ramola watches for a reappearance of its scraggly form, checking the mirrors in a clockwise pattern. After looking at the fourth and final mirror, she decides to spin through the circuit one last time. Then she checks them again.

Natalie asks, "You see something back there?"

"Making sure it's gone."

Natalie says, "I can't believe I'm saying this, but you might want to slow down a little bit. Whole bunch of curves ahead. Coyote Cujo won't catch us."

"Sorry."

As though on cue, the ambulance lurches too fast through a dip in the road, giving Ramola that dropped-stomach, roller-coaster sensation. She slows to 30mph. Bay Road narrows and winds, following a typically New England path that was trod before pavement and town planning. The surrounding forest grows thicker, the houses more infrequent. The northeastern border of the expansive Borderland State Park is less than a mile ahead on their right. Thigh-high, lichen- and moss-colored walls of stacked stones run along both sides of the road for stretches before randomly turning and disappearing into the woods. The walls are a holdover from the 1800s. Farmers would clear the impossibly rocky soil and used the stones to build over 100,000 miles of walls throughout New England.

Natalie prattles on about Coyote Cujo and how it should check its ambitions, downsize to leaping at compact cars or motorcycles, leave attacking ambulances to rabid rhinos or rabid circus elephants. There are elephants at the Southwick Zoo maybe thirty miles west, and Natalie hopes those fuckers are on lockdown.

They pass the torn-up carcass of a raccoon in the opposite lane, supine on its back, paws clenched into black stones, stomach and chest flattened and red. Ahead on the shoulder, another animal, what appears to be a dead opossum, its body seemingly intact. From Ramola's drive-by vantage there is no way to determine if the opossum is the victim of an accident, animal attack, or has succumbed to the virus.

Natalie sighs as though annoyed with her own ramblings, picks up her phone, presses buttons, and says, "Hi, did you miss me? Ah, fuck this." She hits more buttons and slams the phone

down into her lap. She says, "This sucks. This all sucks. Fuck."
She pauses and then asks, "This might sound totally random,
but do you know what movie I hated that everyone else loved?"

"No."

"*City of Men*. No wait, *Children of Men*. I always mess up
the title. The one where the world was fucked because no one
could have babies anymore but Clive Owen finds one preggo,
blah, blah, blah. I mean, fine, I guess it's a well-made movie, but
women as incubators to repopulate and save the world is bullshit, you know?"

Trying to elicit a smile from Natalie, or even better, a subject
change, Ramola says, "I like Clive Owen. He was wonderful in
Gosford Park."

Natalie ignores her. "Paul loved it, of course, and would randomly text me pics and GIFs from the movie. He thought he
was so funny. Which, he kinda was. When we decided to try
getting pregnant I told Paul there would be no *Children of Men*
bullshit for us. If the world was falling apart—more so than it
already was—he had to promise I was more important than the
kid. I had to live. If anyone needed saving, or whatever, it was me
first. He thought I was joking. I mean, I was, but I also wasn't."

"I take it you both promised that your relationship would remain as important—"

"Ha-ha! No, just me. I made him pinky-swear I would always be most important, and if it came down to it, he'd save me
first. He wasn't happy about it, but he did it—" Her voice cracks,
tears are close but she doesn't give in.

Ramola stares ahead. The winding road narrows further; the
forest closing in on them.

"He wanted me to swear back that I'd save him." Natalie

coughs, the sputtering noises transforming into weary, heart-breaking laughter. "I wouldn't do it. I rubbed it in his face. I told him there was nothing I could do, once I was a mom the kid would always come first, isn't that what everyone says? Oh, he got so pissed and tried to take back his pinky-swear, but you can't take it back. Those are the rules. You can't take anything back." Natalie pauses. The pause becomes three deep breaths. "And here I am; the fucking incubator."

"No, Natalie—"

"Paul and I tried to save each other today. We both tried. We fought hard. We really did. But we failed."

"That's enough! No more! I can't imagine what you went through and I know you're suffering and frightened—"

"Don't. Don't say it."

Ramola has to say it, even if she knows deep down it isn't true. "But you are going to live, and so is your child. We're going to arrive at the new clinic in less than ten minutes and they're going to help and take care of you."

Natalie says, "Wow. I can't believe you yelled at me."

"Well, I'm sorry, but you deserved it."

"No, I love it. But you're either a liar or, as we know to be true, a terrible jinx."

Ramola clucks her tongue and waves a dismissive hand, oddly aware the I-give-up gesture is one her mum frequently employs.

Natalie says, "*Gosford Park* is meh, by the way. A movie about rich British assholes."

"Now you're being a prat."

"The characters aren't rich British assholes?"

"They are; however, that's the point of the movie, isn't it. Are there any other films you'd like to besmirch?"

"Where do I begin—oh, hey, you see that? What are they doing?"

Ahead, on a short stretch of straightaway, is a side street on the left. Two people wearing bike helmets, bulky backpacks, and dark hooded sweatshirts ride BMX bikes, pedaling furiously toward Bay Road. They cut the corner, darting between a giant fir tree and an undulating stone wall. They dump their bikes and packs, and they crouch behind the stones.

Ramola slows as the ambulance pulls even with the side street, eyes only for the huddled bike riders.

Natalie yells, and a large white blur smashes into the ambulance's rear. Their back end slides right, as though hydroplaning, and Ramola initially turns into it. The ambulance rumbles along the brush-filled shoulder, which slows them down and allows her to wrest some control. She cuts the wheel, turns them back toward the street, and pumps the brakes. The back end remains rooted to the shoulder though, and as they come to a surprisingly smooth stop, the front grille and windshield faces across the street at an almost forty-five-degree angle.

The two women share a moment of blinking stares.

Ramola peels her hands away from the steering wheel and asks, "Are you all right?" She does so quietly, as though afraid of the answer.

Natalie says, "Yeah. I think so. Well, I'm the same as I was before. Nothing new hurts. I think I peed a little."

A boat-sized white sedan is latched onto the ambulance like a lamprey, its crumpled nose buried into the driver's-side rear wheel well. The car's back wheels spin, whine, and smoke. It bullies the ambulance's back end, pushing it over the road's shoulder, into the brush, and pins the passenger's-side rear bumper and tire against a rock wall. The ambulance is now turned so as to be almost perpendicular to Bay Road. The cab rocks from side to side.

Ramola checks the mirrors but can't yet see the driver. Knowing it'll be futile, given the ambulance's rear axle is likely mangled, she presses the gas pedal. The engine complains, revs high, but they don't go anywhere. She tries the lower gears, shifts into reverse, and then back into drive, but nothing catches.

"I didn't see anything but I assume we were hit by a car and not rammed by a rabid circus elephant, or Dumbo's mom. One of the few Disney animal moms who doesn't die. They put her in a cage instead. Said she'd gone crazy. They always say that."

As Natalie continues on about cages and other Disney moms, Ramola shifts into park, unbuckles her seat belt, and reaches for the door handle.

"Hey, whoa, where are you going?"

"Out there to—"

Natalie finishes for her, "Out there to talk to the nice person who crashed into us and is pushing us into the woods?"

"The gas pedal could be stuck. The driver is likely hurt and needs help."

Natalie yells, "No! N-no! You know! You know what—what the driver is! You—you know!" She gets louder the more she stammers, and her eyes go satellite-dish big the more frustrated she's clearly becoming with herself. "You know, Rams!" The outburst isn't as shocking as her sudden confused countenance.

The bike riders spring from their hiding spots and sprint the short distance down and across the road to the accident. They are boys likely in their late teens; one brandishes an aluminum base-ball bat and the other carries a thin, sun-bleached wooden pole, almost as long as he is tall. In addition to their skateboarder-style helmets and hoodies the teenagers are wearing jeans and black high-top sneakers. Red bandannas cocoon their necks. Each has three water bottles hanging in front of his chest, dangling from a yoke of cords. The taller teen has long dark curly hair spilling out from under his helmet; the straps are unfastened and dangle on both sides of his chin and neck. The other boy's helmet is so tightly worn as to be a carapace.

They give the sedan's rear end and its hissing tires a wide berth. The shorter one waves to Ramola and continues to wave until she raises a hand. He gives a thumbs-up and then cups one hand around his mouth, and shouts. The other teen shouts too. Ramola rolls the window halfway down to better hear them.

"It's okay!" and "We're healthy!" and "We're friendlies!" and "Yeah, friendlies!" and "We're gonna help!" and "We got this!" and "We're zombie experts!"

"Bloody wankers." Ramola turns and says to Natalie, "Call 911. If you can't get through . . ." She digs out Dr. Awolesi's card. "Even if you do get through, call Dr. Awolesi. Or text her. Tell her where we are and we need a new ride."

Ramola opens the ambulance door and steps down onto the street. Natalie objects, says something about taking a weapon. Ramola doesn't respond and shuts the door.

The sedan's rear wheels stop spinning. The teens bob and weave, approaching and then retreating from the driver's-side door like children chasing receding ocean waves and running away when the surf surges back to shore. They engage in rapid-fire commands, insults, inanities, retorts, and it's all so quick as to almost be of one voice.

"The driver's some old guy."

"Smash the window."

"I can't see what he's doing. Wait a second."

"Nah, guy. Smash it now."

"You fucking do it then."

"I can't. Not with the staff."

"What?" which is pronounced as an elongated, affected "Wut."

"The staff is not made for window smashing."

"What's the staff made for? Polite tapping?"

"Don't question the staff."

"Are you going to say 'the staff' every time you refer to it?"

"The staff abides."

Ramola interjects, "Hello, gentlemen—"

"*The staff* blows."

"The staff doesn't blow."

"The staff is *the* bad."

"You're right. It's *the* good."

Ramola tries again. "Hey, guys?"

"You should've just taken one of these." The shorter teen waves the bat over his head.

"You're gonna have to get too close to zombies with your stumpy-ass bat. And I'll keep 'em all at more than an arm's length. I'll be out of range."

"*Keep 'em all . . . at arm's length* is a great battle cry."

Ramola shouts, "Guys! Hey! Over here!"

The teens back away from the car and stare at Ramola. They are both thin and lithe. The taller one with the long hair is a couple inches shy of six feet. His brown eyes are sunken between rounded cheeks and below thick, crayon-scribble eyebrows. The shorter teen might be only a handful of inches taller than Ramola; he's certainly not taller than Natalie. He has sharper, more severe facial features, olive skin, and eyes so dark as to almost be black. He says, "Hey, what's up, Doc?" He smirks and looks to his partner for a reaction or approval. The taller one flashes looks between the car and Ramola.

The Bugs Bunny quip notwithstanding, Ramola speaks before the two of them can start again, hoping her acknowledged medical status inspires gravitas. She says, "Tell me you're not planning on assaulting the driver, who probably needs help, just like my friend and I do—"

"Yeah, okay, Doctor Who. Listen: the driver has been trying to run us down for, like, the last ten minutes."

"He followed us for more than a mile, swerving all over the road and shit, driving after us on sidewalks. He even followed us through a couple of backyards."

"The driver's clearly a zombie."

"You can't help a zombie, Doc."

"A zombie driving the car. Can you believe it?"

"I know, right? This timeline is glitching out."

"So hard."

Ramola says, "The driver may very well be infected, but he is not a zombie." She walks between the teens and as she gets closer to the sedan one of them mumbles, "Same diff." She crouches, peering inside the window. The driver is an elderly white man with thinning but stubborn wispy tufts of white hair. Foamy saliva bubbles around his mouth. He sways in his seat, shakes his head, and rubs his eyes with the back of his hands. His movements are herky-jerky, frames missing from stop-motion animation. When he sees Ramola, he slaps the window with open hands.

The taller teen says, "I think we have his attention."

"Tap the window with the staff just in case we don't."

"Fucker."

Ramola backs away from the car, unsure of what to do. When she first climbed out of the ambulance, she had visions of commandeering a damaged-but-not-totaled sedan and driving Natalie and the presumably injured (but hopefully not infected) driver the approximately two miles to the clinic. She can't think of a way to get the infected man out of the car without endangering everyone, the elderly man included. She is not going to allow the teens to bash and batter him with their weapons. She cannot tell if the teens are too gleeful at the prospect of violence or too clueless to fully appreciate the situation into which they've inserted themselves. Likely a combination of both, as the flame of violence is generally fueled by ignorance. Should they instead barricade the old man into the vehicle somehow, particularly if they are forced to start down the road on foot? They would also have to slash the tires to further disable the sedan, making sure he couldn't drive after them. Perhaps she should check in with Natalie, to see if 911 or Dr. Awolesi has responded.

Ramola briefly explains to the teens that her friend Natalie is pregnant, the baby is due in a matter of days, and they need to get her to the Ames Clinic as soon as possible. Ramola purposefully does not tell them Natalie has been exposed to the virus and is possibly infected. She has never been a skillful liar, including lies of omission. While she thinks it's doubtful the zombie bros have the wherewithal to detect she isn't telling them the entire story, the shorter one looks at Ramola, his head slightly cocked, as though he's picking up on what she isn't saying. That he might not trust what Ramola is telling them makes her trust *him* a bit more.

The shorter one says, "Never been to the clinic but we know Five Corners well."

Ramola asks, "We need a car. Do either of you live close by?"

The taller teen shakes his head. "Our apartment is in Brockton. You could walk to the clinic and back in the time it would take for us to bike back, get a car from a friend, even if we could get one."

They look too young to have their own apartment, but Ramola files that nagging thought away. "Is there anyone close by in Ames you could call, ask for a ride? Another ambulance might be on the way, but I would prefer not to wait too long."

The shorter teen smirks. "Nah, sorry, no one we know around here would want to help us, I don't think."

"Yeah, we're not too popular in these parts."

An odd set of answers that makes Ramola mentally step aside from the manic at-all-costs quest to get Natalie to the clinic and analyze the danger inherent in being alone with two strange and quite possibly unstable young men carrying weapons.

The sedan's door opens. The dented metal pops and creaks. The old man shouts, "Top off!" and laboriously pulls himself out of the car and onto his feet. He's dressed in slacks and a beige dress shirt, some buttons in the wrong holes, other buttonholes skipped over.

"Top off! Half done!" He blinks like there's sand in his eyes. He briefly smiles; the face of someone's kindly grandfather. His mouth goes slack, gapes open; the face of madness.

The teens laugh, and shout, "Oh yeah!" and "Let's go!"

The old man does not move quickly, but he is shuffling toward them. His right leg lags behind as he lurches forward, and he reaches for his hip with each shuddering step.

The taller teen says, "Wait, wait, wait!" He tucks his staff under an arm, most of the length of pole trailing behind him. He unhooks one of the clear water bottles from around his neck; a hard plastic polycarbonate bottle athletes and hikers favor. "Let's have a test."

"Nah, guy. No fucking around."

"Look at him. He's slow." He unscrews the bottle's lid. He steps toward the elderly man.

The shorter one backs away a few steps, and his hard look softens.

"Hey, gramps. Have some. Water is *the* good."

The shorter teen laughs but laughs too hard. He's clearly nervous and scared, but he doesn't want to admit it, and/or (one does not preclude the other) he's on the verge of losing control.

"Top off! Half done! All gone!" The elderly man's voice wavers and is full of gravel.

The teen holds the bottle out in front of him, a vampire hunter holding forth a cross. Water sloshes over the bottle's rim and splatters on the pavement.

The old man's arms jerk. His body shakes and convulses. He coughs and retches.

The taller teen says, "Oh shit, it really works. He's freaking out. The power of Christ compels you!" He laughs, lunges forward, and splashes water onto the old man.

The old man recoils, stumbling back into his car, but he rebounds and propels forward. He lashes out with a closed fist, knocking the bottle out of the teen's hand.

The teen panics, his arms windmilling as he scrambles backward. His staff falls and clatters to the pavement. His feet get tangled with each other, crashing him to the street. His helmet pops off and rolls past Ramola. She runs to his aid.

"All gone! All gone!" The old man's voice is deep and ancient, the weary, inevitable groan of tectonic plates. His broken strides, like those of the coyote, impossibly carry his bulk.

Ramola crouches, grabs the prone teen's left arm, and attempts to pull him onto his feet and away from the approaching old man. The teen half sits up and crab-walks backward. She instantly calculates he is not moving quickly enough for him to get away. Ramola lets go of the teen's arm, reaches, and grabs one end of the wooden staff. She flicks the other end up and pushes it between the elderly man's ankles. She pushes hard right on the staff, as though flipping a lever.

The man's right leg crumples, and the old man lists and falls left. As he does so, the shorter teen rushes in, swings the bat with two hands. Had the old man remained upright, the bat would've struck him in the head; instead, with his right leg giving out and his body already in the process of collapsing, his head dips and his left shoulder rises up, which is where the teen lands the blow. The contact is solid but happens later in the swing's arc, which throws the teen off balance. He falls hard onto one knee but is quickly able to gather himself and regain his feet.

The blow spins the old man to his left, sending him careening into the ambulance. His head bounces off the side panel and he slides to the road.

Ramola rises from her crouch, the staff held in both hands.

The taller teen scoots backward until he's behind Ramola. He laughs and shouts, "The staff is the good!"

The shorter teen limps around in a couple of tight circles, shaking out his lower leg. He swears and talks to himself. Tears stream down his cheeks.

The taller teen stops laughing, serious now, and says softly to his friend, "Hey, guy. It's okay. I'm okay."

"Fuck you! Fuck this!" He wipes his face on his sleeves.

The elderly man rolls over onto his back. A gash has opened on his wide forehead. Hands flutter at his eyes and they smear the blood around, turning his face red. His breaths are watery and hiss like a tire leaking air. Mixed in are heartbreakingly clear ows and whimpers. He attempts to get up, putting weight on his lower leg, which is bent at an unnatural angle at the knee. He screams and melts back to the pavement.

The taller teen asks Ramola, "Hey, um, can I have my staff back?"

The shorter teen stomps toward the old man, bat cocked. He's still crying but he's also grunting and breathing heavy like a bodybuilder gearing up for the big lift.

Ramola, staff in her hands, intercepts him. "Stop. Slow down, wait. Hey, what's your name? You can keep calling me Doctor Who if you like, but my name is Ramola." She hopes to calm him down with an exchange of names, a reminder of their humanity.

The teen pauses his advance. His bat is still cocked but his snarl is gone. He says, "Luis."

"Hello, Luis. And your friend's name?"

"Josh," answers the other teen. He retrieves his helmet and holds it in the crook of an arm.

Luis lunges forward. He says, "We need to do this. We have to—"

Ramola fully steps into and blocks his path. "Look at his leg."

Josh says, "Oh, that's nasty." He half covers his face with a hand, groans, and makes assorted that-is-so-gross noises.

Ramola continues, speaking in pointed and short sentences, as though she is delivering difficult news to a parent of one of her sick patients. "He's not getting up. He will not come after us. You don't need to hit him again."

Luis flutters looks between Ramola and Josh. He says, "He's a zombie. We need to kill him."

"No. He is not a zombie. He is a *man*. You would be killing a sick man. You're not a killer, Luis. You and your friend Josh aren't killers."

Luis shakes his head. "We killed someone before—"

"Hey, guy, hey, no . . ." Josh says, and puts the helmet on. His head sinks between his shoulders and he pulls the helmet's crown over his eyes, as though he can't bear to watch.

Luis says, "He was old." He isn't looking at Ramola, but he isn't looking at the old man either. "Wasn't all our fault. We didn't know what we were doing." The defeated tone of his voice belies the boast or threat inherent within the we-killed-a-guy confession regardless as to whether it is the truth or a lie. Is he saying they killed another infected old man?

She says, "This would be different, Luis. You know what you are doing because I'm telling you. You'd be choosing to kill a man now. There wouldn't be any doubt or question."

"We'd be helping him. Putting him out of his misery. There's no cure," Josh says.

It's clear to Ramola this is empty posturing on Josh's part. Or maybe it's what she wants to believe. Ramola unleashes her most withering look, and Josh dries up, shrinks, and suddenly discovers the tops of his sneakers to be fascinating.

The moment of potential further violence has passed. Ramola feels it, like an easing of barometric pressure. She says, "You don't get to decide that." Ramola tosses the staff into Josh's chest.

He catches it and mumbles, an admonished child, "Neither do you," but again, doesn't dare return her glare.

The old man has stopped moving. His breathing is labored and arrhythmic. His eyes are closed.

The bat sags in Luis's hands, a flag gone limp. He nods at Ramola and walks over to his friend. Josh pats him on the back, mumbles belated commentary about Luis "pillaging the zombie's cut" with one swing.

Ramola walks past the huddled, whispering teens (their annoying bro lingo all but indecipherable) to the ambulance door and opens it. She begins to ask if Natalie was able to get through to 911 or communicate directly with Dr. Awolesi, but stops. Natalie isn't in her seat.

Ramola climbs into and inspects the empty cab as though she might find Natalie crouching or hiding on the cab floor, folded neatly into the center console. She throws a panicked look into the rear of the ambulance, but she isn't there either. Ramola shouts Natalie's name as she slides out of the ambulance, landing awkwardly onto Bay Road. She slams the driver's door shut.

"Rams. Hey, Rams!" Natalie is in the street, standing adjacent to the ambulance's front grille. She says, "I'm right here," as if to say, *Where else should I be?* As raggedy as a child's favorite hand-sewn doll her arms are drawstrings dangling loosely at her sides. The unzipped halves of the too-small yellow sweatshirt are an open curtain for her protruding belly. Most of her hair has fallen out of her ponytail but not all, the stubborn elastic not willing to surrender when all is about lost.

Apoplectic with fear, worry, and exasperation, three questions crowd in and issue out of Ramola all at once. "Why did you—Did you climb—What are you doing out here?"

She says, "Sorry. I really had to pee. I almost didn't make it. Or, I mostly made it."

Ramola sighs. The teens go quiet. The old man has stopped breathing.

Natalie asks, "So how did the zombie fight go?"

NATS

Psst, hey, kid. I tried calling 911 like Auntie Rams said, but it's not picking up. Same for Dr. Awolesi's phone. I sent her a text, and I think it went through but she hasn't answered back, which is a problem because we need a new ride. There's heavy shit going down out there. I can't really turn around in my seat to see without less-than-mildly excruciating pain. Oh don't worry, it's not you, it's me.

I hear Rams talking to two boys. Can you hear them?

Sorry, I don't know why I'm whispering. Feels like the thing to do. Hey, life lesson: if it feels like the thing to do, then do it. Trust your gut. A cliché adults say all the time. Okay, we don't say it all the time, but we say it a lot. I mean, we're not walking into Dunks, buying coffee, and randomly saying to the guy with a cruller, *Hey, trust yer gut,* like it's the secret adult password. You know what, it might as well be the password. Not enough adults tell kids to trust themselves, trust their wee guts. My parents never said it. They only told me what not to do and what to do. Mostly the first thing. No teacher ever told me to trust your gut either. Which is stupid. No one needs to hear it more than kids do. Instead you're told the opposite. I don't have to tell you, right? So many of them make you do stuff you don't want to do because of convenience or laziness or they want to take advantage of you. They'll say you don't know better, you don't know what you're doing, you don't know who you are yet. That's a big one. And it's such bullshit. So, listen, only you know you, and if something doesn't feel right and you can't explain why, who cares. Trust your gut. Team Guts. Gut trust, all the way. You're in my gut right now, so it's like you are already telling you to trust your gut. You are your own gut. It's like the *Inception* of gut here. Okay, I'll stop saying "gut."

Whoa, did you hear that? Something just banged off the back of the ambulance. Shit. . . .

I wish I could see. No one is yelling or screaming? That's good, right? Hold on.

Back. I can see Rams in the other side-view mirror. Goddamn, I wish I could turn around. Maybe I should go out there too. She's talking with one of the boys. I'm going to make this quick.

This might sound weird—especially with the now-you deep-knee bending whenever I do these messages—but as I talk, the you I'm imagining is at least a year, maybe two years older than the you I imagined during the last recording. Wait. Do you get what I'm saying? In my head, it's like you age with each message I record. Time doesn't really work like that, but at the same time it does. Yeah, I'm moving time around because I can. You're growing up right before my eyes, or my mind's eyes. It's kind of cool? Maybe?

Actually it's not cool at all. It's horribly sad and horrible. Horribly horrible. I'm not trying to be funny. There's no way for me to describe how brutally terrible it is your dad died in front of me, like, a little over two hours ago and that not only am I not going to be around for you, but I have, um, foreknowledge of this.

It could be worse?

Yes, I'm crying now.

I hope to at least hold you before I'm gone. But I don't know, it's starting to feel like I'm never getting to a hospital or if I do get there, it'll be overrun like the others or it'll be too late for me to still be *me* by the time they yank you out and plop you into the middle of this hopeless, hellish existence.

Yeah, I'm fun. Sorry. Things are kind of darkest right now, and I've always been a bit of a pessimist. Glass not full. No messing around with halves and halve-nots. Again, not my best joke.

Okay, now I'm gonna trust my gut. Or bladder. I'm going outside. I gotta pee.

Love you.

Sassafras and lullabies.

RAMS

Josh says, "Is she, like, pregnant?"

Luis groans. "Guy. Doctor Who already said she was pregs."

"Right, but it's a shock seeing it, you know, right there, in your face."

Natalie says, "Rams, it's a shame you couldn't save those two from turning into zombies. It's so sad. Almost a tragedy." She shuffles toward the group while looking past them at the dead man on the road.

Josh says, "We're not zombies."

Luis groans again. "Guy. You are the bad."

Ramola says, "Please don't encourage them. Josh and Luis, this is Natalie."

They say, "Hey," and both lazily raise a hand in quarter-hearted greeting.

For her own comfort as much as her friend's, Ramola takes Natalie's left hand, careful to not tug or pull, anything that would put pressure on her wounded forearm. Natalie's skin is warm going on hot despite the autumn chill. A fever could mean she is infected or it could be a side effect of the vaccine, if she does in fact have a fever at all; Natalie has always claimed she runs a little hot.

"Your hand is cold," Natalie says, challenging Ramola to say otherwise.

Ramola pulls her hand away and hides it in her coat pocket, in case it decides to tell the truth.

"Okay, what's the plan? No fucking around." Natalie recounts her inability to get through to 911 or the Ames Clinic, and Dr. Awolesi hasn't responded to her texts.

The teens investigate the old man's car, reporting both front tires are flat and the driver's-side front rim is bent. Even if they could separate the two conjoined vehicles, the sedan isn't drivable. Ramola chimes in to say the obvious; the ambulance isn't going anywhere either.

The teens jog back to their roadside hiding spot for their bikes and backpacks.

Ramola stands in front of Natalie so they are face-to-face. Were the sun shining, she'd be completely engulfed by her friend's shadow. She says, "You know what I'm going to ask."

"I feel worse. It's like the flu. I'm cold and hot at the same time. Light-headed. My arm kills. My head pounds. My throat burns." Her voice is froggy and her skin is pale, wan, and purple and puffy under her eyes.

Despair swamps any and all thoughts of hope and reason. Ramola breaks eye contact and stares off into the woods. She wipes a hand across her forehead, as though checking her own temperature.

Natalie adds, "Don't worry. I promise not to bite anyone. Unless those two really piss me off."

"No noshing the teens, please. With that rough segue in mind, are you hungry? Did you pack any snacks?"

"Only a couple of infant-formula travel packs. I'll pass."

The teens rejoin the women, coasting in circles as they stand on their pedals. Josh's staff juts out of his pack, a flagpole without an emblem.

They say, "We got you" and "Your protection" and "Lots of zombie animals out there" and "We'll scout the road ahead" and "You're lucky we're here" and "We're experts." They sound as ebullient and full of bravura as they did before the old man emerged from the car. They drone on in their endless, witless banter. "This is the part in the zombie movie when the heroes team up with randos" and "They fight to survive together" and "Can't do it alone" and "The first rule of the zombie apocalypse" and "But then the group has a hard time getting along" and "From different walks of life and shit" and "Sometimes they break up" and "Sometimes they don't" and "Then randos get picked off one by one" and "It always happens" and "The brown guy always goes first" and "Guy, you aren't brown" and "The fuck I'm not" and "We'll be all right. We're the heroes" and "Nah, heroes always die" and "Hey, this might sound crazy but we could give you two a ride. Sit on the handlebars" and "Guy. Let them stand on the rear pegs" and "Right. We'd go slow. Totally safe" and "We used to—"

Natalie says, "You're right. That sounds crazy. So, what are we going to do?"

After a brief discussion, Ramola and Natalie decide one of the teens should bike the two miles ahead to the clinic and send back someone to pick them up.

Josh says, "Makes sense but 'don't split up' is, like, the number-two rule of the zomb apoc."

Luis says, "Guy. Don't. I hate it when characters say 'zombos' or 'walkers' or something else so *writers' room*. Just fucking say 'zombies.'"

Ramola shouts, "There are no zombies! This is not the apocalypse! You must stop saying that. It's not helping."

Josh ignores her and says to Luis, "Shrugs, guy. Shrugs."

Luis says, "Whatever. So which one of *we* is going to the clinic?"

The two of them argue. Luis makes a crack about leaving Ramola the staff because she knows how to use it better than Josh. Somehow they achieve a bro-speak consensus ratified with a complicated handshake routine.

Josh says, "Tell me to keep off the moors and stick to the road," quoting lines from a movie that's more than twenty years older than he is.

Luis obliges.

Josh pedals down the road flanked by towering pine, birch, and oak trees, the highest branches shivering in the wind, peacocking their greens, reds, and browns. Leaves fall, whirling in invisible eddies, their individual paths balletic, unpredictable, until they land, as they must, and join the autumnal mob usurping the shoulders of the road, massed against stone walls, blanketing the forest floor. Ramola, Natalie, and Luis silently watch until Josh disappears around a bend.

Ramola checks her phone and is unable to connect to the Internet or get through to 911. Her texts to Dr. Awolesi also go unanswered. It appears they are relying on Josh. If it takes him ten to fifteen minutes to bike to the clinic; maybe another five to ten to convince someone to send a vehicle back in their direction; a fiveish-minute drive down the narrow, windy road; another five to ten minutes (estimate includes crossover time spent getting her and Natalie into the vehicle) on the return to the clinic; and then however long to be screened and prepped for the C-section, they are looking at, all told, close to an hour total. If Natalie is indeed infected (the memory of the warmth of Natalie's skin is a physical one), do they even have an hour? What is she going to do if Natalie succumbs to infection prior to arriving at the clinic? She imagines Natalie with eyes as dead as a cadaver's, her mouth an animal's snarl, and saliva running down her chin. Maybe riding on the handlebars isn't such a ridiculous idea.

As though reading her mind, Natalie says, "Fuck this. I'm not waiting here. Come on, Rams, grab our bags." She steps out into the road.

Luis says, "Whoa, where you going?"

"Heading toward the clinic. Just in case."

Ramola and Luis plead with her to stay at the ambulance. Ramola maintains that it isn't safe to be out walking the road. Luis asks what if they're walking and she gets attacked by a rabid animal?

There's time enough before Natalie's response for Ramola to wonder if she's going to say it doesn't matter if an animal bites her, she's already been exposed. Looking and speaking to Ramola and Ramola only, Natalie says, "We saw what a fucking zoo Norwood Hospital was. What if there are no available emergency vehicles at the clinic or they don't have any staff available to leave the building or, I don't know, what if they don't believe Josh?"

Ramola chimes in to say they should've had Josh take a picture of them and the ambulance with his phone to show the clinic.

Natalie says, "Sure, right. Look, all I'm saying is there's no guarantee Josh will get help. He'll probably be fine but, sorry, what if something happens to him on the way? What if he doesn't make it? I'm not waiting around for what-ifs. I'm walking. If he gets an ambulance, which he probably will, then great and it'll still see us and pick us up as we're walking down Bay Road. And we'll be that much closer to the clinic. And we can knock on doors and ask for a ride along the way too. Worst-case scenario, we walk the two miles. I'm not waiting around to be saved."

Luis says, "Nah, I don't like it."

"Then you can stay here, *guy*. Keep playing pretend zombie hunter." Natalie heads down the road, straddling the double yellow lines, listing from side to side like a ship in a choppy sea, her right hand under her belly.

Ramola isn't sure if this is the best idea. But how can she be sure? How can anyone be sure given unprecedented, impossible circumstances? Natalie's desperation—now manifested by her willingness to march two miles despite obvious pain and distress—plus the notion of moving closer to their destination, even incrementally, sends Ramola into the ambulance cab to quickly consolidate their two overnight bags. After transferring a few of her items, Ramola slings Natalie's bag over her shoulder and jogs to catch up to her friend.

Natalie says, "Okay, Luis. Talk to me. Take my mind off how much walking sucks. Where are you from?"

"I live in Brockton with Josh."

"What are you doing out here? Aren't you guys getting a little bit old to be playing *Stranger Things*?"

Luis chuckles, pedals ahead, and circles a loop around the women. "We grew up in this area. On the other side, the west side of Borderland State Park. With everything ending, we thought it would be, I don't know, fitting to come back."

Ramola says, "Everything isn't ending. Civilization is more resilient than people think."

Natalie adds, "For better or worse."

Luis says, "When we were younger, we would ride into Borderland—we had a special spot—and hang out and make plans about what we'd do in case of a zombie apocalypse. So here it is and here we are." He pauses, as though honoring the memory with reverie and regret. "Turns out it's probably not a good place to be."

Ramola says, "We'll get through this. We will."

Natalie snorts a short laugh. "Luis, how many zombies have you seen so far?"

"Not many. We've put down a couple of cats—"

Natalie laughs. "Sorry. Didn't mean to laugh. It's terrible. Poor Mittens and Mr. Bigglesworth." She says the latter name in her faux British accent.

Luis says, "White foam, walking like drunks, the whole bit, but they charged us. The second one got its head stuck in the spokes of Josh's rear tire. We had no choice."

"You two are indeed heroes. Sorry, I'm being a jerk. Any non-feline zombies?"

"A raccoon, a skunk, and two coyotes."

"Did you put them down too?"

"Nah, they were mostly dead, barely moving, so we just rode away."

"Any people zombies?"

There's a pause, and then Luis talks slowly, like a sputtering engine afraid to commit to the internal combustion. "In Brockton. He was an uncle of someone we used to be friends with, but I, um . . . it was terrible and I don't want to talk about it. And that old guy driving the car was number two. A zombie driving a car. I still can't believe it." He laughs, though to Ramola's ears, it sounds forced, fake.

His responses to Natalie's questions came off as natural and genuine until this answer about a former friend's uncle. Ramola flashes to her previous we-killed-a-guy-before conversation with Luis. She studies the now nervously smiling boy, one who isn't that much older than some of her pediatric patients. Children and teens (and, of course, adults too) lie, especially when put under tremendous stress. At her job she's become quite proficient at sussing out hidden or obscured truths from her young patients and their parents. Ramola concludes Luis was lying earlier or is lying now, but not both. Reflecting on what Luis and Josh said and now Luis not wanting to talk about this *former* friend's uncle, she can't shake the nagging insistence the two teens spoke as though they'd killed a man prior to the outbreak. Ramola wonders if she should attempt to come up with a reason for Luis to join Josh and leave them be.

Natalie says, "We've seen a whole bunch of people zombies. We even had one shooting a gun at us."

"Get the fuck outta here. Seriously?" Luis laughs and claps his hands together once, rides without holding the handlebars.

"This timeline, man. It's so messed up." He pulls up his bike next to Natalie, on her left. His feet drip off of the pedals and spill onto the street. He rolls himself forward with little languid push-offs.

With her raconteur's verve and flair, Natalie recounts their harrowing hospital escape. She does not embellish or exaggerate while omitting their having received vaccinations. Ramola smirks at her brief but curiously strong pang of jealousy that she is not the intended audience of Natalie's spirited retelling.

Luis, utterly charmed and rapt, laughs and spews exclamations of disbelief. Ramola notes he doesn't ask why they were at the hospital. He likely assumes impending birth is reason enough.

Ramola checks for texts and keeps an eye on the road, which elongates ahead of them as though they've made zero progress. "Natalie, let me know if you need a break."

"I'm okay." She doesn't sound okay. Her voice has gone from froggy to desert-wanderer. Her pace is slowing and more labored, favoring her left leg.

Luis says, "So the guy was probably not a zombie before he picked up the gun, right? Or was he? Like the old guy in the car. Was he a zombie before he got into the car? Or was he driving along somewhere and then he turned while he was driving? I don't get it."

Ramola says, "You don't get it because they're not zombies. Both of you need to stop discussing the victims as such. They're people infected with a virus that interferes with communication between brain cells, shutting down inhibitions, causing extreme aggression, confusion, terrible hallucinations."

Natalie says, "I read about some rabies patients, when they get toward the end, they experience moments of lucidity. Almost like a remission, and they're who they were again, but only for a short time. Maybe that's what happened with the car guy. He was gone, but then he came back to himself, and he tried to drive somewhere for help, and went away again, lost in his own malfunctioning brain. It's fucking horrible."

Luis says, "Be right back," returns his feet to the pedals, and zooms off. About fifty feet ahead, he brakes and hops off his bike in one athletic motion. At the same time, a furry dark shape launches from the brush. Luis backs away, reaches behind his head, and pulls the bat out of his backpack as though pulling a sword from a scabbard.

A large raccoon, with its telltale burglar's uniform and black mask, spastically scrambles over the bike's metal frame, hissing and barking. Luis bludgeons the creature with four quick, compact swings.

Ramola stops walking. Natalie, unfazed, continues marching forward.

"Natalie, shouldn't we wait here a moment?"

"Machine's moving. Can't stop it. Too hard to start again."

Luis belatedly covers his mouth with the bandanna as he watches the motionless animal. He gives it a nudge with the bat and quickly backs away. The raccoon doesn't react. He edges the bat's barrel underneath the creature and flings its body toward the side of the road. Muttering to himself (Ramola can't be sure, but she thinks she hears him say, "Sorry, fella."), it takes him two more tries before the raccoon is returned to the brush, a shadow sunken in the leaves and tall grass. Luis wiggles his backpack free, removes a can of disinfectant, and sprays the bike frame, his bat, his hands, the tops of his shoes. Next, he pulls out a plastic canister of wipes and cleans the bat and bike. By the time both are sanitized to his satisfaction, Natalie and Ramola catch up to him.

Cleaning items returned, he re-shoulders the pack, sheathes the bat, pulls the bandanna down, and says, "I, uh, saw it moving in the grass." Hand gestures mimic the animal's approach. His voice is hushed and not in any way self-congratulatory. He avoids eye contact, acting sheepish and embarrassed. Ramola wonders how much different a recounting of the event would be for Josh.

Natalie arcs around Luis and the inkblot puddle of the raccoon's blood. "What are you gonna do when a rabid elephant comes at us?" Natalie giggles and continues walking.

Luis doesn't have an answer. He climbs onto his bike and rides next to Natalie, scanning the brush and perimeter of the state park to their right. Ramola trails a step or two behind. Natalie's breathing is heavy and openmouthed. No one talks.

They walk and they walk. Wind skitters leaves across their path. Tree branches shake and rattle. Birdcalls and the imposter-owl hoots of mourning doves echo; so too the icy, faraway cries and howls of coyotes.

The road ahead is dotted with dead animals; two rabbits, gored but not consumed, another raccoon (a juvenile judging by its size), and a fox. The fox lies on its side in the opposite lane, orange-red furry back to them as they approach, fluffy tail between its legs, no visible injuries or traumas. It could be asleep, readying a surprise pounce, living up to its trickster reputation.

Ramola is not religious or spiritual and rightly scoffs at the notion of things happening for a reason. Her faith is placed within the fragile hands of humanity's capacity for kindness and service. However, given her childhood obsession with the fox, it's difficult not to divine nihilistic meaning from the dead animal or view it as a portent of terrible things to come. Ramola has an urge to carry the beautiful creature into the forest, lay it to rest at the base of a tree, and cover it with leaves and pine needles. Part of her wants to transport it elsewhere, to where there is no sickness. As they pass the fox, Ramola turns and walks backward to fully view its front. Paws are held tight at its midsection, the snout tucked into its chest, and eyes clenched shut as though it can no longer bear to see. Ramola spins back, her gaze returning to Natalie and the winding road through the forest ahead, where all manner of tooth and fang await. In her mind she briefly returns to her childhood bedroom in South Shields, this animal with its still-vibrant, playful, glowing coat is sprawled across her bed, her shabby stuffed foxes (imposters; pale, ugly ducklings by comparison) posed around it in respectful vigil. As a young child, she insisted her parents repeatedly read her favorite Grimms' fairy tale "The Wedding of Mrs. Fox." Her dad used funny voices and was careful to linger on each word, never rushing through, keeping to a rhythm that would lull her to sleep. Her mum often recited the tale by heart, she'd read it so often, and would test and pique her persnickety daughter with dark and goofy ad-libs to the story. Like Mrs. Fox, Ramola professed that when older she would reject all suitors who weren't wearing red trousers or didn't have a pointed face. Lines from the tale run through her head now: "She is sitting in her room, Moaning in her gloom, Weeping her little eyes quite red, Because old Mr. Fox is dead."

Natalie eerily echoes the finishing line, swapping genders, mumbling, "Poor Mrs. Fox is dead."

No ambulances or cars pass them. There aren't even any sirens bleating in the distance.

Ramola checks her watch again. They've been walking for sixteen minutes. Josh should be at the clinic by now.

A mint-green Borderland State Park sign is visible about two hundred paces ahead. The main entrance is on the other, western side of the park. This sign marks an alternate entrance and a small, corner dirt lot in which people who purchased a yearly pass are allowed to park. Two trails lead away from the lot. Bob's Trail is thin, winding, its path veined with tree roots and glacial boulders shrouded by the forest canopy. The other trail has no name and is a two-lane dirt access road, which hikers and bikers are allowed to traverse; a padlocked wooden gate prohibits the public from driving into the heart of the park. Abutting the lot is an intersection. Lincoln Street and Allen Road spoke off in their easterly and westerly directions. Beyond the intersection, houses are again perched along Bay Road.

Luis says, "Josh is taking his sweet-ass time."

Natalie coughs. It's a dry, painful sound, full of dust, and after, she has difficulty catching her breath.

Ramola says, "You're pushing yourself too hard. Let's take a break. A short one."

Natalie says, "I'm fine. I mean, my boobs hurt and my back kills and my hips are pulling apart. But I'm good." She coughs again, then growls, as though she might scare the coughs away.

Luis rides a handful of paces ahead of Natalie, spins out the bike in a neat little move so that he blocks her path and is turned to face her. He says, "I'm a dumbass. Sorry, I got water to spare." He offers game-show display hands in front of the bottles hanging over his chest. "Choose wisely."

Ramola, without thinking, says, "Yes, you'll be no good to anyone if you get dehydrated, least of all yourself or your child. You need to drink."

Natalie comes to an abrupt halt and shouts, "Do I? You think so?" Her teeth are gritted, eyes wild; a look of unadulterated anger. During their university days Ramola mockingly delighted, documented, and cheered sightings of Angry Nats, such appearances generally reserved for unreasonable professors, rude bar patrons, and man-boy twits who insisted Natalie could not turn down having a drink in their company.

As Natalie holds her in a stare, Ramola recognizes the look as not necessarily one of anger, or solely of anger, but one of betrayal and resignation. Natalie blinks rapidly, as though she might start crying. She turns so her back is to Luis, and says, "Rams?" like a question. She bends her left arm and winces.

"Are you okay?" Luis asks.

Whether or not Natalie has succumbed to infection, it's clear she fears having a hydrophobic reaction to water. A high temperature and flu-like symptoms, for the time being, doesn't have to equate to infection and could be vaccination side effects. Hydrophobia is as classic and telling a symptom as foaming around the mouth.

Ramola rubs her friend's right shoulder and considers whispering, *We need to know*, which would feel selfish in a way she cannot explain or abide. She instead whispers, "It might be okay." Can it still be a lie even if it is not a declarative statement?

Natalie says, "It won't."

"You need to try." Ramola wishes she had something better to say, something with more resolve and more hope.

Natalie closes her eyes, shakes her head, and coughs. "Fucking ow." She shrugs Ramola's hand off her shoulder and turns to face Luis. She says, "Hey, guy, I can't wait to drink the delicious neck water you got there. Splash that shit over here."

Ramola walks over to Luis, who is totally confused, sitting on his bike, frozen in place. She says, "May I," and sets to removing one of the water bottles from the cord around his neck. "These are in fact filled with water, I presume. Drinkable water."

"Yeah." Luis lets Ramola untie one of the bottles. "Filled them this morning."

"Did you fill them with love in your heart?" Natalie is freaking out. Tearful begging and pleading would be less disturbing than her desperate humor and the low-wave frequency of panic amping in her voice. Natalie adds, "Make sure you pick the one that doesn't have rabid raccoon guts on it. That's not my thing."

"I'm choosing a clean one." Ramola frees a bottle, unscrews the lid, and takes a quick sip. The water is cooler than she expects. It has that hard taste of water having been in a plastic bottle but is also undeniably refreshing. Her body craves more but she will wait.

Natalie says, "Is this filtered water? Tap water? Brockton's kind of a big city. Do you know the nitrate levels? Do you have the city's water report handy? I'm drinking for two and all that."

Ramola faces Natalie with the bottle cradled against her chest, small hands wrapped closer to the top of the bottle, attempting to obscure the view of the water line. She says, "The water tastes fine."

"You can taste lead, nitrates, sulfates, and all the other –ates?"

Natalie is only a few steps away from Ramola. "Yes, I'm a doctor." She wills Natalie to look at her face and not the bottle.

A wry smile falters and flickers away. "You're not a water doctor."

Ramola wanders to Natalie's right side instead of camping directly in front of her. Still gripping the bottle in both hands, she slowly extends it to Natalie.

"Fine. But this is just going to make me have to pee on the side of the road again." Natalie reaches for the bottle with her right hand, a hand that is shaking. She drops her hand to her side. "Sorry, I guess I'm a little shaky from the walk."

"You've had a day," Ramola says, being her friend's agreeable chorus.

Natalie reaches for the bottle again. Shakes become tremors as her hand gets closer to the bottle. A high-pitched whine leaks through her lips, apparently involuntary, judging by Natalie's shocked expression.

Ramola steps closer and guides Natalie's hand to the bottle. Natalie closes her eyes, but it doesn't prevent the tremors from spreading into her arm, shoulders, and head. She jerks her hand away. Water spills, slapping on the pavement at their feet, but Ramola keeps hold of the bottle.

Natalie, out of breath, says, "I—I can't."

Ramola says, "Let me help. It's all right. You're exhausted. Dehydrated." She employs the same tone of voice she uses with her sickest patients. "Relax. Breathe." Ramola attempts to dampen her inner emotional turmoil by imagining what she needs to do and say next as a clinical list of instructions and procedures handwritten in black marker and in her own precise script on a large whiteboard; a stress technique she adopted during residency.

She tells Natalie to breathe and to leave her arms by her side while lifting the bottle up to Natalie's face.

"It fucking smells awful. Can't you smell it?" Natalie's tremors have not lessened. Her eyes remain closed and she pinches her nose shut, a terrified child prepping to jump into water over her head as callous adults goad her with mocking you're-a-big-girl platitudes.

Luis suggests drinking from a different bottle, but he trails off, the words disintegrating into meaninglessness.

Ramola reads from the list on her mental whiteboard, calmly directing Natalie to tilt her head down and then open her mouth.

Natalie's quivering lips part. Ramola tips the bottle. Water runs into Natalie's mouth. Ramola pulls the bottle away. Natalie's eyes pop open and her cheeks distend. She swallows and her face scrunches, twisting and collapsing into itself, an expression of pure disgust, as though she were forced to consume the foulest matter. She turns away, gasps, and coughs, which is still, somehow, a dry, brittle sound, like snapping sticks. When she spins back and sees the water bottle, Natalie retches and gags.

When finally able to speak, she says, "Get that shit away from me. Why'd you make me?" Natalie is bent over as far as her belly will allow, her hands on her thighs, and loose hair hanging in front of her face.

Ramola darts to Luis and hands him the bottle, the water agitating and spilling at its rough treatment. She goes back to Natalie and rubs the base of her neck and between her shoulder blades with her own shaking hand. She has returned from her clinical mental space without any clue of what to do next.

But there is a definitive diagnosis. The undeniable expression of the oddest symptom of rabies, hydrophobia, means the virus has passed through Natalie's brain barrier. Either the vaccine was not effective against the new, more virulent strain or, more likely, it was not administered in time. Natalie is infected. There is no longer any doubt, just as there is no cure. The virus is one hundred percent fatal.

Ramola alternates hushing her friend and saying, "I'm sorry. I'm sorry . . ."

Natalie abruptly stands up straight, wiping her eyes and brushing the hair out of her face. She exhales and says, "Stop being sorry. It's not your fault."

Luis is sitting on his bike, holding the bottle and sniffing its contents. When he notices Natalie watching him, he dumps the water out and tosses the bottle toward the road's shoulder. It comes up short, bouncing and clattering against the pavement, drumming out hard but hollow percussive notes.

Natalie says, "I didn't tell you about the first zombie I saw. It was—what, not even three hours ago?—he came into my house, killed my husband, and bit my arm. I got vaccinated, but looks like that happened too late." She's calm, composed, as though relieved the truth, as awful and final as it is, has finally been revealed. "Can I have a couple of those cleaning wipes?"

Luis digs through his pack and pulls out white cloths, one after the other, a magician performing the endless-kerchiefs gag. He asks, "How much time before—?"

Natalie cleans her hands and says, "Before what?" She waits for Luis to finish for her. He doesn't. She adds, "I don't know. Do we know?" She doesn't pause here and instead answers her own question. "Another hour? Maybe two? Delirium and hallu-cinations first, right? But how will I know they're hallucinations when I'm having them?"

Luis adds, "And the baby?"

Natalie says, "The virus goes up nerves directly to the brain, doesn't travel in the bloodstream. No one knows for sure, but the baby could be okay, not infected. Right, Rams?"

Ramola answers, "Yes, that's correct."

"So we really need to get you to the clinic," Luis says. "Where the fuck is Josh? I should've gone . . ." He takes out his cell phone, attempts contact.

Natalie says, her admirable if not eerie calm evaporated, "If we get my kid delivered and she's okay, who's going to raise her? Who's going to be her mom?" She coughs, then looks around wildly as though the new mom might emerge from the woods.

Ramola says, "You'll always be her mom," which feels like the worst thing to say as soon as it's out of her mouth. But what could possibly be the best thing to say?

"My parents are too old, and even if they weren't . . . No. Just no. No way. You know. I don't have to tell you that. And I don't want her with Paul's dad, and I don't want her with either of his siblings. They're both total messes. But I don't want her with random strangers either." She covers her face with both hands, issues a wavering sigh, and then blurts out, "Will you do it, Rams?" She takes her hands away, exposing her eyes, which are Mars-the-angry-planet red, and she blinks a desperate code. "Will you adopt my kid?"

Ramola stammers, the question itself is another virus shut-ting down her brain. "Oh, well, I'm not—I don't know if—"

Natalie grabs Ramola's hand. Her skin is damp and on fire. "I know it's not fair of me to ask. Not now. None of this is fucking fair. Is it? And it probably won't come to that, as we're all going to fucking die so yay and none of this will matter. But it does matter, right? Some of this has to matter. Doesn't it? I'm sorry, Rams, but will you do this for me? I know this is a big fucking ask. The biggest. But you have to do this for me. Please, Rams. If you say yes, it'll get me through this. I promise I'll get through this. All the way to the end."

Ramola hesitates—there is no way she can answer with *No, but I'll make sure your child is placed with a good family* even if she wants to—then says, "Yes." At this moment she would've said yes if Natalie asked her to cut off her own head, but she regrets it as soon as it's out of her mouth. This "yes" feels like the heaviest, saddest word she has ever spoken. She repeats her answer, trying and failing to make it sound like an affirmation.

Natalie repeatedly says, "Thank you" and "I love you." She releases Ramola's hand and retrieves her phone from a sweatshirt pocket. Her birding fingers hover indecisively over the screen until one finger pecks at a button. She nearly shouts, "This is Natalie Larsen of 60 Pinewood Road of Stoughton, Mass. I am of sound mind, and this is, um, my last will and testament, or whatever I'm supposed to say to make this legally official. It is my wish—no—I want, I demand Dr. Ramola Sherman of Neponset Street, Canton, have sole custody of my soon-to-be born child." She pauses and scans the others. "I have, um, two people here with me. Witnesses of my legal declaration. They're going to say their names."

She jabs the phone in Luis's direction. He leans in and like a nervous witness on the stand says, "I am Luis Fernandez."

Natalie pivots and points the phone at Ramola, who obliges with her full name and address.

Natalie hits a button on the screen, presumably shutting off the recording, and says, "I'll haunt motherfuckers if it doesn't happen."

Luis laughs, but then sheepishly hides it, pulling his bandanna over his mouth.

Natalie points at Luis and her belly, and says, "If you say something about the movie *Alien* I'll rip your face off." It's supposed to be a joke, but the rhythm is off, and sounds mournful, a lament. She adds, "Okay, if this is going to happen, let's go. We gotta go."

Natalie sets off ahead of Ramola and Luis, who scramble to re-shoulder their bags. Natalie will not get very far ahead of them, but Ramola wants to shout, *Wait!* even though she knows she can't.

NATS

Hey. I want to say this before they catch up and can hear me. It's official. I'm infected. I know I was talking and acting like I knew I was all along, but I—I was really hoping these messages would work like a reverse jinx and I would be okay. But I'm not okay. So, yeah. Soon all that'll be left of me are these recordings.

No. *You* will be left of me. Am I saying that right? Do you know what I'm trying to say? My tongue is slow and I'm getting dizzy. That's supposed to happen because I'm infected.

I'm a part of you, so the recordings aren't all that's left of me. You have parts of me. Auntie Rams has parts of me with her. Make her tell you all those parts. Even the bad parts. I know I can be a lot.

(male speaks, inaudible)

Do you mind? I'm talking to my kid.

That was Luis. He rides a bike that's too small for him and makes jokes about zombies driving cars like those are the craziest things the universe has to offer—it's not even close—and he jokes about this being a different and ridiculous timeline because why? Crazy, awful stuff happening. Pfft. Horrific shit has always happened, is *always* happening. And everywhere! And will happen! It won't stop. There aren't any other timelines, and this one has always been a horror. I'm not saying this to scare you, like the sun rising and falling each day shouldn't scare you.

I'm not going to be me for much longer. How am I supposed to wrap my head around that? What makes me *me*? Who or what will I be? Am I a different me with each passing second? I don't feel different, but how can I tell when I am?

I won't be able to worry about what's going to happen. That's kind of a weird comfort. I wish I was going to be around to always be worrying about you.

(silence)

Auntie Rams says she's going to take care of you. Be nice to her. The nicest. She's—

(silence)

I know you can't always be nice. No one can.

And you're going to think bad thoughts, appalling things, things that if you actually said or did people would think you're a monster, but it's normal. No one ever tells you that it's okay to think hideous stuff and that everyone else does too. I used to cultivate elaborate daydreams about getting into arguments over the silliest, inconsequential bullshit with coworkers and friends, even Rams. Who does that, right? Who fantasizes about getting pissed off?

"Is that Josh?"

But when I'd start I couldn't stop and I'd feed my anger like a bonfire until the scenarios got so big and out of control, burning everything down, then after when I finally would come out of the daydream I'd be all worked up and upset with myself for even thinking that way and I would be convinced I was a terrible no-good person and I'd slip into a self-hatred spiral, but that's what people do, we prepare for the worst and think our worst but then we try our best.

"What the fuck is he doing?"

Everyone has the worst inside of them but some of us try to make something beautiful out of it anyway. I sound like an insane Hallmark card. Have I changed already? Am I not fully *me* anymore?

(Luis and Ramola speaking at once, inaudible)

Sassafras and lullabies.

And love. The kind that's so good it hurts and will always hurt. A great and most terrible love. I'm sorry.

Bye.

RAMS

"Do you mind? I'm talking to my kid."

Listening to Natalie again speaking to her unborn child, Ramola wants to send a message to her mum and dad, to tell them she is sorry, but for what she cannot say.

Natalie's verbal patterns are off, and her delivery, and syntax. It's not every sentence, but there are missed connections, thudding halts, shifts, awkward restarts.

"There aren't any other timelines and this one has always been a horror. I'm not saying this to scare you, like the sun rising and falling each day shouldn't scare you."

Ramola assumes Natalie implies the horrors of existence are as common and everyday as a sunrise and sunset, but "I'm not saying this to scare you" makes it difficult to fully parse the intended meaning or what tattered shred of hope or inspiration might be elicited.

"Auntie Rams says she's going to take care of you. Be nice to her. The nicest. She's—"

Under the weight of Natalie's pause, Ramola looks away as though she has been caught in a lie. Her heavy eyes fall to the pavement briefly, then unmoored they float up and she stares at the lazy undulations of the surrounding foliage. She guiltily thinks, *I'll try*, which does not equate to *yes*. "I'll try" are words she studiously avoided as a medical student and resident because they granted permission to fail.

Luis says, "Is that Josh?" His question is both rhetorical and incredulous.

At the edge of their vision, emerging from a bend in the road, a person rides a bike toward them. It is clearly Josh in his black helmet and too tall for the bike, one end of the staff in his pack rising up over his head. He pedals furiously, standing up for better leverage.

"What the fuck is he doing?" Luis veers his own bike left, away from Natalie, and he wobbles to a stop using his outstretched sneakers rubbing against the pavement as brakes.

Ramola searches the road beyond Josh for an ambulance or a car, anything, hoping the teen is the head of a cavalry, that he's a fabled dog leading rescuers to Timmy in the well.

She and Luis simultaneously speak to, at, and over each other: "Where's the ambulance?" and "Why is he riding by himself?" Neither one answers the other, nor do they dare acknowledge the implications of their questions.

Natalie finishes recording and puts her phone back into her sweatshirt pocket. Ramola urges her to stop walking, to wait a moment, to hear what Josh has to report.

Josh sprint-pedals until he's with the group, skidding to a stop in front of Luis, their front tires almost touching. He dramatically hunches over the handlebars, head dropped, back rising and falling as he pants for air.

Luis knocks hard on Josh's helmet. "Hey, where's the ambulance?"

Between gasps, he manages, "I didn't make it . . . all the way . . . to the clinic. How'd you get out here? Why aren't you guys back—"

Luis interrupts, "Wait. What do you mean you didn't make it to the clinic?"

"Guy. We are in the shit. The shit. Like, a half mile from here, maybe less, there's a big group, at least ten, headed this way—"

"I knew it. A fucking zombie herd." Luis's mouth drops open, a can-you-believe-it almost-grin. He rubs his hands together as though he can't wait to see it.

"Nah, guy. They're not zombies. It's worse. They're like a militia or mob or something. Not the National Guard or police or anything official like that. Some of them are just weekend-warrior dads, you know, wearing khakis and beer bellies, but most had weapons and there were two ginormous dudes in head-to-toe army fatigues, faces painted, crossbows, scary-ass—"

Luis interrupts. "I don't get—"

Ramola says, "Let him finish."

Josh continues. He tells them the group didn't see him coming and he hid behind some trees next to an old graveyard to watch what they were up to. There was a slow-rolling red pickup truck following behind the men on foot, and they fanned out and knocked on doors of the houses on both sides of the street. No one answered as far as he could tell.

Ramola breaks in with, "Hold on. Did I hear you correctly? They have a pickup truck. Did you ask them if they could give Natalie a ride?"

"Fuck no. When they got close to the graveyard I booked it outta there. Rando militia types are always way worse than zombies. I've already seen this movie a zillion times."

Natalie laughs, says, "Too young to live, too dumb to die." Her laughs turn into coughs.

"Bloody hell, you watch too many movies. This isn't a movie!" Ramola shouts.

Luis piles on. "Seriously? You didn't talk to them, didn't go to the clinic? You just came back here?"

"I'm telling you, they're bad news. When I was riding away they yelled after me and it wasn't like, 'Hey bro. What's up? How can we help you?' They angry-yelled at me. They were all like, 'Stop right there!'" Josh gives a deep-voiced, mocking impersonation of male authority. "Let me translate that for you. It's not hey-guy-we-want-to-help-speak. It's give-us-your-supplies-and-maybe-we-won't-wear-your-skin-speak."

Luis groans and says, "I knew I should've gone."

"Guy. I can't believe you're not with me on this."

Ramola says, "Both of you be quiet for a moment, please." She spins herself in circles, her hands on top of her head, too tired, angry, scared to do anything more.

Natalie mutters to herself and walks past the teens, tracking the yellow double lines. Her inefficient gait is deteriorating and is more painful to watch, a robot doomed to shake itself apart. Her previously upright posture is melting; left shoulder is slumped and not level with her right.

Josh says, "Where's she going? We gotta hide. Or up ahead, before they get to us, we might be able to take a left down Lincoln Street, head toward the center of town, get help there."

Ramola says, "No. We're going to the clinic. There is no other option."

"Facts. Natalie has to get there, and, like, now," Luis says to his friend, as though he's sharing bad news.

Ramola is about to suggest Luis bike ahead to ask the group for help and/or go on to the clinic if they decline, when she spies the metal pegs sticking out from the axles of their rear wheels. Earlier, when the teens suggested they hitch rides on their bikes, she hadn't seriously considered it, given Natalie's pregnancy. But that was before Natalie's hydrophobic episode and her infection became inarguable. The clock moves in triple-time now. The pegs jut out perpendicularly from the axle, are essentially sections of pipe of a two-to-three-inch diameter, and are at least five inches long, certainly longer than their feet are wide. They would make adequate footholds. Standing astride the rear wheel while the bicycle is moving would be a fall risk for Natalie, obviously, but Ramola doesn't want to risk sending Luis ahead and have him come back without any help, losing both time and shortened distance to the clinic in the process.

Luis says, "I'll go. I can convince them they have to help."

"Nah, bro. Bad. Bad." Josh throws nervous looks over his shoulder at the road behind him.

Ramola says, "We are all going."

Natalie stops walking and turns around.

Ramola continues. "We're all going so they can see Natalie and so I can do the talking. If Natalie and I stand on those rear pegs"—she points at Luis's bike—"you're confident you can remain balanced with our extra weight?"

Without hesitation, Luis says, "Oh hell yeah."

Ramola says to Natalie, "If those men want to help us, give us a ride, great, but if not, we keep going to the clinic ourselves. No more waiting around."

Natalie nods, but her look is distracted, faraway.

Josh says, "Trash idea. We need to—"

Her fists clenched, Ramola turns on the teen and yells, "There's no other idea! She has to get to the clinic now!"

Given Josh is approximately twenty-five pounds heavier than Luis, they split up the total weight load for each bike. Natalie will ride with Luis, Ramola with Josh.

Ramola stands behind Natalie, her arms out like a gymnast's spotter, but Natalie doesn't need help. Natalie puts her hands on Luis's shoulders and steps up and onto the pegs with a surprising spryness and confidence, or, overconfidence, which Ramola fears is a result of the infection interfering with her brain's ability to curb inhibition and assess risk. The rear tire sinks under the added weight, but doesn't completely flatten. Ramola worries less about the tire's integrity and Natalie's feet slipping off than she does her ability to hold on with an injured left arm.

Natalie's belly rests against Luis's back. She asks, "You sure about this, guy?"

"I've had heavier on here."

"Ain't you sweet? I won't bite you in the neck until we get there."

"Stay leaned forward, I can take it." The strain in Luis's voice communicates the opposite. "Don't step off until I stop, and one foot at a time." He pushes the bike forward, grunting with each of the four lunging strides of his legs, working the bike up to a speed with which he can place his feet on the pedals. They wobble and shimmy from side to side for a heart-swallowing moment, but then straighten out and glide smoothly down Bay Road.

Ramola jogs over to the rear of Josh's bike, clamps onto his shoulders, and climbs onto the pegs. The step up is only about a foot off the ground but the elevated position already feels precarious and unstable. She says, "We need to catch up to them, but in the safest possible manner."

Josh doesn't say anything and slowly pushes them forward. She feels him pouting and sulking beneath her hands. His listless affect is a full-body eye roll, his silence a no-one-ever-listens-to-me protest. She wants to scold him again—it felt good to do so earlier—perhaps teach him some choice British slang in the process. However, she reminds herself he is not an adult and he is within the age range of her patients. The displays of bravura do not fully mask the lost, frightened, and confused young man he clearly is.

She leans forward, as far as she dares, and says, "Thank you for this, Josh."

Josh pumps his legs and accelerates them down the road. They gain on Luis and Natalie. Ramola's unbuttoned coat billows open and the blast of cold wind waters her eyes. She presumes it feels like they are moving faster than they actually are given her unaccustomed perspective hovering above the rear tire of a bicycle. She suppresses the urge to request that he slow down.

Josh says, "I still don't get why we shouldn't avoid those guys, take a different route, just in case. I mean, is she going to have the baby, like, right this second?"

Ramola realizes Josh doesn't know Natalie is infected. She tells him, plainly, and adds, "She doesn't have much time."

Josh makes stuttering vowel sounds, eventually evolving into speech. "Ah, oh, uh, does Luis know? Is he in danger?" He pedals faster and for a moment, Ramola fears he's aiming to smash into Luis and Natalie, a harebrained attempt to rescue his friend by toppling the pregnant zombie off the bike.

Racing to get all the words out, she says, "He knows, he knows! And we weren't keeping it from you. We didn't know— none of us knew until Luis gave her water and she reacted. Natalie was bitten late this morning but we hoped she had been vaccinated in time."

Josh doesn't respond. He pulls even with the others as they glide past the Borderland parking lot and the Lincoln Street/ Allen Road intersection.

Natalie towers over a determined Luis. Not a big kid to begin with, he's scrunched in his seat as though being accordioned by Natalie pressing down on his shoulders. There doesn't appear to be enough tire rubber and metal frame to hold them up. They're a circus act in which a comically small bike will shed parts as a lead-up to a crowd-pleasing crash and pratfall. Natalie holds her head tilted to the left, as though her neck is stiff and hurts. Ramola wants to call out to her, talk to her, but doesn't want to distract her or break her concentration.

Josh calls to Luis, "You good, bro?"

"I'm *the* good." He's out of breath, but he continues pedaling. "Where's your postapocalyptic crew? Witness me!" Both teens laugh. Natalie laughs too and repeats the "Witness me" line.

Ramola says, "I've seen that one," inordinately proud of herself, although encouraging more movie references or comparisons is not what she should be doing with this lot.

After the brief outburst, the group goes silent. Beneath Ramola's feet the rear tire spins and the blacktop blurs. Every bump and rut they pass over sends a jolt into her ankles and knees. She worries about the level of physical stress and strain Natalie must be experiencing.

Beyond the state park and intersection, there are again homes dotting the wooded roadside. From Ramola's vantage, it's impossible to know if the homes are occupied, as there are no lights on and the windows are dark. Do the empty driveways mean cars are hidden inside garages? Did all these residents flee the area days ago, ahead of the statewide quarantine? Now that they are about a mile from the clinic, if they are to come across a house showing clear signs of occupation, is it worth the added time and chance to knock on the door?

Josh asks if they can turn left ahead; he knows a way to bypass a big section of Bay Road. The group answers with a resounding no.

Luis asks, "Hey, where are all the big scary men?"

Josh's "Farther down" might as well be a "Fuck you."

On their right, marking an elbow bend in the road and on the corner of Rockland Street is the Ames Baptist Church. If not for the large cross on the side of the building, it could be a sprawling, painted-white New England Colonial-style house, or a converted funeral home. It sits on a sizable plot of land, including a wide, sprawling front lawn and empty L-shaped parking lot, which is being explored by a small flock of turkeys.

Luis asks, "Should we be worried about turkeys in this timeline?"

Ramola answers, "Only mammals can get rabies."

"Lucky us," says Natalie.

They roll past the church. Its white announcement sign at

the street corner, near a crumbling, moss-covered stone wall, lists emergency-contact phone numbers and the stark message, "Pray."

High-pitched, ululating shrieks, eerily childlike in their voicing, are joined by deep growls that sharpen into piercing, relentless barks. Unlike the distant cries they heard earlier from the edges of Borderland, these unseen, mortally engaged combatants are close, either on the church grounds or within its immediate environs.

Josh and Luis clumsily veer their bikes into the opposite lane at the unexpected apocalypse of sound and exchange nervous banter.

Ramola says, "Keep it steady," takes her right hand off Josh's shoulder, and turns her head to better look behind them. She doesn't see any animals charging down Bay Road, nor can she see the turkey flock. Out of sight, the brutish battle cries continue and now include alarmed turkey clucks and gobbles, the heavy whoops of their beating wings. Ramola returns to her fully forward-facing stance, awkwardly pushing hard onto Josh's shoulder as she does so. Josh shouts a complaint. Ramola apologizes and says, "Nothing coming after us that I can see. We are *the* good."

Luis says, "Cheers. All right, mate." His accent is fully Australian.

On their left they pass a residential street called Pheasant Lane. Ramola spies cars in a handful of the driveways, which brings a sense of comfort that not everyone is gone. Although they now must be less than a mile from the clinic, she wonders if they should stop and ask for a ride, particularly if the teens are getting fatigued.

They pass another residential side street on their left and then round a bend that becomes a long stretch of straight road.

Josh says, "There they are."

About one hundred yards away is the red pickup truck, straddling both lanes, its chrome grille designed to be a toothy, wiseass grin. If it's moving, it's going at a speed imperceptibly slow from this distance. Two men walk beside the vehicle, carrying what appear to be shovels, and there are others along the road's shoulder, one carrying a hunting rifle. The truck honks its horn twice and more people spill out of the wooded periphery onto the road. In the lead, maybe twenty-five yards ahead of the truck, are two large men dressed in head-to-toe camouflage gear, stepping in time, their crossbows held across their chests, a pledge to future violence.

Luis says, "Jesus. That one dude is big as a fucking tree."

"He is the Tree," says Josh.

Ramola has to admit this hodgepodge group of men and the manner in which they approach is unnerving if not outright frightening. Having been concerned solely with getting Natalie onto the fabled pickup truck and to the clinic, other questions nag: For what purpose are these men breaking quarantine laws? Why are they, as Josh claimed, going door-to-door?

She says, "Don't stop until we are within their number. I will talk to them."

"Good luck talking to the Tree," Josh says.

The men in front, the ones wearing camo, split from the road's double lines, each filling one lane. They wear polarized sunglasses and the parts of their faces not covered in coarse hair are smeared with black and green greasepaint. As the bicycles approach they hold up black-gloved stop hands. The pickup truck continues its slow creep behind them. Other men veer off onto driveways in groups of two or three.

The teens coast to a smooth stop and both Ramola and Natalie step down from the pegs without issue. Luis looses a groan of relief and rolls his shoulders.

Natalie says, "Gee, thanks, guy."

The tallest one—Ramola cannot think of him as anything other than "The Tree" now that Josh pegged him with the nickname—says, "You're not supposed to be out here. You should go back to your homes. It's not playtime." He stares at Josh as he makes the latter statement. "And you should've stopped when I said to."

The other large man in fatigues opens and closes his hands around the crossbow, clearly enamored with the crinkling leather sound his gloves make.

Luis laughs, leans left between the bikes, and whacks Josh in the shoulder. He says, "Guy, I take everything I said back. They are the bad."

"Facts."

"Excuse me?" Ramola announces, and walks in front of Josh and Luis. The two men in camo don't move. She points to her ID badge and says, "My name is Dr. Ramola Sherman and we are in desperate need of your help. My friend Natalie here—"

The other man in camo interrupts: "Oh Christ, has the UN landed already?"

Ramola is dumbstruck by the question. "I'm sorry, the UN?"

The Tree takes off his sunglasses and glowers at Ramola. "What country are you from? Don't lie."

Natalie sidles up next to Ramola, steps in front of her, and shouts, "Listen, you racist fucking wannabe rednecks. Rams—

Dr. Rams to you—lives in Canton, and if you give her any more shit I'm . . ."

Ramola says Natalie's name and variations of *relax* and *calm down* and *it's all right* as she gently pulls her away from the expressionless men. The teens break into giggles, and why not? The whole world has gone mad.

The red truck pulls up directly behind the two men. A bearded driver steps out and says, "Hey, nice day for a bike ride, right?" and laughs at his own non-joke. He's a solidly built, early middle-aged white man, of less-than-average height, with a head of coarse hair worn short, coming to a widow's peak. Distinct patches of white form an archipelago in the sea of his light-brown hair. He wears tan carpenter pants, a blue jean jacket buttoned up to the neck, work gloves, and black boots. Coffee-stained teeth mushroom out of a charismatic smile; his cheeks hide his eyes. "I'm Dan, and—so, yeah, what's going on? I gotta say you make an, um, unexpected group. What are you guys doing out here?" He steps between the men in camo and stuffs his hands into his front pockets. A move, Ramola assumes, supposed to communicate *Aw shucks, I'm harmless* and *I'm in charge.*

Ramola starts over. "I'm Dr. Ramola Sherman. We desperately need help and we don't have time—"

The Tree interrupts, "Do you hear her?"

The second camo guy says, "Looks like we already have foreign government interference—"

Ramola says, "For fuck's sake, that's it. Natalie, back on the bike. Come on." She walks behind Josh's bike and flails a hand in the direction of the other men. "You daft bellends stay out of our way."

The camo duo mumble vague none-shall-pass threats, which

are less threatening as they sidle and shrink away from Ramola and toward the pickup truck.

Dan taps each man's shoulder, and says, "Okay, Richard, okay. Stanley. Hey, let's calm down." His "calm" has no *l* in it, and is replaced with an *ah*. His Boston accent is so pronounced, like Josh's British accent attempt, it sounds faked.

Josh says, "Dick and Stan. Who will ever forget them?"

Luis laughs. "Ooh, let me guess which one is Stanley."

The Tree snarls a fuck-you, though it is not clear if his name is Stanley. Before either teen can guess as much, Ramola makes one final attempt to ask for help. A potential ride to the clinic is only a few feet away.

"I am a doctor at Norwood Pediatrics. Natalie and I were in an ambulance on our way to the Ames Clinic. A car blindsided us about a mile back. We were not injured. The same cannot be said for the other driver. Our ambulance is no longer drivable, we have not been able to get through to emergency services on our phones, and no new ambulance has been sent for us. These two young men witnessed the accident and are kindly helping transport us to the clinic so that Natalie and her child can be tended to properly." As she speaks she walks toward Dan and the two men. "Will you give us a ride to the clinic? It's in Five Corners, less than a mile away. We'd be eternally grateful and you'll be back doing whatever it is you're doing in no time at all."

Calls of "What's going on?" and "You guys all set?" from the other men in their group (five in total) who mass ten to twenty yards behind the truck. Two men wear dark-colored fleece vests over tan button-down shirts with large orange patches on the left sleeve. They are standing too far away for Ramola to read the script on the patches. They carry long, skinny poles with some sort of corded loops at the ends. Unlike Richard and Stanley in camo, two of the remaining men wear typical northeast suburbanite male autumnal garb, designer fleeces and flannels, and they carry shovels. One short, balding man swims in a too-big New England Patriots varsity-style jacket and carries a small-caliber hunting rifle.

Dan turns and holds a thumbs-up and then waves to the group behind him. He says to Ramola, "Oh, okay, yeah. You know that clinic isn't very big. It's not like a full hospital. Is it even open, functional? I don't know. We haven't gone by there, so I don't know. But yeah, of course. I'll give you a ride."

Richard and Stanley sigh, spin away, and toss up their hands, generally reacting like spoiled brats whose parents won't buy them a candy bar at the grocery store.

Dan ignores them. He cups his hands around his mouth and shouts to the other men behind them, "Go ahead! You can keep knocking!" The other men disperse into two groups, one tan-shirted man with each group, walking up driveways on opposite sides of Bay Road. The man with the rifle remains behind and mills about in the middle of the street.

Dan says, "It's Natalie, right? You can ride in the cab with me. The rest of you can sit in the truck bed if you want."

Josh says, "Hell yeah. You'll be getting us closer to home."

"Yeah, we're done out here," says Luis.

Ramola thanks Dan, takes Natalie's hand, and leads her between the silently apoplectic camo pair. As they scoot around to the passenger side, Natalie whispers into Ramola's ear, "What's in the trailer? Can't be good." It wasn't visible until they walked around the front grille, but there's a small rectangular, two-wheeled trailer hitched to the truck. Its four side panels are metal, painted black, and maybe two feet in height. A large green drop cloth is draped over whatever its contents may be.

Ramola rises up on her tiptoes but only sees more of the lumpy canvas. "I don't know." Questions of what these men are doing and why they are knocking on the doors of local homes are neon warning signs flashing in her head, but she isn't going to ask them. All she wants is a ride to the clinic. She tries the truck door handle, and it is locked.

Josh and Luis walk their bikes to the truck saying, "Excuse me" and "Beg pardon" and "Right-o" and "After you" and "I insist" and "Hardly" and other random acknowledgments and apologies using obnoxious and dreadful British accents.

The Tree steps in front of the teens, preventing them from lifting their bikes into the cargo bed. He whines to Dan, his voice increasing in pitch as he talks impossibly fast and without a pause for a breath. "Did you read the Reddit I sent about the UN conspiring with the deep state to manufacture and spread the virus so they can swoop in and save the day with new vaccines to fool the public into thinking the other vaccines they force on us are safe and how they dropped the green bait packs and used veterinarians and pediatricians to spread this virus and continue to monitor the progress in hospitals?"

From his jacket's deep pockets, the other camo man pulls out a couple green rabies vaccination bait packs, ones the Wildlife Service has been dropping locally for weeks now. He says, "We've been telling you, Dan. These damn things even have French instructions on them. This is global biological warfare." He steps toward the teens and shakes the packs inches from Josh's head.

Luis says, "Watch out, he's gonna give you the government rabies."

Dan shakes his head and says, "Guys, come on." Ramola notices a physical resemblance among Dan and the camo men beyond their bearded middle-aged white-maleness. If they're not brothers, they're cousins. Regardless, Dan now seems less like their leader than a person with a truck, a hitch, and a trailer. He adds, "I'm not arguing with you over this. I'm giving a pregnant woman a ride." He walks around to the back of the truck.

The Tree says, "And she just happens to show up with a foreign doctor—what are you doing?"

"I'm unhitching the trailer, leaving it here if you need it. We'll reattach when I get back."

Natalie says, "Let's go. We need to go." She yanks on the door handle. "It's locked."

Dan pauses his work with the trailer to unlock the door with two chirps from his key fob.

Natalie opens the door, and as Ramola helps her into the car seat she talks to herself. "You're okay, you're still here, this is happening, out of the woods, over the river, through the woods . . ." and her mumbles deteriorate into repeated words that don't build into phrases. Stray words further devolve into throat clearings and hard, empty swallows.

Ramola says, "We're almost there. I promise," and remembers what Natalie said earlier about the value of promises.

"I'm really tired." Natalie's slow head nods morph into palsy-like shakes. She stares out the windshield.

Ramola drags the cranky seat belt across Natalie's front, making sure the lap belt is below her belly, and buckles her in. Instead of another verbal check-in, pep talk, or feckless well-wishes, Ramola quickly backs out of the cab as though being chased. She shuts the door. She's tired too.

Dan has dragged the small trailer to the road's shoulder and he and the camo men are in the middle of an argument.

The Tree says, "You act like you're above us all. Treat us like we're dumb and crazy."

"That's because your conspiracy theories are dumb and crazy," Dan says.

"So your Twitter guy is better than our Reddit?"

Dan walks away from the trailer and yells, "I am better than your goddamn Reddit."

The other camo man says, "You're wrong, Dan. Head in the sand like always. This is just the beginning of an attempted overthrow. But an army of patriots is on their way to stop it and keep the virus from spreading. They're gonna do what needs to be done and we should be doing more to help them."

Josh and Luis take advantage of the argument to climb into the truck and stow their bikes. Standing in the truck bed, each with one foot up on a side panel, the teens push themselves up higher for a better view of the other men approaching the houses. Luis calls out, "Hey, Dr. Ramola, those guys in tan shirts are animal control."

Why is Luis telling her this? She doesn't need to know that; she needs to get Dan in the truck and get the truck turned around. The rest of whatever fascist fantasy nonsense these men are up to can go on without her and Natalie. She says, "Dan! We must get Natalie to the clinic, now. She's overtaxed, dehydrated—" She pauses. What if Dan offers Natalie water in the truck cab? She won't be there to prevent him from doing so. And there are Josh and Luis with their water bottles still hanging around their necks. What would these appalling men do if they witnessed Natalie's hydrophobia? Ramola stammers to a pleading finish. "She needs an IV and care. We simply must go without any more delay."

Dan says, "Yes, I'm coming," and jogs away from the camo men huddled near the trailer. He passes Ramola and rounds the truck's front end to the driver's side.

The Tree says, "Why don't you tell your new pals what we're doing? Tell them those are your animal control shirts the other guys are wearing, and all this is your idea. See if they still want a ride."

Ramola taps the passenger window twice. Natalie doesn't turn her head and continues staring out of the windshield.

The other camo man lifts a corner of the drop cloth in the trailer and says, "Say hello to my furry friends." Richard and Stanley laugh.

Ramola doesn't look. She runs to the truck's rear. Placing both palms flat on the rear gate she simultaneously pushes down and jumps up, lifting her right leg, and gains a foothold. She scrambles onto the gate despite the two teens grabbing at her arms, their dangling water bottles knocking into her head, making the climb more difficult. Once fully inside the truck bed, they quickly rearrange the bikes and gear. Ramola shuffles over to the cab's rear window so she can see Natalie.

Muffled but loud barks explode from the house to the truck's right. Men shout: "Hey, we got one!" "It's pissed!" "He's a big one." "He wants to dig right through that door."

Standing on tiptoes, Ramola is able to see over a row of hedges to the modest Cape-style home, painted yellow with white trim, single-car garage attached. Two dormers rise out of the charcoal-black shingle roof and a single redbrick chimney splits the home in the middle. An American flag and a yellow Gadsden flag with its coiled snake flank the front door. Also on either side of the front door are two of Dan's men, their faces pressed against the sidelight windows. A third stands on the brick front landing.

Dan is half-in, half-out of the truck. He asks, "Are people home?"

"No one's answering! Car might be in the garage." The man in the tan shirt bangs on the door with an open palm and shouts, "Hello, this is Animal Control. We'd like to have a word. Hey, anyone home?" With his other hand he holds the pole with the loop at the end.

The dog's barks are heavy and deep, varying in rhythm; quick staccato yaps mixing with longer, haunting bays.

Dan steps back from the truck then stops, unsure of where to be. He says, "Okay, if they answer, be up-front. Don't lie to them. It'll go better. If no one answers, um, just wait. Wait until I get back. I'll make this quick." He ducks into the cab and shuts the door.

Luis says to Josh, "Are those assholes doing what I think they're doing?"

The Tree laughs, beams an I-thought-you'd-never-ask smile, and says, "You want to stop this virus? You need to give it less places to jump to, right, Doc?" He says "Doc" as though it's a slur. "Quarantine the humans, cull the animal vectors. Sorry to say, pets are animal vectors. It's not nice work, but—" He lets the "but" hang, lets it linger. It's typical, reactionary, barbaric reasoning, all too familiar, and historically proven to fail time and again.

Dan starts the engine and backs up slowly. The truck bed vibrates under Ramola's feet.

Ramola says to the Tree, "Killing healthy animals has never been effective in halting rabies outbreaks. Vaccinating them has."

The truck's horn blasts twice and simultaneously the truck stops short, pitching Ramola, Josh, and Luis toward the bikes and rear gate. Ramola keeps her feet but the two teens stumble and fall next to the bikes. There are two more horn blasts, loud and piercing. Ramola scrambles back to the cab and peers through the rear window. Dan and Natalie are arguing. Ramola knocks on the window then realizes there's a sliding panel of glass about the width of her head surrounded by a black, metal frame. She works it open.

Natalie presses the horn one more time with her left hand, and points out the windshield with her right and says, "Big bad coyotes."

Two mangy, battle-scarred coyotes trot down the road toward the truck. One is considerably larger than the other. The big one trots with a noticeable limp. Ramola stands for a better look over the cab. The longer she stares at the bigger animal the more she is convinced, despite the improbability, it is the same one that dove into their ambulance. The sight of this sick, wounded, undeterred animal fills her with near-incapacitating dread and awe; an emotional-level recognition, or reconciliation, that the gears of the universe will always grind its adherents—apostles and apostates alike—in its teeth.

The Tree whoops, shouts, "Game time!" and fist-bumps his partner. They leave the trailer and walk into the middle of the road, in front of the truck, readying their crossbows.

The coyotes' front shoulders are in a permanent up-shrug,

heads lolling low to the ground, their mouths dripping saliva. They snarl, bark, and cry. When their weaving paths overlap they snap at and bite each other, which doesn't slow their progress. They continue inexorably forward as a recombinant organism, driven by their relentless new instinct.

Ramola says into the cab, "Dan, we can still go, correct? Surely your friends can handle this," hoping it's the right thing to say to get the truck rolling again. Her hand taps a hurry-up SOS on the cab's roof.

Natalie says, "Where coyotes? There coyotes," and laughs.

Dan begins backing up again, aiming for the mouth of the yellow house's driveway.

One of the camo men shouts, "Dan, you're gonna miss the fun part!"

Two men, including the one carrying the hunting rifle, trot down the opposite shoulder, toward the approaching coyotes. Josh and Luis have pulled out their own weapons and are conspicuously quiet.

As the truck's rear end crawls up the inclined drive, the men at the yellow house back away from the front door, shouting and pointing at one another. The front door opens and the dog's barks increase in volume exponentially. A tan-and-black blur launches from the darkened interior of the house, knocking the man in the animal control shirt onto his ass. It's a muscular, broad-shouldered German shepherd, jaws snapping, white-and-pink spittle spooling from its mouth. The dog pivots right and attacks one of the shovel-carrying members of Dan's group, clamping onto his left calf, biting its way higher up the leg. Undaunted by two solid shovel blows to its side, the dog forces the flailing, screaming man to ground. With his quarry down, the dog tears into his neck and face.

A white man, presumably the one who opened the front door, follows the dog out of house, lurching between the flags and onto the stoop. He is as tall as the Tree, but likely at least a decade younger, and he is awash in blood; arms, legs, torso, cheeks splashed and stained red. There's so much blood on him it can't all be his, though some of it must be, as one leg of his joggers is torn and so too one of his shirtsleeves. He shouts, "Where you come from? You must say," repeatedly, but it sounds like one word, and with improper intonation, as he sets upon the animal control officer on the stoop, who is caught in mid-attempt to regain his feet. He has no chance. The mauling is brutal and efficient. The infected man rains hammer blows upon the officer's head, then grabs and briefly lifts him so they are face-to-face, biting his neck and cheek before dropping him to the ground. As he coughs and frantically wipes his mouth (making gargling noises that to Ramola's ears sound like he's saying "from hell") the infected man kicks and stomps the head of the animal officer, who, but for arms and hands fluttering helplessly, doesn't move.

Too stunned and frightened to come to either man's aid, the third of the yellow house's exploratory group yells for help and backs down the slate stone walkway toward the drive. He does not move quickly enough. The dog and the infected man converge on him. Fangs, hands, and teeth.

The truck is stopped. Everyone is shouting, including Ramola. Luis and Josh bounce on their heels, asking if they should jump off the truck and help, but the attacks are so one-sided and final the outcomes are decided as soon as they begin. Ramola grabs one of each of their arms, anchoring them to the truck bed for a moment, telling them, "No!" and "Stay here," and "You can't help them." Then she crouches by the open cab window and shouts, "Go, go, go!"

In two strides the German shepherd bounds from the walkway and into the drive. It leaps against the truck, clawing and scratching at the metal. The dog lifts onto its hind legs, its bloody front paws and barking, snarling head hanging over the side panel. Josh swings his wooden staff and connects, but it's a glancing blow the dog shrugs off. If anything, the staff strike antagonizes the already-frenzied animal. It hops up and down on its rear legs, trying to push its bulk over the side and into the bed.

The truck's engine finally answers with its own roar and lunges forward. Only Ramola is prepared for the sudden acceleration as the teens are sent backward. Luis smartly goes low and down, squatting in next to the bikes and in front of their gear. Josh fights to remain standing, using his staff as a balancing pole. Ramola holds on to the open frame of the rear window and watches out the windshield.

The truck charges into Bay Road going too fast for the change in pitch (from elevated drive to flat road) and for such a tight left turn. Two men, including the one with the hunter's rifle, are unexpectedly in the truck's path, either caught in mid-retreat or running to the aid of the others at the yellow house. The surging front grille clips the rifleman, sending him rolling onto the opposite shoulder, and the swinging fishtail of the truck bed slams into the second man, batting him airborne. He lands bonelessly on his back.

Dan jams on the brakes. Ramola is pressed flat against the cab's rear window. The bikes, gear, and Luis slide up the cargo bed. Josh cries out as he tumbles over the driver's-side wall, his dropped wooden staff drum-rolling on the pavement. The stopped truck is a diagonal slash across the road's center lines. Dan opens the door and gets out of the cab. Luis grabs both loops of the water bottles and climbs over the side of the truck to Josh, who is on his knees, rubbing his chin and checking his hand for blood.

Natalie's door flies open, recoiling to halfway-closed on its hinges. Ramola reaches through the rear window, grabs a fistful of sweatshirt at Natalie's shoulder, and yells, "No! You are not going anywhere. Close the door."

Natalie turns her head and offers Ramola a dismissive, completely out-of-character sneer. She twists out of her grip, leans out of the truck, and pulls the door closed.

The dog is already biting, shaking, and thrashing about the prone man in the middle of the street. It quickly moves on to the rifleman on the road's shoulder, gnawing at the hands and arms bunkering around his head. The man's groans turn to high-pitched screams. The rifle is strewn between the truck and the man. Ramola puts one foot on the sidewall, considering a mad dash for the gun. The dog turns and unleashes a volley of barks as though it hears her thinking.

There's a high-velocity whoosh and an arrow chunks into the rifleman's right hip. His screams increase in volume and are pitched at a frequency that rattles the truck's loose rear sliding window in its frame. He reaches for his leg, and as the dog takes advantage of the opening, burrowing into his unprotected face and neck, his cries quickly weaken to watery gargles.

"I'm sorry, I'm sorry!" shouts the other camo man, Richard or Stanley, Stanley or Richard; he holds his aimed crossbow in front of his body as though memorializing the ill-fated shooting pose.

The Tree is ten feet behind his partner and engaged in a struggle with the larger coyote. He swings his crossbow like a cudgel at the animal's head, which is clamped down on his pant leg. Despite the arrow sticking out of its left shoulder, left leg limp and dangling, the coyote's ferocity and the effectiveness of its attack are not compromised. The Tree is in danger of being chopped down. The smaller coyote is twenty or so paces beyond them, lying dead in the road, three arrows sticking out of its pincushion body.

Having quickly dispatched the rifleman, the German shepherd, its dark coat gone darker with blood, sprints for the other man in camo. Its speed and might is as mesmerizing as it is frightening. Teeth bared, focus singular, there's almost a sense of joy or freedom in the bounding, athletic attack; it is finally fulfilling a long-ago animal promise, one that will not be broken.

There is a chorus of yelling on the other side of the truck, but Ramola only has eyes for the rifle on the ground now that the dog is entangled with the other camo man. She climbs out of the truck, jumping down to the pavement. The weapon is only steps away, but time slows as though she is running in a nightmare; the distance expands, the ground upon which she runs becomes a bog. She snatches the rifle by its stock and quickly points the barrel out and away from her body, preparing for an attack. But she is not really prepared, as she's never shot, much less held, a firearm. Both camo men continue to grapple with the two animals. The German shepherd is upright, full weight coiled on its hind legs as though two legs are indeed better. Its front paws scratch and probe the man's chest, pushing him backward and dangerously off-balance; the rabid animal has already re-learned the imperative to get his opponent to the ground. Even if Ramola were comfortable shooting a weapon, she does not have a clear shot and fears hitting one of the men.

Behind her, Josh and Luis are yelling to each other. She turns and takes two running steps. On the other side of the truck, the rampaging infected man run-walks in that now familiarly awful broken gait, but he is retreating from Luis instead of advancing. Luis has both sets of water bottles hanging around his neck. Two bottles are in his hands, and he splashes spooling waves of water at the infected man. Josh, his chin bloodied, is a couple steps behind Luis and halfheartedly carrying his wooden staff.

The infected man yells, "No!" and he sounds teary, desperate. He says, "Please," splitting the word into two, overexaggerated syllables. *Pluh-eeze*. He coughs, gags, and he waves his hands.

Luis shouts taunts and expletives as he splashes more water. He quickly sheds one empty bottle for the next full one, forc-ing the man to continue backing his way down the street and away from the truck. "Get in! Get in," Luis commands, and he climbs over the rear gate. Once inside he throws more water at the infected man, who has stumbled beyond Luis's range. Josh is likely concussed, given how slowly he moves. Starry-eyed, he stands at the back of the truck all but ignoring Luis offering a hand, urging him up.

The infected man wipes his face, working it over like it's a stubborn mask that won't come off, his hands webbed with blood, saliva, and mucus. With each pass of his hands over his nose and mouth, he says, almost conversationally, "I smell the blood." When his arms abruptly drop to his sides and he locks eyes with Ramola, her personal barometric pressure plummets. Dizzy and nauseated with fear, she lifts the shaking rifle, steadying the stock against her right shoulder, trying to convince herself to shoot. Aiming low, for a leg and not for a kill shot, she pulls the trigger. The kick isn't as strong as she anticipated, but she still misses badly; the bullet rips through the yellow house's row of hedges at least ten feet to his right. He rushes toward her. An ecstatic, beatific smile, a zealot's smile, splits his face.

Somewhere, way too close to her left, the German shepherd bays and howls, as though in victory.

Josh charges out from behind the truck and hacks at the infected man's left knee with his wooden staff. The knee buckles. He doesn't fall but is brought to a halt.

Ramola runs toward the truck. Natalie's door is still thankfully closed, and she is an impassive, darkened shape behind the tinted passenger window. Dan stands in the truck bed, urging her on. Aiming for the junction of the cab and the bed, Ramola throws Dan the rifle and then, using the rear tire as a push-off with her left foot, she jumps. Simultaneously, she pulls herself over the side and tumbles into the cargo bed. Quickly scrambling onto her feet, she finds the scene outside the truck has fast-forwarded, or skipped frames, like the virus has gone quantum and is infecting reality itself.

There is an arrow sticking out of the infected man's right shoulder. He tries to pull it free, but his blood-slicked hands slip off the shaft. Josh leadenly backs away, one halting step at a time, and wipes his bleeding chin. He's not wearing his helmet; it must've fallen off in his tumble out of the truck. Luis is still where he's supposed to be, where he was before Ramola climbed into the cargo bed, and he is in the same position, offering a hand to Josh. The German shepherd is latched onto the Tree's left forearm and it yanks and pulls the man in an undulating circular arc. The other man wearing camo lies on the pavement, curled on his right side, posed like the fox they passed earlier, blood and bubbles geysering from his mangled neck. Dan is crying and has the rifle aimed at the infected man, and he shoots. A red splotch explodes between the infected man's shoulder blades. He sinks to the ground, bending his legs, extending his hands, as though he's choosing to sit, to rest, to lie down on his stomach and put his head down. Josh now faces the Tree and the dog. Instead of joining that particular fray he stays on course, walking backward until he knocks into the truck. He drops to one knee, right below Luis standing with his hand out, forever out. The big coyote appears, wrapping around from the other side of the truck like it's a shark that has been circling for as long as Ramola and everyone else lost track of it. Or maybe it's returning from the yellow house's front yard or driveway after it wandered over there to finish off anything that needed finishing, and now it's coming back, coming to where it is meant to be. Josh doesn't see the big coyote (where coyote, there coyote) and its arrowed shoulder and one limp leg and three-working legs and its long, thin snout, which opens, opens wider than should be possible, showing its red mouth and its white teeth. It strikes high, biting Josh in the head, teeth fishhooking into cheek and ear. The sick, wounded coyote isn't as strong and powerful as the berserker dog, the scythe reaping through this group of men. The sick, wounded coyote is nearing its end. Josh boxes the animal's ears and punches the body. The sick, wounded coyote releases and limps away, pained whines alternating with choking sounds, as though the tongue is blocking the throat. The coyote briefly sniffs at the body of the rifleman and transforms again into the smooth shark, swimming and disappearing into the brush. Ramola and Luis jump down to the street and rush to Josh's aid. They each loop an arm through one of his arms. Josh isn't yelling or screaming in pain. He has both hands over his eyes and he cries. He sobs and he bawls and he wails; the chest-hitching, breath-stealing tears are of a bottomless, bereft, hopeless grief. Ramola and Luis are crying too and they say, "It's gone" and "Let's get out of here" and "I'll take a look." They do not say, "It'll be all right." They lead him to the rear gate that Dan drops open, and the three of them lift Josh (openmouthed, incapable of words) into the cargo bed. Ramola steps up onto the gate, afraid and suddenly sure she's too late and the German shepherd is behind her, in midair, eager to show her all its teeth. The rear gate closes, she spins around, and the dog is not there. The Tree is still in the road, standing next to his camo partner but not looking at him. He leans and wavers, a weeping willow in an autumn wind. He cradles his arm, the crossbow an offering at his feet. His head is down. A weary penitent. Beyond him, the dog's dark shape recedes as it sprints down Bay Road, triumphantly barking in full throat, running so fast it could be floating.

The truck is finally moving. Dan is driving, Natalie in the passenger seat, and Ramola, Josh, Luis, the Tree, and the bikes and gear arranged in the cargo bed like puzzle pieces. It's a matter of minutes before they will arrive at Five Corners and the clinic.

Using a disinfectant wipe, Ramola finishes cleaning Josh's facial wounds, a constellation of small red holes leaking a watery red. She doesn't tell him what she said to Natalie only hours ago, that a quick and thorough cleaning post-exposure is sometimes enough to destroy the virus. The Tree, sitting with his back against the rear gate, his arms around his knees, refuses her help when she offers. Ramola only asks once.

Luis is in Josh's ear, keeping up a manic one-person banter about the clinic and vaccines and rides to hospitals and help, getting him help.

Josh holds his bandanna against his cheek and says, "Hey, um, Doctor Ramola, that, um, person you know who got bit in the arm." He pauses, leaving space to signal and honor that he's talking about Natalie in code.

"Yes, Josh."

"How long before, um, that person became infected and, like, showed signs?"

Ramola tells him the truth as she now knows it. "Less than an hour."

"And the closer the bite is to the brain, then, it'll take even less time."

"Yes."

Luis looks at Ramola and blows out a long sigh, puffing out his cheeks, then sends his watery eyes down to the truck bed.

Josh says, "Yeah. Okay." His expression freezes, and Ramola wonders again about a possible concussion, or if he's gone inside himself to check for symptoms. He turns to Luis, who will not look at him, and says, "Guy. This isn't our movie. This isn't our story. It's theirs."

Luis shakes his head, wipes his eyes.

Josh continues, "We should've seen it before. I mean, it's fucking obvious now. You and me aren't the heroes. We're the randos, yeah?"

Luis looks up, then flips the helmet off his head and over the side of the moving truck.

Ramola cannot help herself. "This is not a movie. And you are both heroes helping Natalie get to the clinic."

Josh says, "We tried. This time we tried. That counts for something, right?"

Ramola doesn't hear Luis's response as the truck emerges from the wooded residential area to the end of Bay Road and the commercially developed, strip-malled intersection of streets called Five Corners. To their left and across Route 123, sandwiched between a CVS and Shaw's supermarket is the Ames Clinic; one building, two floors, not appreciably bigger than a Colonial-style home. A fleet of police cars, blue lights flashing, fill the clinic's lot and choke Route 123 down to one passable lane. Parked along the building's front entrance are two coach buses. Gowned clinic staff lead pregnant women and women carrying newborns onto the buses.

Ramola says, "Oh fucking hell, where are they going?" She hops out of the truck the moment Dan pulls to a stop in front of a police officer holding up an outstretched hand. She opens Natalie's door, and tells her they have to hurry. Natalie unbuckles herself but is moving in slow motion. Ramola says, "Sorry," then forcibly tugs the seat buckle out of Natalie's hand and pulls the belt from under her belly because the auto-recoil is too slow.

The officer is at the driver's window, recognizes Dan, and tells them they can't stay, can't get help here. By the time Dan is asking, begging really, where they can go, Ramola has Natalie out of the truck and walking away.

Josh calls out as he runs in front of the women, holding out Natalie's bag and his backpack. "Take mine, please. I don't need it. You might."

Knowing refusing his pack might result in an argument that slows them down further, Ramola accepts and says, "Thank you." She says it twice because she can't bear to say, *Good luck*, and she leads Natalie away from the truck, toward the clinic.

Police attempt to stop her, but she does not stop. She shouts her name, medical ID badge held out like a shield. Eventually, one officer leads her and Natalie toward the buses.

Briefly stopped at a bottleneck, Ramola throws a look behind her. The truck is gone. Luis and Josh are on their bikes and pedaling back down Bay Road.

You Will Not Feel Me
Between Your Teeth

This is not the end of a fairy tale, nor is it the
end of a movie. This is a song.

* * *

Natalie's face is almost blank. There's only a little bit left of
her. Luis doesn't know the real her, of course, and he realizes
this, and within that realization, a horror: there's only a little
bit left of the Natalie he met less than an hour ago. He wonders how much of that Natalie was already a compromised,
diminished version. Luis thinks the dimming or leaking away
of who you are is the worst thing that can happen to anyone.
He is right, but there are many worst things that can happen
to anyone.

Josh gives Ramola his backpack and she thanks him and she leads Natalie away.

Josh says, "Let's just go."

Luis says, "You first." He shoulders his pack, swapping out his baseball bat for Josh's wooden staff.

They go back the way they came, retracing their paths down Bay Road, back under the canopy of trees where it's darker and more foreboding. You are not supposed to go back, you can't go back, and if you attempt a return you will be forever lost. Luis knows this, but they're doing it anyway.

They don't slow at the yellow house and the four dead men in the road. They glide through, the scene already like a memory, one that's unreliable. Luis doesn't grieve for the men. If anything, he hoped to find them shambling aimlessly, arms outstretched, mangled faces a comic parody of death, of ridiculous, messy, capricious death, so it would be easier to pretend they are in a zombie movie. He will still pretend.

They ride past the white church. Two dead turkeys are in the parking lot. A pillowful of loosened feathers are massed and they rise and fall in the wind, new birds learning to fly.

Josh's riding is erratic. He weaves and abruptly jerks his bike at hard angles when the road is clear. He shouts at shadows and he shouts at trees. He lists until Luis calls out his name, then he lists some more. Luis knows Josh will not be Josh for much longer. Perhaps he already isn't Josh, or the new non-Josh is growing, metastasizing, laying claim. Regardless, Luis will follow Josh and follow him until he cannot lead anymore.

There is no discussion about going back to their Brockton apartment, the one they've lived in for six months, the one with a single bedroom and a futon couch. They've been making rent with the help of their haunted parents, who are happy to have the almost-grown-up ghosts of their sons out of juvenile facilities and their court-mandated youth programs, and who are equally happy to have those ghosts out of their houses.

Luis knows they cannot go home.

* * *

What Luis does not know: The virus doesn't herald the end of the world, or of the United States, or even of the commonwealth of Massachusetts. In the coming days, conditions will continue to deteriorate. Emergency services and other public safety nets will be stretched to their breaking points, exacerbated by the wily antagonists of fear, panic, misinformation; a myopic, sluggish federal bureaucracy further hamstrung by a president unwilling and woefully unequipped to make the rational, science-based decisions necessary; and exacerbated, of course, by plain old individual everyday evil. But there will be many heroes, too, including ones who don't view themselves as such. Dr. Awolesi will be proven correct in her epidemic forecast: the exponentially increased speed with which this rabies virus infects and progresses will aid in its own containment and control. Nine days after Josh and Luis meet Ramola and Natalie a massive pre-exposure vaccination campaign will finally begin in New England for both humans and animals. In concurrence with the quarantine, the vaccination program will be wildly successful and will return the region from the brink of collapse. In the final tally of what will be considered the end of the epidemic [but not, to be clear, the end of the virus; it will burrow, digging in like a nasty tick; it will migrate; and it will return all but encouraged and welcomed in a country where science and forethought are allowed to be dirty words, where humanity's greatest invention——the vaccine——is smeared and vilified by narcissistic, purposeful fools [the most dangerous kind, where fear is harvested for fame, profit, and self-esteem], almost ten thousand people will have died.

* * *

Luis follows Josh to Borderland's satellite entrance, past the gate, onto the mile-long dirt road, an artery into one of the many hearts of the expansive park. The knobs on their tires kick and flip small stones. Josh shout-sings a nursery rhyme as they ride deeper into the park, as they become more alone with themselves. The road cuts a rolling swath through the green and growing. The dead and the dying are in hiding, are not showing their empty stares and rictus grins, but they never remain in hiding for long. The sky is a strip of dark gray, another road.

The forest yields and the road empties into open fields boasting dry grasses as high as the teens' waists. Ahead is an empty, historic [as designated by the state] blue house, tilted and randomly placed as though it had tumbled off the side of the narrowing dirt road. To their right is a crooked footpath through the field. Josh wobbles on his bike and falls into the grass next to the park information sign encased in glass and framed in brown wood. Luis dumps his bike next to Josh's and he helps his feverish friend onto his feet. Josh begins a new rhyme. It is unfamiliar to Luis and he feels ashamed, as though he doesn't know his friend like he thinks he does. Josh ties his bandanna over his mouth, making a gag. The red cloth peels his lips away from his front teeth, showing the future. Luis takes a coiled rope out of his pack. Josh clasps his hands, as if in prayer, in front of his stomach. Luis wraps and loops the rope around Josh's wrists just like he saw them [who are them? characters? actors?] do on a famous television show. He ties it all off as best as he can, leaving enough rope for a ten-foot lead. Josh walks and Luis trails behind carrying one end of the rope and the wooden staff.

Danger skulks undercover in the fields; the tall grass bows and waves, whispering of the epic battle to come. The zombie foxes are the first to attack. The scent of their musk announces their stealthy approach. The zombie raccoons are next. Their snorts and chitters fill the air, broadcasting their immutable intentions. Luis wields the staff expertly, vanquishing the smaller animals using acrobatic parries, focused strikes, and cagey counterthrusts. Despite his limitations, his weakening hold on both physical and mental health, Josh heroically sallies forth, defending with spastic but brutal kicks and double hammer blows. The teens more than endure the tiny terrors, they revel as though there never was and never will be a sweeter time, a greater moment. If not an apotheosis, this is them at their best, and they laugh and they boast and they shout and they live and they know there is no future.

Danger crashes through the woods, snapping branches and overturning rocks, impatient for the teens' arrival, thirsting for their introduction. Blocking the entrance to the forest, a zombie deer greets them with a storm of hooves. The teens' defense is impregnable, however. The deer soon fatigues, and ultimate, inevitable defeat arrives when her reed-thin foreleg shatters at the dull swipe of the wooden staff. Her epileptic convulsions and contortions communicate a dire warning and judgment: their time was brief, their time is over. In the forest where the path thins into ruts and the branches above overlap like entwined fingers, there is no more gray sky. Something follows the teens from the cover of the opaque brush. Judging by the ruckus and upheaval, perhaps it's the forest itself stalking them. Josh slows, and staggers more than he walks. Luis urges him on, the rope limp and dead in his hand. The zombie bats appear next, a mini-tornado of wings, claws, and needle-sharp teeth. There are too many bats for Luis to deflect; it would be like fighting rain. Luis freezes up but Josh knocks his friend to the ground and shields him with his body. The bats are left to satisfy themselves with Josh's skin and blood. They begrudgingly accept the tainted offering, but they do not linger. The teens push deeper into the forest, following the paths they traced and memorized years ago, when their summer adventures and tragedies happened here. They are still kids, of course, but they have already lost their childhood. A zombie coyote as large as a wolf finally crashes through the brush ahead of them. It allows the teens to gape at its glorious all-ness before the attack. In the gray, dulling afternoon light, smothered by the conspiratorial canopy, the animal's great head appears to be floating disembodied over a mass of dark-brown fur. It has glowing, hot-coal-red eyes, all the better to see them with. As it creeps forward, within pouncing distance, impatient lips reveal an overcrowded mouth and dripping stalactite canines. Its paws don't pad as much as they gouge, each step scalloping a mini-grave. Close enough, its body now fully seen, brawny muscles flex and ripple. The standoff with the teens lasts only a few seconds, and it lasts a geologic age during which glaciers grind and birth the landscape around them. Then it finally leaps. Josh steps into the arc, taking the brunt. The coyote's bear-trap jaws snap onto his forearm. There is no grace to this battle. It's savage and dirty and desperate. Josh, strangely quiet but for heavy breaths and short grunts, knees the animal's rib cage and stomps on its paws. Luis swings the wooden staff, and he pokes and jabs, but the weapon is ineffectual. He abandons the staff for a heavy stone he raises with two hands and bashes into the side of the coyote's head, and then the top of its skull. There's a crack and a uniquely canine whimper; red eyes shrink and dim. The coyote deflates, goes slack, releases Josh, and wobbles down the path on quivering legs, veering into the brush without so much as a ripple or snapped twig.

Danger lurks inside the teens, thrashing through one's heart and the other's mind. In a circular clearing, ringed by boulders and tree stumps, a hub spoked with alternate paths marked by carved wooden trail markers, Josh stops walking. He turns, and he *has* turned. This is the reveal of Zombie Josh, the zombie teen with red coyote eyes, lips a ragged drawn curtain, foam and saliva fauceting from his gagged mouth. Luis cannot help but stare at his friend's teeth, as though he'd never really seen them before, seen them for what they can be. Hands still tied together, Zombie Josh rushes at Luis. Thus begins a dance that will last into the night. Luis will not hurt Zombie Josh, even though he's seen all the movies and knows all the rules. Instead, he will duck and he will dodge and he will sidestep and he will run. He will leapfrog onto the boulders and tree stumps and he will wind around the wooden posts of the park signs, centrifugal force aiding in acceleration and changes of direction. He will use the staff as a pole vault and he will use the staff to deflect, to block, and to steer Zombie Josh away without ever striking him. He will pull and then slacken the rope lead tethered to Zombie Josh's hands and wrists, puppeteering his friend into an arcing, orbiting trajectory, one that will not intersect with his. Luis's plan is simple: to outlast. It is in this manner, with the watchers watching from the trees and the shadows that Luis and Zombie Josh dance their shoes to pieces.

* * *

If Josh had his druthers, were still capable of having druthers, they would've made it to a giant calved boulder called Split Rock. Josh has succumbed to physical exhaustion and the late stages of the virus. He is sitting on the ground in the clearing, half-propped against an oblong, couch-sized boulder. His eyes are closed. His breathing is arrhythmic and shallow.

They didn't make it, but they are home.

Luis's eyes are open wide, light-starved in the dark. His breathing is even and controlled. Luis is crouched next to his near comatose friend. Luis wonders where Ramola and Natalie are. He wonders how long ago Natalie ceased being herself. He wants to think that he and Josh did something good today, something that, if it doesn't balance the cosmic ledger for the irredeemable sin of their past, it at least tilts the scale back toward their favor. But then he remembers the last time he saw Natalie's face, and he fears their help might've been too late, might've been for nothing.

The irredeemable sin of their past: the inexplicable [even now, especially now] complicity in a brutal beating resulting in the death of an old man, and the silence after, and the terrible price of that silence: the disappearance and death of their best friend.

We will not intrude on Luis here, not for much longer. His past, particularly his regrets and recriminations, belong to him. We know enough and we will never know enough to understand what he will do next anyway.

Luis slips his hands under Josh's head and unties the gag. The sopping-wet bandanna slides easily out of his slack mouth. Luis drops it to the ground. He does not wipe away or clean the crusting foam from Josh's lips. Josh coughs once, a dusty memory of a functioning body. Luis rolls up his right sleeve. He cannot see his own smooth, unblemished skin in the dark. It's hard to believe it gets this dark every night. Placing a thumb on Josh's chin, Luis pulls down the lower jaw, opening the mouth. He takes his thumb away. Josh's face and body tremors, but he doesn't wake and his mouth stays open. Luis places the soft underside of his forearm into Josh's mouth, the inside of which is as hot and damp as a sauna. Luis positions his left palm under Josh's chin and pushes, closing the mouth, forcing his friend's teeth against his skin. It hurts, but he doesn't know if the teeth have broken through yet. He pushes harder and Josh convulses, perhaps because the body's main airway is being blocked. There's still a spark of life within the engine. His jaws contract once, and hard. The pain is an electrical storm, and stars explode in Luis's vision. He retracts his arm. When he finds the dark holes in his skin, he wipes the area with his fingers, mixing the saliva and blood together. Luis sits with his back against the rock, shoulder to shoulder with his friend. He initially planned to run and rampage through the forest like the monster he will become, but he doesn't want to leave Josh alone, even if he's already gone.

Luis has sweat through his clothes and he shivers as the temperature continues to drop. His teeth chatter. He hugs his knees into his chest, trying to keep warm. His wounded forearm throbs with his heartbeats. The times between Josh's shallow breaths expand until the final, infinite time. Luis is then left alone to listen to the forest's night sounds he's never really heard before, a beautiful and sorrowful secret he will not have the privilege of carrying for very long. Luis closes his eyes, leans into his friend, and waits for the fire to burn through his head.

DO YOU BECOME A ROSE TREE, AND I THE ROSE UPON IT

RAMS

Police cars slowly creep away, their drivers unsure of direction and purpose beyond clearing a path for the buses to roll out of the clinic's parking lot.

A brown-haired, middle-aged clinician wears a white lab coat over jeans and a dark-blue button-down shirt. She holds a clipboard against her chest. Without an introduction she says, "We've been holding the buses for you, but we weren't going to hold them for much longer"; an offhand accusation, attributing the irresponsibility of their lateness to Ramola. It's not fair, and it feeds the roots of a forest of shame, sadness, and rage that she is not able to save Natalie.

"Thank you, and sorry, we were in an automobile accident." Ramola shakes her head but not because she says anything wrong. It's an impatient tic of hers, one that was more prevalent when she was a stressed-out medical student. Ramola and Natalie are not yet on the black-and-purple bus. They are still standing in the street, looking up at the woman stationed between the bus's folding doors.

She asks, "Are you injured?"

Police officers shout, "Let's get rolling" and "Time to go," and punctuate with car-door slams.

Ramola says, "No, we're fine."

"Have either of you been exposed to the virus? We cannot risk—"

Ramola places a foot on the bus's first step and says, "We have not. May we come aboard? The officers are telling us we have to go." She climbs onto the second step, sure that the woman knows she is lying. How can she not? Ramola's voice is a reedy screech and she overcompensates with a crumbling smile and a tractor-beam stare. Lying might be the wrong decision; perhaps if she tells the truth they'll still be allowed on this or the other bus (gray, its doors already closed), or a police officer would take them to another hospital still open to the general public. With the memories of Norwood and how long it took to wade through the throngs and eventually get treatment cobwebbing her head, Ramola is determined to get on this bus by any means, medical-school oaths—and herself—be damned. Still, there's a part of her that wants to be caught in the lie now, because being caught later is inevitable.

The clinician backs up, almost into the lap of the bus driver, to allow Ramola and Natalie passage. She complains they don't have time to store Ramola's bags under the bus and they'll have to be placed in the overheads, if they fit.

Ramola positions herself so that she or her bags block her view of Natalie as she climbs onto the bus. As the clinician peers over her shoulder, Ramola asks, "What is your name again?"

"Dr. Gwen Kolodny."

"Thank you, Doctor. And where are the buses taking us?" The police officer who led them to the bus already told her where it was going. The question is to keep Kolodny talking and not focused on Natalie shuffling into the aisle. Ramola tries to catch Natalie's eye but her head is down, hair hanging loosely over her face.

Dr. Kolodny sputters a distracted answer, a fully secured hospital, transferring unexposed maternity patients and newborns, near the border of Rhode Island, and she mentions the town of North Attleboro as the bus driver's two-way radio spews static and coded chatter. She turns to talk to the driver. The doors swing closed and the bus rolls forward before Ramola finds her seat next to Natalie.

Natalie is turned and facing out the window. Ramola assumes she's doing so purposefully, to avoid being seen by other clinicians in white coats flittering up and down the aisle like hummingbirds. Perhaps it is time for Ramola to stop assuming fully rational decision-making in regard to Natalie's behavior. She's going to begin to suffer from cognitive deficiencies and delusions soon, if it isn't happening already.

Ramola asks, "Are you all right?"

"I'm peach," Natalie says. Not "peachy."

The bus rocks from side to side as it crests the elevated lip of the lot exit. It turns left, goes straight through the Five Corners intersection, following one police car, blue lights flashing. A low murmur ripples through the bus's passengers now that they are moving. Across the aisle from Ramola are two young pregnant women. They are both staring ahead, faces frozen in worried expressions, hands folded on top of their swollen bellies. The one by the window mutters something that makes the other woman laugh nervously.

Ramola has put these women and all the others sitting in

front of and behind them at risk by getting Natalie onto the bus. She has compromised her pledged medical ethics and knowingly broken federal and state quarantine protocols and laws. She's sick with worry, fear, grief, and disappointment at how easy it was to lie and to actively endanger the well-being of others. And for what, ultimately? Natalie cannot be cured, and they are at least twenty-five minutes away from an operating table, assuming this next hospital will even admit them. Ramola takes out her phone to send a text to Dr. Awolesi. She writes, "Per your instruction we arrived at the Ames Clinic." Ramola rescans the text, says it in her head so it reads as *Look at what you made me do, should someone else get hurt it'll be your fault too*. She erases the text and starts again. "Arrived at the Ames Clinic. All patients being transferred via bus to North Attleboro. Natalie has not been seen by OB/GYN yet." She hits Send, then types, "I don't know what else I can do for her." She erases that one too.

"Hey, Rams?"

"Yes, I'm right here."

"I'm scared."

"I know."

"Thank you for knowing."

"You're welcome."

"Everyone in here knows about me."

"No, they don't."

"They do. And they're not going to bring us where they're supposed to. I can almost hear them thinking about what they're really going to do. They think in small voices. They hide their small voices behind smaller hands. Baby hands, but not hands that belong to babies. But I stopped listening hard enough. I don't want to hear them."

"Natalie—"

"Sorry. Can you say yes again? I need to hear it."

"Yes?"

"No, a real one."

"What am I saying yes to?"

"I need to hear the yes you gave me back on the road. It has to be the same exact one, or it won't work. I'm worried I'll forget it and I need it to get me through to the end. Right, remember? When you said yes, I said I'd go all the way to the end. I need to hear it one more time."

"Yes."

"Please. Again."

"Yes."

The driver shouts and the bus slows. Not quite a slamming of the brakes and tire-screeching halt, but the rapid deceleration is enough to propel everyone forward, hands grasping the seatbacks in front of them. Passengers gasp and the pneumatic brakes hiss. Once the bus comes to a full stop, Dr. Kolodny and another person wearing a white coat rush up the aisle to the front. The bus idles in a residential, wooded area. A large white house is directly across from Natalie's window. Ramola looks at her watch. They've been riding for about five minutes.

Ramola and Natalie are four rows back from the driver. The clinicians obscure most of Ramola's view through the windshield, but the police-escort car has stopped perpendicular to another vehicle, a mammoth white SUV, parked across the middle of the road.

The chatter up front is clipped, agitated, and sets off a chorus of "What's going on?" and "Why did we stop?" throughout the bus.

Ramola stands, one foot in the aisle. It does not improve her vantage. She asks Natalie, "Can you see what's going on?"

"The Tree's buddies are here. Whole bunch of trees."

Ramola leans across and over Natalie. From her angle she can't see the police car or the SUV in front of the bus, nor does she see any people initially. Then a crouched man runs out from behind the white house's garage. There are gunshots, rapid small-caliber pops mixing with loud, singular explosions. Ramola dives back, away from the window. Screams and shouts fill the bus, along with shrieks from newborns. Ramola almost forgot there are babies on the bus too. Everyone leans away from the windows, tries to make themselves smaller in their seats, everyone except Natalie. She sits tall and has her hands and face against the glass. Ramola grabs her right arm and pulls her away. Natalie's complaint is subverbal, a growl.

It's unclear if the driver is given an order from Kolodny, from police on the two-way radio, or acts on his own. The engine revs and the bus lurches forward, titling left as its passenger-side wheels climb the elevated shoulder. There's more yelling, more gunshots, and stomach-dropping moments of weightlessness as the bus leans farther left, and Ramola is sure they're going to tip onto their side, Natalie and her window mashed into the pavement. The police car and SUV roadblock roll by Natalie's window, the scene dreamlike, as though contained within a terrarium, and the odd, elevated and angled view vertiginous as they float by. Men wearing dark or camouflage clothing hide behind another SUV stashed in a driveway. Others are positioned behind trees or flat on their bellies at the stone walls. They fire at the policemen huddled behind their car and they fire at the buses. Bullets thud into the side panel but none hit the windows. Another moment of weightlessness, lifting Ramola out of her seat as the bus comes off the shoulder, then all tires are back in contact with the pavement. The cabin shakes like a wet dog, straightening as the bus accelerates. People in the back rows yell about the gray bus left behind, not moving, windshield shattered. Clinicians run up and down the aisle checking with patients, reassuring them. The bus driver speaks over the intercom but the babies are crying and other patients are shouting, talking over him; no one is listening. Ramola attempts to slow her breathing and still her shaking hands. She watches out Natalie's window and through the windshield for more roadblocks and men with guns.

This initial firefight lasts only five minutes, but a standoff with the Norton police and eventually the National Guard will go on for five hours, further ensnaring lines of communication and consuming most of the local emergency resources. Nine members of the Patriot Percenters militia will die, along with four policemen, the driver of the gray bus, and one of its passengers, a woman who gave birth less than ten hours prior to having a bullet punch through a window and into her neck. Right-wing conspiracy devotees will insist the civilian and policemen deaths are fakes and the entire event a false-flag operation. Like the Tree, the Patriot Percenters believe the deep state is purposefully spreading their lab-created virus to push vaccination agendas, attempt a coup as America is distracted and succumbing to the health crisis, and then decree a permanent state of martial law. The Percenters are convinced Phase 2 has begun: exporting the virus to surrounding New England and Mid-Atlantic states via busloads of infectious patients and deep state–controlled medical personnel, most of whom are foreigners, as reported on the most notorious and popular hate-fueled conspiracy website.

Ramola counts the seconds as they tick. She measures the expanding distance from the attack. She smiles at every staff member and clinician who walks by to ensure they focus on her and not Natalie. She looks out the window, waiting for the next calamity to show itself. She watches and listens to Natalie, losing count when she thinks she sees a quiver and curl of her lip. She starts over at one and begins counting again. Five minutes pass in this manner.

As their bus powers down the quiet wooded road, no vehicles follow. Frenzied chatter within the cabin has receded in volume, but it remains an insistent murmur, waves lapping shores at low tide.

Natalie shudders into a coughing fit; a dry, throaty blast of three barks lasting four cycles. When she finishes, the bus goes quiet and still. Ramola can't and won't look into the aisle or at people in other seats, afraid of what she'll see and afraid others will see a confession on her face.

Natalie wipes her mouth on the back of a sleeve. Is she shedding the virus now? Natalie mutters to herself, twists to more easily look out the window, her head tilted, eyes wide and blinking.

The new silence lingers, and Ramola has to break the spell, to make their presence on the bus seem normal and nonthreatening. She taps Natalie's shoulder, whisper-repeats her name, and asks how she's feeling, how she's doing.

Natalie shrugs and she shakes her head. Her right hand spelunks into one of the yellow sweatshirt pockets and returns with her cell phone.

NATS

(muted, low voices and the hum of an engine)

"Excuse me, I haven't had a chance to check in with you yet, Natalie. How are you feeling?"

Sassafras and lullabies.

"Oh, we're doing quite well over here. Thank you."

RAMS

Natalie flips through app screens, presses a purple rounded square, a capital cursive *V* in its middle. A home screen opens with the script heading *Voyager*. Natalie thumbs through menu options until the screen is a blank purple color, red Record button at the bottom. She presses that, too, bringing up a horizontal, quivering white line. She leans left, her head and shoulder resting against the bus window.

Ramola twists, her back to the aisle and facing Natalie. Her view of the phone screen is blocked.

Natalie's right hand alternates between tucking hair behind her ear and hovering over the phone, index finger extended. A trace of a smile on her face, though upon closer inspection, it's not really a smile. There's no upturn in her lips, no exposure of teeth, but instead a softening of expression, facial muscles relaxed, eyes half-lidded, almost sleepy, eyebrows slightly elevated, unguarded. It's the ghost of a look of contentment.

Ramola has stopped counting, even though time stubbornly goes on without her marking it. She continues closely observing her friend, afraid of witnessing the point-of-no-return transformation, afraid she missed it already. In the tinted window glass, there is a near mirror-quality reflection of Natalie's face. In this reflection there are no tear and dirt stains, no puffy circles under her eyes, no feverish red splotches on her cheeks. Trapped in the glass's amber is Natalie's younger face: Ramola sees the Natalie she first met in college and the one she shared an apartment with and the one from those nights sitting on the kitchen floor and the one she secretly cried over when she moved out and the one in that bachelorette-party photo, her favorite photo; the Natalie she'll always remember until she cannot remember anything anymore. This reflection of younger selves rest their heads against the Natalie of now, the one who showed up bloodied at Ramola's townhouse, the one who fought and is fighting valiantly, the one who is dying despite her defiance. The split images are representatives of the past and present, and together, the horrible future. Both sets of faces are only inches away from each other and they are in sync, staring and blinking at the phone screen, opening their mouths to say something, but they do not speak.

If Natalie looks up now, what will she see? What will Ramola see?

"Excuse me, I haven't had a chance to check in with you yet, Natalie. How are you feeling?" asks Dr. Kolodny. She's a sentinel in the aisle wearing rubber gloves (was she wearing them earlier?), and she only has eyes for Natalie. Her professional veneer, already haggard and worn at the edges, collapses.

Ramola jumps out of her seat and stands between Dr. Kolodny and Natalie. She turns forward and back, opens and closes her white coat, wipes her face, and glances at her watch, desperate to somehow keep the Natalie-is-healthy lie alive until they get to the hospital in another fifteen minutes. Is that all the time they will need? Is that all the time they have?

Natalie says, "Sassafras and lullabies." Her voice is low-pitched and airless. She sits up from the window, breaking away from her reflection.

Ramola says, "Oh, we're doing quite well over here. Thank you."

Natalie hits a button on the phone and puts it back into her pocket. She says, "I'm tired. A tired peach." She lowers her chin into her chest and runs one hand through her hair, which falls out from behind her ears and blankets most of her face. The gesture is purposeful; she's hiding from the awful world.

Dr. Kolodny speaks sternly, a teacher trying to shame a churlish student sleeping in the back row. "Natalie, I need to take your temperature. We were supposed to screen you prior to leaving the clinic, or right after leaving, and I was on my way to do so but then everything—is it okay if I slide by, Dr. Sherman? Thank you." Dr. Kolodny shimmies into their row, nudging and edging Ramola into the aisle with her hips.

Ramola says, "Of course. But I could—is there anything I can help with?" She folds her hands together, unsure of what to do beyond snatching the thermometer from Kolodny's hands and throwing it off the bus.

Natalie says, "Is that the right thermometer? It doesn't look right. It's small. That's a baby one. What are you trying to do?"

Dr. Kolodny inserts the temperature wand into the rear of the device, covering it with a disposable sleeve. "This is not an infant thermometer."

Natalie says, "The baby ones don't work on adults. They run

hot. Hot, hot, hot. Right? You do know I'm pregnant too. Pregnant women run hot."

Ramola adds, "I can attest her body temperature is normally in the low-to-mid ninety-nine degrees."

"I'll keep that in mind. Open your mouth, please, and keep this under your tongue."

Natalie tilts her head back, her brown hair parts, a sly smirk flashes, and she opens her mouth as wide as she can. Once the thermometer makes contact with her tongue, she snaps her jaws shut as though a trap is triggered. Dr. Kolodny flinches and Natalie giggles.

"Please keep your mouth closed."

Natalie mutters around the mouthful of thermometer. "Sorry. Me laughing is stress. I'm stressed, so stressed. And I run hot. Wicked hot. Scalding hot iron shoes."

The thermometer beeps and Dr. Kolodny doesn't look at the reading. "Your mouth must remain closed, please. Just for a few seconds."

Before the thermometer goes back in her mouth, Natalie grabs Dr. Kolodny's hand and pushes it toward her belly. "Feel her moving around in there. Feel her. I want you to. Do you want a living creature or all the treasure in the world?"

Ramola intervenes, calls out Natalie's name, separates their hands, and coos lies to Natalie (instead of Kolodny), "Let go. It'll be okay." Natalie gives a watery-eyed look of betrayal and slumps in her seat. Ramola's heart splinters and cracks. Tears sting her eyes. The first tears always sting the most.

Dr. Kolodny threatens to have Natalie restrained. Other staff and clinicians congregate around their seats. Whispers and chatter swells from the other patients.

Natalie shouts, "All right. I'll be good. Just let Rams do it and get it over with."

Dr. Kolodny yields the thermometer. Ramola holds the wand in one hand and the readout device in the other. How can she fool the machine? How closely are the others watching?

Natalie says, "They're not going to like it," and opens her mouth. Her brown eyes are wide, glassy, red rimmed. The wand goes under Natalie's tongue. Her mouth closes, lips form a tight seal. Natalie and Ramola stare at each other, making their silent confessions.

The thermometer beeps—102.8 degrees.

Dr. Kolodny quickly huddles with staff, and before they break up and disperse she orders them to distribute respirator masks to everyone on board. One staff member stays with Kolodny, the largest one, a young, baby-faced Latino man standing well over six feet tall. He stares at Natalie as though he's terrified of her.

The doctor says to Ramola, "What do you know? You have to tell us."

Natalie shouts, "No!" Both hands rest atop her belly. Her teeth are gritted, lips pressed tightly together though they flutter, wanting to peel away. Breathing heavily through her nose, head tilted, downcast, not making eye contact with anyone, glaring hard at the seatback in front of her.

The large man and a clinician with a respirator mask in her hand worm past Ramola and speak to Natalie, their instructions droning and monotone. Patients vacate the seats directly in front and behind.

Natalie shouts, "No!" again but doesn't lift her hands away from her belly, doesn't resist their putting the mask over her nose and mouth.

Could Ramola convince any of them Natalie has the flu or any number of other viruses that cause fevers? Kolodny will surely insist upon submitting Natalie to a full examination and find the wound on her arm. What lie will Ramola tell then?

Ramola leans in, grabs the doctor's arm at the elbow, and whispers, "Natalie was bitten on the left forearm by an infected man more than four hours ago. She received the first round of vaccine approximately an hour after exposure. She's been present-ing symptoms of infection for at least an hour, possibly longer."

Dr. Kolodny says, "Let go of me," and attempts to twist out of Ramola's grip.

Natalie barks, "No!" into her mask. The two staff members remain in the area in front of Ramola's seat, with the large man resting one knee in her chair, and ask Natalie more questions.

Ramola, no longer whispering, says, "I'm sorry we—we had to get on this bus and it was wrong of us—wrong of me to tell you she hadn't been exposed, and I know she can't be saved but her child still can. She needs a cesarean section as soon as possible—"

Dr. Kolodny holds up her hands, shakes her head. She twists free and darts up the aisle, almost knocking a woman to the floor.

Ramola calls after her, "You must call ahead. Tell the hospital to prepare for her arrival. Please, this is our last chance."

Natalie continues yelling, "No!"

Dr. Kolodny is next to the driver and shouts something to him. Whatever she tells him, he does a double take. She repeats herself. The driver does not hand Dr. Kolodny the two-way ra-dio as Ramola hopes. The bus slows and the pneumatic brakes again become hissing snakes.

It's a smoother, more controlled stop than earlier, although because Ramola is standing she pitches forward and latches onto the headrest of the now-empty seat in front of hers to keep her feet.

Natalie continues yelling. As they rumble to a stop, other passengers fearfully peek over the rows of seats.

Dr. Kolodny walks back down the aisle announcing, "This stop is only temporary. There is no issue on the road ahead of us. Please stay calm. Keep your masks on. We will be on our way soon." When she reaches Ramola and where the staff continues struggling with quieting Natalie, she says, "Please help Natalie get off the bus safely."

The rest of the bus goes quiet but for Natalie still shouting, "No!"

Ramola says, "Please. I'm sorry and I should've told you—"

"The driver is alerting the police that we are dropping you here, using the home address on the mailbox we parked next to. You and Natalie will be picked up very shortly." Dr. Kolodny says this while looking at some other area of the bus that neither Natalie nor Ramola occupies.

"We can't. It'll be too late. Please."

"Federal quarantine law is quite clear on this. We cannot risk her infecting others on board, including our six newborns."

"Doctor—"

"And even if I let you stay, the hospital we're going to will not take her, and they wouldn't take us."

The last part sounds like a lie, has to be a lie. Or is it? Would Kolodny and staff physically remove them from the bus if she refuses to budge? Ramola shouts and appeals to other clinicians on board, all of whom wear the same blinking, blank face of disbelief, of *This isn't supposed to be happening.* Ramola then turns to the terrified patients, masked women and their crying babies. Ramola knows the horror on top of the horror is that she and Kolodny are both correct: this bus is Natalie's child's last chance and they cannot in good conscience continue to risk the other patients without their consent, particularly as Natalie has become more agitated, more dangerous. Ramola envisions asking each patient if Natalie can stay. Many if not most would say yes, but all of them?

Natalie shrieks in pain as the two staff members yank on her arms, trying to pull her to standing.

Ramola, swollen with a righteous rage at everything, including herself, yells at them to stop and she pounds on the backs of their shoulders with closed fists until they do. Ramola pushes and shoves her way past them to her friend.

Natalie clutches her injured forearm. The fingers on her left hand spasm into a gnarled, arthritic fist. Her eyes roll around the bus's interior as though she doesn't recognize where she is, how she got there. She shouts, "Y-You can't eat her! I know your names!"

Ramola tries to soothe and calm her down, saying, "I'm here. It's me," and rests a hand on Natalie's sizzling forehead. Natalie lifts her head, twists and shakes the hand away. With the mask covering her mouth, Ramola doesn't know if Natalie attempted to bite her.

She repeats Natalie's name, leans in so their faces are mere inches from touching. She feels the unremitting heat of Natalie's corona of fever on her own face. Natalie finally locks eyes with Ramola, blinking rapidly as though focus is difficult to maintain. Her shouts decay into a breathless, muttered mantra. Ramola slowly peels Natalie's right hand from her left arm. Hand in hand, Ramola gently urges Natalie onto her feet and they shuffle into the aisle. She squeezes Natalie's hand. Natalie does not reciprocate.

The large man holds the two bags Ramola brought on board. He wears a mask now too. He says he'll carry them outside for her.

Natalie says, "You can't eat her. I know all your names, all of them . . ." at a conversational volume, though it is not her voice anymore. It's a voice that belongs to someone else.

Needing fuel to go on, Ramola feeds the dying embers of her previous rage. She says, "Doctor," spitting out the word, filling it with the leaden weights of despair and disappointment, "what address did you give the police?"

Astride the driver, Kolodny states the address and points out the opened folding doors.

The large man follows closely behind Natalie. As they pass, patients shrink away. Quick, hushed bursts of "We can't just leave her on the side of the road" and "She can't stay. It's not safe" percolate behind them.

Ramola spews questions as they walk the short distance down the aisle to the doors: "Doctor, did the police give you an estimated time of arrival?" and "Doctor, did you tell them Natalie is pregnant?" and "Doctor, how will you be able to sleep at night?" Ramola knows the last question might be cruel, but why not share what she would ask herself.

She pauses at the top step. The cold, late-afternoon air is three steps down. Ramola turns away and says, "Doctor, what if we refuse? Are you going to physically remove us?"

Natalie is next to Dr. Kolodny and the bus driver, who is

standing, a full head taller than Natalie. He wears a mask and gloves. The large staff member looms behind Natalie, the bags slung on his shoulders, his free hands extended and open, as though ready to reach and grab. The way they look at her, the way everyone on the bus looks at her, Ramola knows the answer to her last question.

Natalie aims her face at the doctor, and hisses. "You can't eat her . . ." She slides her hand out of Ramola's and swipes at the doctor, hitting her in the left side of her head above the ear. There isn't much power behind the strike, it's exploratory, an opening salvo, the distant rumble before a storm. But it's enough that the bus explodes into shouts and shrieks. The driver and the large staff member clamp onto Natalie's arms and wrestle her down the bus stairs.

"I know all your names!"

Ramola is forced out of the bus, stumbling backward, and she twists and falls off the plunging final step to the pavement. She lands in the mouth of a driveway, scraping her palms.

The bus driver is next out of the bus and he tugs hard on Natalie's left arm. She is forced to step heavily onto the road. One leg buckles but they prop her up, prevent her from falling. Now on the street, the driver and staff member drag her away from the bus. She screams and thrashes her head side to side, and when the men finally let go, giving her a little shove away from them, they jog back to the bus.

Ramola clambers onto her feet and steps between Natalie and the retreating men. She hushes and holds her arms up in surrender. Natalie quiets instantly, a plug pulled. Her shoulders hunch, her chest deflating into itself. One hand rubs her belly, then drops limply to her side.

With one foot on the road and the other on the first step, the large staff member tosses the two bags near Ramola's feet. He says, "I'll make the doctor call again. This is wrong and I'm sorry. Good luck." The doors rattle closed behind him, and the moment he's inside the bus pulls away.

Where the road meets the end of the cracked and pothole-filled driveway, a black metal mailbox perches atop a crooked white wooden post. The red flag is missing. Ramola takes a picture of the mailbox. She texts the street address and, in a separate text (mindful of the data crunch continuing to compromise the local cellular network), she sends the photo to Dr. Awolesi, who has yet to respond to any messages.

An old white farmhouse is at the other end of the drive, set back from the road about one hundred feet. The dilapidated home squats in a wide field of dry, dead grass, with at least another three acres of land beyond it. Ramola assumes this area was once a working farm that included the vast empty field across the street, its tree line pushed back another couple hundred feet. There isn't another home visible in either direction. The gray sky is low and falling.

Natalie walks and talks in circles, her orbit gradually carrying her up the farmhouse's drive.

"Natalie? Please stay. There will be a car coming for us soon." Ramola can barely get the words out of her mouth without either crumbling or exploding. She swears, shoulders the two bags, looks down the empty road in both directions, and trots after Natalie.

"We haven't had much luck on the road today, have we?" Ramola says when she catches up. "We really should wait by the mailbox so they'll more easily find us when they arrive." What kind of lie is one not of your own fabrication but is instead a repeating of someone else's meant-to-be-broken promise?

Natalie shakes her drooped head, whispers trapped within her mask.

Ramola scoots ahead and blocks Natalie's path again. Natalie walks until she bumps into Ramola belly-first, bouncing her a few steps backward. Natalie laughs a bully's laugh, which weakens Ramola's legs and steals her spirit. She's never felt smaller.

Natalie squeezes her eyes together, holds them closed for a beat, and when she opens them there's a flicker of light, a flicker of who she is or was. She says, "I hurt so much. I'm not doing well, Rams."

Desperate to believe in and take advantage of a brief symptomatic return to lucidity, even as she knows the stolen time will be delicate, finite, and final, Ramola says, "Natalie, please stay with me." She means *Stop walking and stay with me by the side of the road* and she means the impossible, forever kind of *Stay with me.*

"I wish I could. I'm sorry, Rams." The tone and the gravel aren't her voice, but the inflection is hers.

"If the police or an ambulance doesn't come, we'll hitch a ride with any car that passes by."

"You have to get me in the house."

"It doesn't look like anyone is home, how do—"

"It's not safe out here. And you won't be safe from me."

"The house is too far from the road. If someone drives by, they might not see us and I'm not leaving you by yourself in there to watch for cars."

"I need to lie down. I'm about done."

"You can have my coat and rest on the grass."

"You have to take my phone after."

"Natalie—"

"And tell me you'll adopt her. Tell me yes, again, Rams. One more time. Tell me now."

"I will try."

"That's not a yes."

Ramola is tempted to remove Natalie's mask, to see more than her eyes. "Yes."

"Thank you, Rams. Love you."

"I love you, too, Natalie."

Wind gusts and leaves swirl around them. Natalie gasps and full-body twitches as though startled. She quickly looks left, then right, and then ducks her head. "We can't stay out here." She whines at phantoms down at her feet. "You're going to have to do it. When we get to the house." She carefully lifts her feet one at a time, then scurries forward, ahead of Ramola, and says, "The mouses. The mouses are out of the houses."

Ramola rushes to catch up. Natalie doesn't slow down, trudges up the pitched and empty driveway, walking like she's afraid, being chased. Her strides are unbalanced, too long, too greedy. Ramola worries she's pushing herself and will fall. She tries to grab Natalie's right hand but Natalie pulls it away.

Natalie says, "A cat will swallow them down. The way of the world."

Ramola takes a picture of the farmhouse.

The front banister shows off missing teeth. One squared-off baluster spindle leans against its stoic neighbor. Wooden front steps bow and creak under their feet. The porch floor is warped and narrow, with barely enough room for the front stoop and a sitting area. Gray paint peels and flakes away, revealing scars of dark wood. The black skeleton of a rocking chair is banished to a corner and sags against the house. Purely decorative, the chair doesn't appear strong enough to hold up a ghost. Behind the chair are two brooms with white plastic handles, the wire bristle heads all but buried beneath leaves and dead grass.

Natalie sways side to side and prattles on about the way of the world.

The screen door is missing its screen and rattles impatiently. Ramola rings the doorbell, knocks, and calls out, "Hello? Is anyone home?" She doesn't wait long for an answer she assumes isn't forthcoming and tries the doorknob. It doesn't turn, but she notices the door isn't flush within the frame. She leans in and pushes; the door sticks initially but then opens.

Natalie brushes Ramola aside and enters the house first. Ramola stays within the doorframe and whispers after Natalie to wait. Then she calls out to imagined residents and their shadows. Natalie parrots her calls in a high voice. No one answers. There are no approaching frenzied footsteps.

Natalie disappears down a hallway. Ramola steps inside. The house smells of dust and lavender. She turns on a light. In the front entry is a set of steep stairs clinging to the wall like ivy. A mechanized lift rests at the bottom, the seat a smaller version of a dentist's chair. The chair is dust-free, appearing to have been recently wiped down and cleaned. Whoever lives here likely abandoned ship less than a handful of days ago.

Ramola drops her bags next to the chairlift and leaves the front door open so that she might better hear a siren or an approaching car. She texts the photo of the house and a message about their being inside it to Dr. Awolesi. She follows that up with the somewhat cryptic "The procedure may have to be performed here," as though she can't bear to explain or to extrapolate what will happen if no one comes. She dials 911 and leaves it on speakerphone. The call is forwarded to an answering service. Ramola leaves a message.

As she dials and redials 911, hoping to get through to a live operator, Ramola rummages through Natalie's overnight bag: headphones, phone charger, purse, two pairs of leggings, two T-shirts, socks, nightgown, hair elastics, nursing bras, maternity pads, toiletries, a set of infant babygrows, a green fleece coming-home outfit, a hat, booties, nappies, a set of plastic bottles with nipples, and four containers of ready-to-feed formula.

911 kicks over to the message service, which reissues the cold, high-pitched beep. The house is silent but for Natalie's voice echoing from somewhere else on the first floor. She is talking to herself. Ramola swears and shouts at the phone. "Someone answer! We need help!"

She rips open and empties Josh's backpack, contents spilling and thudding to the hardwood floor: a can of Lysol, hand sanitizer, rolled-up red bandannas, a hooded sweatshirt, a pack of disinfectant wipes, a coiled length of white rope (the kind that might be used for a clothesline), a roll of duct tape, latex gloves, painters' masks, a plastic bottle of water, three disposable lighters, loops of bungee cord, a phone charger, and a sheathed hunting knife. The blade is longer than her forearm.

"Natalie?"

She doesn't answer. Footsteps creak from the back of the house.

Ramola ducks into a small eat-in kitchen. She washes her hands at the sink using the almost-empty bottle of dishwashing soap, her scraped-up palms stinging. The window above the sink overlooks the end of the driveway and the grassy side-yard. She cannot see the road from here. After quickly drying her hands on a dishtowel hung over the oven door handle she puts on a pair of latex gloves.

While Ramola checks her phone for return texts or calls (there are none) Natalie shouts and her heavy stomps are accompanied by small smashes and crashes, the breaking of little things.

Ramola says, "Are you all right? Stay where you are. I'm coming to you."

She walks through the other end of the kitchen to the hallway and its beige peeling wallpaper. She passes the stairs and portals to other darkened rooms on the way to a spare room at the rear of the house turned makeshift bedroom. Perhaps the home's owner preferred sleeping here instead of relying on the chairlift each night to get to the master bedroom on the second floor. The doorframe outlined in molding has no door. A queen-size unmade bed claims most of the space in the square-shaped room. The wooden headboard has ornate bedposts as thick as elephant tusks, tapering to oval, egg-shaped knobs. Along the opposite wall are a box-furniture-store armoire and another rocking chair, this one buried under a mound of clothes. Natalie is a silhouette across from the foot of the bed, standing in front of a dresser that partially blocks the room's only window, the gray outside light further dimmed by lace curtains.

Natalie stands in profile. Her respirator mask is gone. She spits out random, monosyllabic vowel-based sounds. She paws through the dresser's dwindling set of knickknacks, small porcelain animals and dolls, and she smashes them into the walls and floor.

Ramola turns on the ceiling light; only one bulb of the two within the domed fixture works. She nearly tiptoes into the room while saying, "Natalie, let's get you in bed, all right? Have a lie-down. You need rest."

Natalie pushes and rocks the dresser front to back, front to back, spilling the remaining figurines. The top drawers slide open and closed like loose, wagging tongues.

Natalie turns toward the doorway, toward Ramola. Saliva drools in a thick line from her bottom lip and chin. Above her top lip is a mustache of accumulated white foam. Her eyes go lidless they open so wide. They are the glistening, reasonless eyes of lunacy, of vacancy and the transformed, of the werewolf and the vampire and the zombie and all the other monsters centuries of folklore and myth have attempted to ascribe to the rabid human face.

Natalie exclaims, "Oh!" and smiles, but it's not a smile. Her head tilts forward, pulled by the same new gravity drooping her shoulders and pulling her chest into kyphosis. Her facial muscles spasm and quake, her lips fissure, upper lip lifting into a *V* over an exposed canine. She rushes at Ramola, angrily shouting.

Ramola holds up her hands and drifts backward toward the doorway. Before she can say anything more than her name, Natalie is on top of her. She grabs a fistful of Ramola's left sleeve and pulls her arm toward her open mouth. Ramola bends her knees, dropping her weight, which straightens her arm and allows her to squirm it out of the coat. She pops back up and spins, attempting to free her other arm as well. Caught mid-turn,

Natalie two-handed shoves her between the shoulder blades. Outsized and outweighed, Ramola is sent tumbling into the hallway, careening into the wall and landing awkwardly on her right side. Her shoulder absorbs the brunt of the collision with a spike of bright pain.

Natalie lumbers into the hallway and kicks Ramola's left leg, mid-thigh, a direct hit but on the muscle and without much leverage behind it. Next, she tries to stomp down on Ramola's knees but misfires, throwing herself off-balance, tilting her weight. Forced to put her hands on the wall to catch herself and recalibrate, Natalie gives Ramola an opening.

Ramola scrabbles onto her feet and sprints down the hallway, to its other end. She pauses in the entryway at the chairlift and bottom of the stairs where most of the contents of Josh's pack remain on the floor. Natalie gives chase but she is breathing heavily and moving slower, her quick-burst attack already depleting her body's energy and strength reserves. At least, Ramola hopes that's the case.

Ramola briefly considers running upstairs, but without knowing the layout she fears being trapped. She also doesn't want Natalie falling or hurting herself or the baby climbing up and down the stairs. Instead she hangs the loop of rope off her barking right shoulder and grabs the roll of duct tape. She waves her hand in a come-here gesture and she talks in the calmest voice she can manage, telling Natalie it's time to go to bed, time for rest.

The sound of Ramola's voice has the opposite of the intended effect. Natalie clambers down the hallway that is either shrinking or she is filling, roaring more nonsense, the nonwords an aural virus, infecting Ramola's head with a near-blinding fear.

Moving too slowly initially, Ramola bumbles into the kitchen, her feet sputtering on the linoleum. Regaining some of her composure, she darts through the room and into the hallway. Backtracking to the rear of the house, Ramola runs at full throttle to expand the distance between her and Natalie.

Returning to the bedroom, Ramola leaps onto the bed and crab-crawls into its middle, crouched but with her legs coiled under her. Her first attempt at opening the duct tape goes awry as the tape sticks to her latex gloves. She tears off a strip and the gloves, tosses them into a dark corner. She rips open another length of tape, leaving one end attached to the roll.

Natalie billows into the room, screaming between gasping breaths. She knocks into the bed with both legs, as though not realizing she can't pass right through it. She leans and stretches and reaches for Ramola, opening and closing her mouth.

Ramola ducks and pivots, avoiding Natalie's grasping hands, scooting back toward the far side of the bed, but hoping to stay close enough to lure Natalie to lean and extend further.

Softly, Ramola says Natalie's name again and tells her to lie down. Natalie snarls, shouts, "Never leave!" and lunges with her right arm. She falls onto the bed, hands first, holding her torso up as though preparing to do a modified push-up. Ramola slaps and sticks the tape to the back of Natalie's right wrist and then quickly slides backward and off the bed. She sprints around the perimeter of the frame to the other side, coaxing herself to move faster. While Natalie is distracted by the tape and still bent forward, Ramola lowers her left shoulder and slams into Natalie's backside.

Natalie pitches onto the mattress, landing on her left shoulder, and rolls onto her back. Her lower legs dangle off the bed.

Ramola is fortunate that Natalie went left instead of right, as the duct tape is not trapped under Natalie's body and is still attached to her wrist. Ramola quickly cocoons Natalie's wrists and hands together. Natalie kicks out at Ramola but doesn't land a solid blow. When she tries to sit up without the aid of her hands, she falls back to the bed with the slightest nudge. Ramola ties off one end of the rope between and around Natalie's taped wrists. She loops the rest of the rope around the closest bedpost, making a pulley, and hauls in rope until Natalie's arms are hoisted over her head, then she ties it off.

Ramola next fights with Natalie's feet and legs, absorbing kicks to her thighs and one breath-stealing shot to the gut. In a war of attrition that leaves both women exhausted and gasping for air, Ramola wins the battle. She muscles Natalie's legs onto the mattress and builds a complex web of tape from ankle to ankle and tethers each to the lower bedframe. Battered and bruised, Ramola returns to the entryway, retrieves the collection of bungee cords, and uses them to buttress the arm and leg restraints. Natalie wriggles against the makeshift but effective shackles. Her back arches and her swollen belly rises with her manic efforts at escape. She screams and shouts and cries and laughs.

Ramola whispers, "I'm not leaving—I'll be right back," and flees the room.

Natalie's unhinged wails chase her down the hallway, out the front door, onto the porch, her feet drumming on the plywood, finally sputtering to a stop on the grass, bent over, gasping for air, hands on knees. The distance is not enough. Natalie is there next to her, screaming into her ear. She needs more distance, to be farther away, maybe walk down to the road to wait for a rescue, or maybe walk to the next house to ask for help and the one after that and the one after that. Would she still be able to hear Natalie? Would she be able to unsee her tied-up form and her heaving, pregnant belly?

Natalie's shouting mercifully ebbs. Ramola straightens and her breathing slows. From the vantage of the set-back, elevated front yard the road is a thin sliver, an ebbing brook between fields. The wind blows and the grass obeys, summoning a phantom in a blue-and-white ankle-length nightgown.

Ramola does not believe in ghosts, but she believes in this one. The phantom is slight, diminutive, as wispy as the bristles attached to a dandelion seed. Her arms are long and thin, built for reaching, tapping, touching. On the other side of the road, she floats through the field of yellow and brown. Her path is chaotic, without direction. Her hidden legs piston, expanding and retracting the bottom of the nightgown as though it is a bellows. She slows to jerking stops that seem permanent until there's a sudden, automatonic restart. Her face is not visible, not even when she looks up across the fields at Ramola standing in front of the house.

Ramola should go inside and lock the doors and windows, draw the curtains, turn off any unnecessary lights. There's a part of her that wants to wave at the phantom, to walk through the fields, to welcome her home.

Ramola remains in the front yard with the wind still blowing, the grass still obeying.

The infected woman either does not see Ramola or is too ill to cross the road and approach the house. She stays in her field and slow dances to a song all of us will one day hear.

The overhead light fixture in the kitchen doubles as a ceiling fan. Its base droops away from the ceiling plaster, exposing wires. Only two of the three bulbs work.

Ramola sits in an unsteady chair at the small table and inspects Josh's hunting knife. The nylon sheath includes a pocket with a sharpening stone the size of her thumb. The handle is hard rubber and the blade is black, curved, and smooth, coming to an exaggerated tip. She sets it next to a spare collection of knives she harvested from the drawers. Most are old, serrated, and have rust spots on their blades, though she did find one paring knife that appears to be in good condition.

After checking and rechecking and dialing and redialing and texting and retexting, Ramola creeps down the hallway to the back room. A pungent ammonia smell of urine hits her a few strides from the doorway. When she enters the room, Natalie reanimates, growling, yelping, and whimpering in pain. The whimpering is hardest to take because she sounds like the real her.

Natalie writhes against her restraints. She lifts and drops her head. Her mouth is fully ringed in foam so thick as to appear fake, sloppy makeup in a cheap horror movie. Her eyes don't focus as much as they roll and spin.

Ramola wants to put a hand on Natalie's abdomen to feel for the child's movements, but as she approaches the bed, Natalie nearly levitates trying to break free. Ramola retreats from the room, to the kitchen, and to her phone. No messages. She slumps back into the chair with warped, uneven legs. It teeters front to back. She covers her face with her hands, rubbing and pushing against her eyes until the dark goes purple.

Ramola transfers items one at a time from the kitchen table and front entryway to the bedroom, placing them on the dresser. With each pass, Natalie calls out in her new language.

When they were inside Norwood Hospital, Dr. Awolesi explained the virus was not blood-borne and would not pass through the placenta to the baby while Natalie wasn't showing signs of infection. She said the post-exposure vaccine Natalie received was safe for both mother and fetus, but there wasn't a lot of medical literature out there regarding what would happen if a woman at her stage of pregnancy succumbed to rabies infection.

She said they would still perform the cesarean section even if Natalie were presenting clear symptoms. Dr. Awolesi was reasonably confident the baby would not be infected.

Ramola remembers the last line clearly, perseverates on it, inspects it from every angle available.

She also remembers Natalie volleying back a quip: *Reasonably confident? Is that like a medical shrug?*

Ramola dumps the clothes off the chair and sits.

Natalie continues to babble and growl and writhe, though her strength appears to be waning.

How long can Ramola wait before she is forced to attempt a hackneyed C-section?

With each second that passes it's likely the risk of infection or illness to the child increases. However, she cannot and will not perform surgery on Natalie while she's awake, feeling pain, and thrashing about. Ramola would most certainly injure or cut the baby. Unfortunately, there is nothing with which to anesthetize Natalie. Ramola is not going to whack her on the head like in a dime-store thriller where one swipe of the butt end of a gun handle conveniently knocks the hero out cold until the opening of the next chapter.

Killing Natalie and then performing the procedure is not an option. A mother cannot be oxygen-dead for more than four minutes or the child will not survive. Those four minutes cannot be negotiated or bargained with. C-section births normally take ten to fifteen minutes in ideal conditions. Given she doesn't have to worry about Natalie surviving the procedure, Ramola should be able to decrease the timeline, but there's no way she can perform it in less than four minutes.

Ramola will wait for help or—if she has no choice but to attempt the procedure herself—wait until Natalie slips into a coma.

Still, while the virus's incubation period and post-infection timeline have exponentially sped up, Ramola does not know how long it will take for Natalie to pass into deep unconsciousness. In addition, she does not know how long her body's basic functions will continue while comatose. What if Natalie were to die in the middle of the procedure, a distinct possibility whether or not she is in a coma? That four-minute clock would again be ticking for the baby.

Ramola leaves the chair, walks to the bed, and says, "Reasonably confident. A medical shrug."

Natalie howls.

Ramola's body is in the chair in the bedroom that is attached to the hallway that is in the house that someone else built.

Inside Ramola's head, she is on the bus to the clinic sitting next to Natalie. There are other people in the seats near them but they are blurry, indistinct, and she doesn't think about them. Ramola is in the aisle seat, facing the window. Natalie leans against the window, gapes at her phone, finger dangling above the screen. Ramola stares at the reflection in the window.

After pacing the length of the hallway with her phone, Ramola goes to the bedroom. To drown out Natalie's cries and the groaning mattress upon which she struggles, Ramola recites a version of the fairy tale "Fundevogel." While she has retained certain key lines, she hasn't committed the entire story to memory as with "The Wedding of Mrs. Fox."

"A forester on his rounds found a child on top of a high tree. She had been snatched out of her mother's arms by a large bird. The forester took the rescued child home to live with him and his daughter, Nats. She named the found child Rams. Nats and Rams got along quite well and loved each other very much. One morning the forester left for a three-day trip. The nasty old cook then pulled Nats aside and told her he was going to boil and eat poor little Rams. Well, Nats wasn't standing for any of that, so she told Rams about the cook's scheme and they ran away and hid in the forest. The old cook sent a group of terrible men after them and they quickly caught up. Only moments before capture, Nats said to Rams, 'Never leave me and I will never leave you.' Rams said, 'Neither now, nor ever.' Then Nats said, 'Do you become a rose tree, and I the rose upon it?' When the terrible men arrived they found only a rose tree and one rose on it. The children were gone. The men went back to the cook and reported finding nothing. Outraged at the men's stupidity, the old cook went out into the woods himself. The children saw him coming. Nats said, 'Rams, never leave me, and I will never leave you.' Rams said, 'Neither now, nor ever.' Nats then said, 'Be a fishpond, and I will be the duck upon it.' The old bumbling cook nearly ran into the pond. Tired and despairing, he lay down at the shore to drink it up but the duck swam to the cook, grabbed his head with her beak, and dragged him into the deep water, drowning him. Nats and Rams went home together, their laughter echoing through the forest, and if they have not died, they are living together still."

Ramola retells the fairy tale from the beginning to keep from crying.

Natalie is tiring, losing to the infection. Her shouts have become the mumbles of a person talking in her sleep. Her eyelids flicker but do not remain open. Ramola wonders if her fading consciousness is the sole work of the virus or of possible aortocaval compression syndrome as a result of her lying on her back for an extended period. Such a position is not advisable for even healthy patients and could be placing stress on the baby, but Ramola cannot safely move Natalie onto her left side.

Ramola places two hands on Natalie's abdomen. The baby moves and lashes out. She says, "I don't know if I can do it."

She thinks, but doesn't say: *I don't want to do this. I can't do this. I won't do this.*

Natalie squirms under her hands. Ramola lifts them away as though she touched a hot stove.

As a medical student, Ramola assisted with more than a half dozen C-sections during her six-week OB/GYN rotation. For most of the procedure she simply observed the attending obstetrician and a resident perform the surgery. She was often tasked with retracting the abdominal wall to give the obstetrician a clear view of the surgical field. The abdominal rectus muscles are generally not cut during the procedure and are instead separated and moved to the side. During her final C-section as a medical student, they allowed Ramola to tie three sutures as the uterus was being closed up.

As a pediatric resident Ramola had to complete newborn nursery rotations and was often on call nights. When summoned to the OR for C-sections her job then was to take the newborn, ensure the baby was stable, and to perform any resuscitation that might be necessary. She was not standing at the operating table in those instances, but in those hazy, overworked, late hours, she would often fight to keep focus by following the discussion/instructions between the obstetrician, the OB resident, and nurses.

Ramola retells the fairy tale. And then retells it again.

"Then Nats said, 'Do you become a rose tree, and I the rose upon it?' When the terrible men arrived they found only a rose tree and one rose on it."

Ramola retrieves Natalie's phone from the sweatshirt pocket. As she does so, Natalie turns her head and opens and closes her mouth like a goldfish. It's a myth that goldfish retain memories for only three seconds.

Getting to the home screen does not require a password. Natalie must've turned off the lock-screen setting prior to succumbing to infection. Her phone's battery is at thirty-one percent, still plenty of charge; a cruel reminder of how little time has passed since Natalie was bitten.

Ramola opens the Voyager app to hear her friend's voice again. She doesn't make it through the first message.

Natalie's breaths are shallow and she is no longer speaking, crying out.

Ramola returns to the kitchen, tries her phone. She sits with her eyes closed, and breathes deeply. Attempting to still her shaking hands and galloping heart rate, Ramola leans on her stress-reduction technique as she did on Bay Road when attempting to get Natalie to drink water. She imagines a whiteboard, this one bigger than any other she's used before. The broad, blank board is there for her now. She was unable to imagine it while in the same room with Natalie.

She begins the handwritten list of instructions using black marker and her careful, looping cursive: The first incision, horizontal near the pubic hairline, a six-inch cut. It could be longer if necessary. (This line is written shakily on the board with the implication that the cut can be longer because Natalie does not have to be stitched up afterward.) The rectus muscles are normally retracted and pulled out of the way. (She will not have that luxury here and her cursive *m*'s and *l*'s are sloppy, indistinct.) Cut through or split the rectus sheath and the muscles themselves. (This will result in more blood loss, which is reflected in her misspelling of "muscles.") There will also be the peritoneum to contend with prior to reaching the uterus. The bladder and intestines might need to be pushed aside. (She cannot just hack and slash her way through if Natalie is to remain breathing throughout as much of the procedure as possible. For the baby to survive, Ramola needs to keep that four-minute oxygen clock from winding down to zero. Because of all this she writes in a harsh slant, the letters avalanching downhill, and she crosses out "intestines" and inexplicably rewrites it in printed capital letters.) Cut through the three layers of the uterine wall without injuring the baby. (Neither hunting knife nor paring knife are meant for the tough, delicate, precise cutting, and this final line is an illegible smear as though she erased it with the flat of her hand.)

Ramola tries to envision a successful surgery resulting in a live birth, and she tries to envision an after. But she can't see anything beyond her dying friend strapped to the bed.

What am I going to do? I don't want to do this. I can't do this. How can I possibly do this?

Ramola first cuts the tape between Natalie's ankles and pushes her legs apart. Natalie doesn't stir.

She cleans Natalie's face with wipes and a kitchen towel. Carefully slipping the elastic band over her head, Ramola covers Natalie's nose and mouth with a painter's mask. Natalie doesn't stir.

Ramola deposits the used tape and soiled towels into a garbage bag along with the leggings, underwear, and blue shirt-dress she scissored away. After spraying Natalie's body and bed with aerosol disinfectant, Ramola returns to the kitchen, de-gloves, washes her hands one more time, puts on the last pair of latex gloves.

Folded sheets and towels Ramola found in a linen closet are draped over Natalie's chest and her legs, edges tucked under her hips and thighs. The two remaining towels are folded on top of a kitchen chair Ramola dragged into the room, a cushioned platform upon which she'll inspect the baby.

Ramola cannot perform the surgery while standing on the floor. Her reach isn't long enough. She hovers at the foot of the bed and watches the slight rise and fall of Natalie's covered chest. What if she stays there, does nothing, and simply watches until there is no more rise and fall? No one would know she didn't try.

She can't do this. She stands and she watches. The house makes creaking and rattling noises, the kinds it saves for when someone is alone.

Her mental whiteboard is a mess of cross-outs, circles, arrows, smudges, and the order of instructions is almost impossible to follow.

Ramola climbs over the foot of the bed. As she settles onto her knees, she sinks into the mattress. Natalie's belly pitches slightly forward. The angle for surgery is not ideal and the weight pressure is surely squeezing the child forward. Ramola's every movement sends quakes through the mattress and jostles Natalie's body. She should've found a way to get Natalie to the hard floor. It's too late to do so now.

On the bed, between the mattress's edge and Natalie's left leg, is a rectangular plastic container. Inside are hand towels and knives. She picks up the hunting knife. It feels top-heavy. The brutish instrument is not an extension of her hand.

She whispers, "I'm sorry, but—" then stops before uttering, *I can't do this.*

"All right," she says instead, then leans forward and allows the quivering mattress to settle. She anchors her left hand halfway up the belly and pushes it away from her. The baby reacts to the sudden force and pressure. Ramola says, "All right" again, this one not meant for Natalie, and she shakily inserts the fearsome knife tip into Natalie's skin at the start of the planned incision line. Blood beads instantly. As Ramola slowly drags the knife to her right, a muffled low moan, one that could be wind outside until it cannot be, builds into a jagged scream from Natalie, and her body flinches and spasms.

Ramola retracts the knife, scrabbles backward, her lower back ramming into the edge of the footboard. She screams, "I'm sorry!" and throws the knife at the wall to her right. It bounces off and clatters on the hardwood.

"Please don't make me do this."

Ramola paces at the foot of the bed.

"Never leave me and I will never leave you. Neither now, nor ever."

Ramola climbs back onto the bed. She places one hand on the belly, the other holding the hunting knife. Natalie's breathing is nearly imperceptible.

As Ramola finishes the initial incision, Natalie's earlier groans and screams ring so clear in her head as to be happening now.

The light in the room is terrible. The clouded overhead fixture, the extra lamps, the flashlight on her phone do not illuminate enough. There is so much blood. Ramola switches out the knives. She switches them again and again and again.

Her mental whiteboard goes blank. The blankness expands, becomes an infinite void of whiteness, one in which she might be lost willingly.

She's through to the thick, fibrous muscle of the uterus. With the mattress shaking, it's impossible to see any rise and fall of Natalie's chest. Has she stopped breathing even though her moans and screams continue in Ramola's head?

How long has Natalie been dead? How long has she been gone?

How long has the four-minute clock been ticking?

Ramola works as quickly as she can. The knives fight against their usage. Her fingers tremor and cramp up.

The last of the cutting is done.   The knives are away.
     She reaches inside and pulls the baby out.

The baby is a girl. Her skin is ghostly gray.

Neither Ramola nor the baby is breathing.

She cries.

No Care and No Sorrow

This is not a fairy tale. Certainly it is not one that has been sanitized, homogenized, or Disneyfied, bloodless in every possible sense of the word, beasts and human monsters defanged and claws clipped, the children safe and the children saved, the hard truths harvested from hard lives if not lost then obscured, and purposefully so.

This is not a fairy tale. This is a song.

* * *

Rising ocean levels conspire with a tidal surge from a storm stalled over northern England and Scotland. The River Tyne breaks over its banks and floods the Quayside in Newcastle. The low-lying area between the Tyne Bridge and the Millennium Bridge is hit the hardest, with floodwaters reaching up to five feet in height. Roads are washed out. Dozens of businesses are forced to close while hundreds must evacuate their homes and seek higher ground. Four motorists and one jogger drown in the flash flooding. It takes two weeks for the Tyne to recede from its highest level in recorded history.

While flooding wreaks similar havoc in ten-year-old Lily's hometown of South Shields, she is most upset——in the charmingly plucky way only ten-year-olds can be——that her school trip to the Newcastle is postponed for two months. It's not that the Newcastle Castle is her favorite castle, not by any stretch. It's actually quite small as castles or forts go, and Hadrian's Wall and the Roman fort Arbeia [both in South Shields] are more impressive, even awe inspiring.

It's the creature that resides near the Newcastle Castle that Lily wants to show her snotty friend Robert. He doesn't believe it exists.

* * *

Poor Mrs. Brehl and the overmatched chaperone Mrs. Budden [Gary's fussy mum, who refers to her son as "Gare Bear"] have their hands full with the class. So, too, the uninspiring tour guide who is dressed as a Roman or Anglo-Saxon or Norman soldier, Lily is not sure which. She did not pay attention when he identified himself, and to be fair, she's distracted by his voice cracking and the dusting of acne on his forehead, which doesn't really lend him soldierly gravitas.

Laird and John race each other from room to room, playing a two-person game of tag. Julia spits over the edge of the railing while on the roof. Lydia throws a wad of tissue into a hidden, nonfunctional pre-medieval toilet. Andy flicks his mates' ear-

lobes as the tour guide drones on and pinches ankles and the backs of knees as kids walk up the stairs. Camille taps on shoulders and then jams her flashlight directly into her victims' eyes. Even Gare Bear gets into the act and repeatedly asks the guide about a ghost named Chaunccy.

The children don't normally misbehave to this extent. The truth is, without being able to verbalize this, they are sensitive to the miasma of unease within the city. They felt it as soon as they stepped off the train: the weight and weariness of the flood and the resigned fear of more and worse floods sure to come. Being in the castle, this living bit of history, is actually ramping up this ineffable fear of the future; this structure that has survived for more than one thousand years now represents the impermanence of the city, of everything. In the face of this, the children react in the only way they can: they laugh and they fool around and they rebel because they have to live forever.

The tour ends in a dark basement with a film and presentation that is to last twenty minutes. As the teacher and chaperone are distracted with the throng of giggling and hand-fighting kids, Lily tells Mark that if the teacher asks, she went to the toilet. Then she grabs Robert's hand. Having been in the castle before and in possession of an unerring sense of direction and place, she leads him from the basement and out of the castle. No one stops her because she walks like she knows where she's going, which is, in and of itself, an accurate assessment.

Once outside in the cool, gray damp air, Robert repeatedly asks what she's doing and where they are going. Last night he had dreadful nightmares in which the black waters of the river swallowed him and the city whole.

Lily says, "Not far. You'll see. Quit whingeing."

They make an odd pair. Robert is fair-haired and creeps along like a rodent in an open field echoing with the hungry calls of hawks and owls. He is a full head shorter than Lily, who could pass for a new teenager. Her long brown hair is woven into a thick single braid that no one dares pull on. Lily-punches hurt the most.

Two streets from the castle they turn right and walk a narrow road behind the sprawling Cathedral Church of St. Nicholas.

Robert whispers, although there's no one around. "This is barmy. We need to go back."

Lily pulls Robert into the middle of the road, stops, and points up. "Have a look."

Across from the cathedral is a set of brick structures associated with the church. They've stopped in front of one building's front door adorned with ornate stone arch work, colored pink and white. Perched at the top, front paws with nails wrapping over the arch, staring down from above a circular window and the front entrance, is the Vampire Rabbit of Newcastle.

Robert laughs once. He looks at Lily as though seeing her for the first time. Then he laughs again. "That's——that's a rabbit, innit?"

Lily crosses her arms over her chest; her smile could power a hydroelectric plant.

The Vampire Rabbit is a stone gargoyle painted black. Its nails and teeth are blood-red. The eyes are wide and menacing. Its ears are long, like a hare's, and if you stare long enough, you can imagine them as bat's wings, or belonging to a demon.

Robert jokes, "Look at its teeth. Does it have *the* rabies, then?"

Lily groans and whacks his shoulder. Lily-shoulder-whacks hurt the most too. Robert doesn't let on how much it smarts by not rubbing his arm. She says, "We're not in America," out of the side of her mouth, as though she's embarrassed to be saying so.

Lily tells Robert a brief and to-the-point story about the city once having had a big problem with grave robbers until there was a night when an actual eight-foot-tall creature shaped like a vampire rabbit [she does not commit to the creature actually being what it looks like] appeared in this same doorway and scared them off. The dutiful citizens then built a gargoyle version in its honor and it has since scared away all other grave robbers. She ends with, "It's working, innit? See any grave robbers lounging about? Unless you're one. If you are, I'd leg it before it nips your neck."

Robert laughs nervously again. "I'm not. Is that the real story?"

She tells him some people think the vampire rabbit could've started as an odd representation of the Easter Bunny, a reminder of spring [Robert interjects, "The Easter Bunny gone mad."], and other people think it's a symbol of Freemasonry and others think it's a cheeky two-finger salute to the cathedral and the Anglican Church in general. She adds, "No one really knows why. It's all sassafras and lullabies."

Robert pulls his gaze away from the rabbit. He says, "Sassa-what?"

Lily turns red. "Sassafras and lullabies. It——it's an old saying. Means everything is bollocks."

"Say it again."

"No."

"Your accent changes when you say that. You sound like someone else——"

"And you sound like a tosser. Always and forever."

* * *

Lily insists she's old enough to walk the ten minutes home from school by herself. She engages in a semiweekly, one-sided argument with Gran. She has taken to employing charts and video presentations accompanied by music and sound effects [she wants to make films one day] outlining increasingly elaborate reasoning as to why this small but earned bit of independence would not only benefit her character in the long run, it would also enhance the lives of everyone within the household. Gran patiently waits and smiles warmly until Lily is done with her presentations before she says, "No." Appeals from Gramp and Auntie, both of whom having been won over [or worn down] to Lily's side, hold no sway with Gran.

Upon returning from the Newcastle trip, Lily walks home from school with Gran. While their battle of wills in regard to the walking-home debate is building to an epic confrontation, if not a conclusion, Lily adores and is slightly in awe of Gran. She lives to make her laugh that closed-eyed, I-disapprove-but-you-are-too-much chuckle.

Lily doesn't lie to or hide things from Gran. She tells her about the school trip and successfully sneaking out to see the Vampire Rabbit. Gran does not approve and tells her as much, but Lily, in describing her unwitting accomplice Robert as being as timid as a dormouse and twice as twitchy, elicits the laugh she craves.

Lily has to work to keep up with Gran. They are soon upon their semidetached home with the brick walls and a white trellis.

Lily asks, "Is Auntie home too?"

"She is."

Lily enters the kitchen first. Auntie and Gramp are in their usual spots, sitting at the intimate round table with the sunny vinyl tablecloth. They both glance over the frames of their glasses, likely reading the same news stories; Gramp clutching his newspaper, Auntie hunched over her tablet. Before they say their hellos and come-give-us-a-hug-and-kiss and how-was-your-day, they smile their wan I-see-you-dear smiles.

Lily goes to Gramp first. He always sits at the end of the table facing out into the room because it's easier for him to get out of that chair, the only one at the table with armrests. His cane leans against his right leg. The arthritis in his shoulders bothers him more than he lets on. Many mornings Gramp will ask Lily if he's become the cute little old man he always wanted to be. She agrees but will include a cheeky quip about his level of cuteness. When younger, she chafed at his describing himself as "little."

After a peck on his stubbly cheek she announces that she saw the Vampire Rabbit. Gran shakes her head but does not tell them of her sneaking away from the group to see it.

Gramp says, "Sounds better than any of my school trips." He fluffs his paper, his own punctuation mark to the brief discussion, and disappears behind it.

Lily shimmies behind Gramp to get to Auntie Rams. She always sits in the chair with her back to the wall, hemmed in between her parents as though resigned to being trapped. While all adults are old, Lily knows Auntie Rams is younger than her nearly totally gray hair belies.

"Come give me a peck, luv." Auntie holds her arms wide. It's the safest place Lily knows to be. Auntie groans like she's squeezing as hard as she can, but she's gentle as always. "You're getting so big."

"Ugh, you say that every day."

"It's true every day."

Lily asks, "Home before me? Did you cut classes again, Dr. Auntie?" She giggles at her own joke. Auntie Rams teaches biology and life sciences at the small marine university. Lily only recently learned that she used to be a children's doctor but gave it up before they moved to England.

"Don't be clever. I only had one lab this morning. No vampire rabbits to be seen, unfortunately."

After a bit more light banter, more for the adults' sake than hers, Lily escapes the table, leaving Gramp, Auntie, and Gran, totems in their spots at the old table. There they will remain until it's time to prepare dinner.

Lily wonders what they will talk about when she leaves, but she will not spy on them today.

* * *

The morning after Lily's birth, Dr. Awolesi finally responded to Ramola's texts. An ambulance escorted by two army jeeps later arrived at the farmhouse. Ramola and Lily were thoroughly screened and transported to the hospital in North Attleboro.

During the first eighteen months post-rescue, with each day that passed——some more frightening, frustrating, and improbable than others——Ramola kept waiting for Natalie's parents or Paul's siblings to lay claim to Lily. None of them did; honoring Natalie's recorded wishes. Still, Ramola assumed someone of authority would eventually step in with a definitive, irrevocable "no," and take Lily away. While she has never and would never admit this to anyone, she desperately wanted to hear that "no."

During those earliest days, while Ramola dutifully filled out the reams of paperwork and participated in countless interviews and hearings, she daydreamed about the various ways in which the final "no" would happen. She felt a mix of guilt and an existential relief at the prospect of failing to keep her promise yet being able to say to herself and to the Natalie she keeps in her head, "I did my best. I tried."

Ten years on, Ramola is still trying and doing her best.

* * *

When Ramola wakes alone in her bedroom, in that liminal dead-of-night space where one exists and where one doesn't at the same time, the surgery Ramola performed often replays in her head so vividly as to demonstrate part of her is still there in that farmhouse. Perhaps it would be more accurate to say the surgery is instead a part of her, connecting wings and floors within her memory palace and it will do so for as long as the structure stands. Accompanying will be a memory of who she was before that day changed her. On these nights, which occur with varying frequency, Ramola sometimes gets out of bed and splashes cold water on her face and does her best to stubbornly bury that which won't remain in the ground, or she walks aimlessly, haunting the hallways and rooms of her childhood house——the one she never wanted to move back to——or she stays in bed and allows herself to wallow and wade deeper into those dark waters, indulging in the loss of her friend and the loss of who Ramola used to be and who she will never be again.

Ten years on, Ramola is still trying and doing her best.

* * *

Lily's bedroom is in the converted attic. She closes the door quietly. Gran would ask [her ask is a demand] that the door remain open unless she is napping.

The walls of Lily's small bedroom are covered with travel posters from cities and countries she's never been to. The first set was a gift from Auntie. Apparently, they had once hung in her American flats. Lily has taken over the collection. She also has a globe on which she places pushpins. Boston has a green pushpin because she has been there, even if she doesn't remember it. Red pushpins represent the cities she wants to travel to with Auntie, and they include Athens and Los Angeles. The blue pins are stuck into the farthest-away places [Easter Island, New Zealand, Antarctica] she'll go to on her own when she's older.

On her unmade bed, waiting patiently by her pillows, is an ancient stuffed-animal fox.

Lily runs across the room and plops heavily into the seat at her wooden desk, undermining her earlier quietness when shutting the door. She can only be quiet for so long.

She wakes her sleeping tablet and inserts earbuds into the bowls of her ears. With a tap and swipe of fingers, she opens the streaming service and then navigates to a private set of recently uploaded audio files.

What Robert said about her sounding different rings in her ears. The very thought of him attempting to take the piss scrunches up her face. There's also this: maybe she does want to sound different. Maybe that's who she'll be.

Lily stares at the list of files on the screen and whispers, "I'm mad at you," but there's no real anger behind it. Only a complex longing and wonder at once what was and will never be.

She opens the first file and presses the Play button symbolized by a triangle fallen on its side.

ACKNOWLEDGMENTS

Thank you to Erin Stapleton and Dr. Jeff Kolodny, for their invaluable research help. Any medical inaccuracies are mine, either through error or convenience. (Don't judge me.) My awesome sister, Erin, especially went above and beyond with this book. First I made her house spooky in *A Head Full of Ghosts* and then I put her to work with this novel. Sorry, Erin?

Thank you to my friends and first readers, Lydia Gittins and Stephen Graham Jones. Their input was invaluable. Extra thanks to Lydia for shepherding me on side trips to South Shields, the Newcastle Castle, and of course, to the Vampire Rabbit. She also didn't laugh at me when I ran the original what-if by her: can a zombie give birth to an uninfected baby?

Thank you to friends Nadia Bulkin and John Langan, who listened, advised, and helped along the way.

Thank you to Stephen Barbara and Jen Brehl, for your guidance and help smooshing this thing into a thing. Thank you to everyone at William Morrow and Titan Books for all you do.

Thank you to friends and family for their love, support, and patience.

And thank *you* for reading.